The
Cape Cod
Conundrum

**Other Penny Spring and Sir Toby Glendower Mysteries
by Margot Arnold**

MARGOT ARNOLD

The Cape Cod Conundrum

A Penny Spring and Sir Toby Glendower Mystery

The Countryman Press
Woodstock, Vermont

Cover design by Honi Werner

This edition published in 2007 by
The Countryman Press
P.O. Box 748, Woodstock, Vermont 05091

Distributed by W. W. Norton & Company, Inc.
500 Fifth Avenue, New York, New York 10110

Printed in the United States of America

10   9   8   7   6   5   4   3   2   1

In loving memory of
Louis Wilder,
gifted editor, gentle man

WHO'S WHO

GLENDOWER, Sir TOBIAS MERLIN, 1st Baronet [created 1992] Archaeologist. O.M., F.B.A., F.S.A., Knted 1977; b. Swansea, Wales, Dec. 27, 1926; s. Thomas Owen and Myfanwy [Williams] G.; ed. Winchester Coll.; Magdalen Coll., Oxford, B.A., M.A., Ph.D; Fellow, Magdalen Coll., 1949–; Fellow, All Souls Coll., 1990–; Emeritus Professor Near Eastern and European Prehistoric Arch., Oxford U. 1 dau. Sonya Danarova, m. Dr. Alexander Spring, 1991, 2 gr.ch. Mala & Marcus. Participated in more than 30 major archaeological expeditions. Author of several books, including *The Age of Pericles*, 1993; also numerous excavation and field reports. Clubs: Old Wykehamists, Athenaeum, Wine-tasters, University.

SPRING, Dame PENELOPE ATHENE, D.B.E. [Civil] 1992, anthropologist. b. Cambridge, Mass., May 16, 1928; d. Marcus and Muriel [Snow] Thayer; B.A., M.A., Radcliffe Coll.; Ph.D., Columbia U.; m. Arthur Upton Spring, June 24th,1953 [dec.]; 1 son, Alexander Marcus, M.D. 2 gr.ch. Marcus & Mala Spring. Lectr. Anthropology Oxford U., 1958–68; Mathieson Reader in Anthropology, Oxford U. 1969–1993; Extramural Lectr. Oxford U. 1993–; Fellow, St. Anne's Coll., Oxford, 1969–. Field work in the Marquesas, East and South Africa, Uzbekistan, India, and among the Pueblo, Apache, Crow and Fox Indians. Author of over twenty books including anthrop. classics *Sex in the South Pacific*, 1957; *Feminism in the 20th Century Muslim World*, 1978; *Modern Micronesian Chiefdoms*, 1989; and *The Fijians*, 1992.

Prologue

"I'm sorry, Clara, I really am. I wouldn't have done this if there had been any other way, I hope you understand that." The hysterical voice was part whisper, part gabble. "But it has all gone too far, much too far. You were right of course, I should have listened to you. Oh my God, yes! When I found out it was all too late and I was too involved. But now it has to be *stopped*, oh yes, stopped—that's right, stopped. Maybe this will show the way to someone with eyes to see and a mind to understand—I can't think of any other way. *You'll* tell them, Clara, won't you? I'm too afraid. For you it's different, but if I came forward now my life would be over, ruined, and I can't face that, you know I can't . . . ."

In the darkened classroom lit only by the dim hall light filtering in through the thick glass panels on each side of the door, the woman made no reply to her frantic companion. She sat rigidly behind the desk, her dim eyes void of expression, her pallid face gleaming white in the gloom, as the frantic voice mumbled on. "The books like so—but I couldn't be too obvious about them, you see. And if you just point like that to the map? Yes, fine, fine! Oh, no!" The voice soared in anguish as the woman took a sudden lurch forward. "No, no, we can't have that . . . string, string—that's it." There was panting and shuffling, then, "Oh my God, there's someone coming!"

There was the faint squeak of rubber soles on the rubber-tiled floor of the hallway. The handle of the door turned but it did not open, then the footsteps continued on.

"Thank God I remembered to wedge it, oh, thank God!" The voice rambled on. "But I can't stay with you any longer. I can't be seen here. I'll have to leave you to it." There was a slithering noise as a map was pulled down on its roller beside the desk. "All set? Books, map—yes, yes, that should be fine, just fine." There was a hysterical giggle. "What I would give to see their faces! But I'll be gone by then. A clean pair of heels. There, it's all set and I'll leave you to it. This is the only way. Forgive me, Clara, forgive me . . . ."

The figure groped its way cautiously to the door and peered out, listening intently. A large object was pushed out of the door in front of the whisperer, who closed the door firmly and scurried off down the long corridor. The light footsteps and a quiet whirring masked a sudden snap and slither within the darkened classroom. Then there was only silence, as the woman sat stiffly at the desk—waiting.

Chapter 1

"I just had to see you before you left, so I thought I'd drop in on my way from the airport to the Cape," Penny Spring said, hugging and kissing John Everett to the quiet amazement of the young secretary who had just ushered her into his regal office in the publishing house of Cosby and Son on Beacon Street. "So Millicent talked you into it after all—you really *are* retiring this time!" Age was certainly not withering him, she noted: he was rounder and more amiable of countenance than ever.

He smiled ruefully at her. "Yes, we compromised. Come and sit down and have a sherry. We have a lot of catching up to do." Out of a heavy cut-glass decanter he poured them both hefty shots into delicate crystal glasses and lifted his in a toast. "To your most excellent fortune!"

"And to yours, also. So where are you off to?"

"Arizona," he said to her surprise. "After the earthquake of '89 Millicent went off her previous obsession with California, but her arthritis has become so bad that the doctors advised a drier, warmer climate and so we settled on Arizona. It's close enough to California that she can pop out and see our son and the grandchildren whenever she feels like it, and not quite such

11

a major trek for me to get back to Boston when the mood strikes—though I am thinking of starting up a small press out there, so I don't imagine the mood will strike all that often."

Penny looked around her at the massive mahogany furnishings and elegant appointments of another age and sighed. "This place will just not be the same without you. I don't suppose I'll ever see it again."

"Why ever not?" he said sharply. "It'll still be here and with a Cosby at the helm too—first time in donkey's years. One of Millicent's young cousins is taking over. And, as one of our longest-around and most distinguished authors, he'll be as happy to see you as I've always been. Not thinking of quitting us are you? Jules would be devastated."

"Jules?" she queried.

"Jules Lefau. Our silent partner for some years now. He says he invested because we turn out such good work, but *I* think he wants it as a tax write-off." John grinned at her. "Anyway, he was as impressed by your new title as I was—*Dame* Penelope Spring, indeed! How did that happen?"

Penny winced and sighed again. "All pretty ridiculous really. But after that affair in Rome the PM was convinced we had saved his precious skin and he tried to make Toby a life peer. Toby had the nerve to turn it down. Said he did not want to be in the House of Lords, not even once! But he hinted strongly that he wouldn't say no to a baronetcy and what about his partner who was equally responsible for the rescue? He quoted all the Americans who had been knighted—like Douglas Fairbanks, Jr. and so on—and pointed out that none of *them* had saved a PM's life. I told him to cool it, but you know how obstinate he is once he gets going. Anyway, after much fluttering in high circles—there hasn't been a baronetcy created in God knows when—Toby got his way and I was made Dame of the British Empire at the same time. After all the fuss he'd made, I could scarcely turn it down, though personally I think my son's remark when he learned of it sums up my feelings exactly. Alex said, 'I always knew you were a dame, but now that it's official, that and seventy-five cents should buy you a cup of coffee.'"

John, who like many a Boston Brahmin was an Anglophile and a bit of a snob, replied, "It's a very great honor and, besides, will look just great on the dust jackets of your books." There was a small silence before he went on, "I know his title doesn't mean a thing to Toby, so I suppose he wanted it to pass on to his grandson?"

"That's about it," she agreed. "Amazing isn't it? You can just imagine what All-American Alex and Sonya—who, at heart, still follow the Party line—think of that, but there's not a damn thing they can do about it, a fact that pleases Toby enormously."

"So he's really wrapped up in the children, is he?"

"When they first arrived he didn't take a scrap of notice of them, other than to peer disapprovingly at them in the hospital and then to show up—unwillingly I might add—for the christening. But once they started to walk and, above all, to talk— well, it has been a very different story! The man is besotted, not so much on Marcus, as one might have expected, but on *Mala*. A female has finally captured him, heart and soul. You know how he used to be about coming to America, all moans and groans? Well, I swear he's given more lectures over here since the twins had their first birthday than he has in England. I think he must be supporting the Concorde single-handedly, he uses it like a bus!" She sounded faintly aggrieved.

John tactfully changed direction. "And on top of all this you also are a woman of means now? How exactly did that happen?"

Again she winced. "That's even *more* ridiculous than the title. It happened this May. I was over in New York for the American Anthropological Association's meeting—and to see the family, of course." John suppressed a grin as he helped himself to another sherry and replenished her glass. "And at the

13

meeting I ran into this old student of mine who is now a professor at the University of Virginia. He took me out to dinner to catch up on the news and we both got a bit looped in the process. It was my birthday, so he insisted he had to get me a present. So we went into this little dive off Times Square and he bought me a bunch of lottery tickets—the pay-off that week was something fantastic so *everyone* was buying them. Well, the next thing I knew I was notified that I was one of the winners! There were about twenty of them that week. But to make a long story short, my cut, after taxes, was $350,000 dollars."

She slid an apologetic glance at her attentive listener. "And I don't mind telling you, John, that it is a heaven-sent windfall; without it I could not afford to retire, and I've been thinking more and more about retirement of late, ever since Toby retired from his professorship and went off to All Souls. I was beginning to feel quite sorry for myself, wishing I had taken your advice years ago and taken one of the fat professorships I'd been offered over here, with all their nice retirement benefits and such, instead of hanging on at Oxford, which is high in prestige but a little skimpy on things like pensions. Not being able to afford to retire, I thought I was really up the creek. Pitt-Rivers just isn't the same without Toby around, though his successor is a nice enough young man. And Jessup has been even more aggravating than usual with all the fuss about our titles and him with only an OBE. So I was getting pretty fed up with things and then, like manna from heaven, this money falls into my lap."

"So are you going to move back here?" John asked hopefully. "Come and join us in Flagstaff!"

She shook her head. "No, I'm too entrenched in Littlemore and there are certain benefits in staying in England when you're my age. National Health for one, which actually works. But it does mean I can step aside gracefully now and have enough money to finish off some old projects, maybe even start some new ones, and travel when and where I want—like now, for instance. Sonya and Alex have this fantastic deal from some Cape doctor, who credits Alex with having saved his life when he keeled over with a heart attack at some convention. He has a place right on the sea in Hyannisport and he offered it to them for free while he and his wife went off to Europe. Sonya jumped at it—perfect for the children, and Alex flies up from New York on the weekends. He's hoping to get a whole week off after Labor Day."

"And will Toby be joining you at all?" John lifted the decanter and looked enquiringly at her, but she shook her head. "No, no more thanks. I have to drive to the Cape and the traffic this time of year is frightful so I'll need all my wits about me. Toby's already down there."

His eyebrows shot up. "Then why didn't he meet you at Logan and save you the hassle after this long trip?" he demanded.

She smiled faintly. "We did discuss it, but it's a bit of a conspiracy, I'm afraid. You see Sonya has only just learned to drive. She never had the chance in Russia and there has not been much occasion for it in Manhattan, but now they've decided to move out of the city she has finally learned. Toby is *very* apprehensive of her skills, particularly with all the congestion on the Cape just now, so *he* insists on doing all the driving. But he thought we could use a second car down there and the only tactful way to do it without making the whole thing too obvious would be for me to rent one and drive down."

John chuckled. "Still the same old Toby, I see."

Penny's gloom returned. "Not really, he's changed a lot, mellowed quite a bit. Happy as a lark at All Souls writing a definitive work on the Age of Pericles, his favorite period. It is one book I think he actually will finish. No, everything has changed. I'm getting so I hate the very sound of the word."

"Coming from an anthropologist, that is about the silliest damn statement I ever heard." John Everett said with spirit.

"Come off it, Penny! Change is the very meat and drink you live by."

Her attractively ugly little face lit up with a sudden grin. "I don't know what it is about you, John, but every time I come in here I seem to unload all my moans and groans on you. You're right, of course. I suppose what I am trying to say is that beginnings are always more fun than endings. And I know I ought to be ashamed of myself. I've nothing whatever to complain about." She got up. "Well, I must be on my way. I'm sure you must be up to your ears in last-minute business."

"Oh, don't rush off," he pleaded. "God knows when we'll get the chance to chat like this again."

"No," she was firm. "I must go. They'll start to worry if I don't show up soon."

He smiled sadly at her. "No qualms about returning to the Cape after our last go-around there? I often think of that. Weird as it may seem, I think that was one of the most exciting and enjoyable times of my whole life."

"Good heavens, no! It was all years ago and no one is going to remember me and my misdoings. This time I'm keeping well away from policemen. Toby and I both swore off after Rome. No, this will be strictly fun in the sun with the family," she assured him. His intercom buzzed urgently, and so, with a quick peck on his rosy cheek and a "God bless! Remember me to Millicent," she made her escape before he could protest further.

To her, Route 3 and the Mid-Cape highway seemed un-changed, as she sped along in the endless stream of traffic heading for Cape Cod, but when she turned off on to Route 132 at the Hyannis sign and headed for downtown Hyannis, she felt she had entered a new and alien landscape in which few remembered landmarks were visible. Thankful for Toby's meticulous directions, she fumbled her way down Sea Street and along the shore road heading for Craigville Beach. When she was almost in sight of the beach, she spotted two small flags—a Union Jack and a Stars and Stripes flapping in the light breeze. A small sign with an arrow was pinned to a wooden post; "Down here, all the way," it read.

She obediently turned on to an unpaved road that led, bumpily, through a dense thicket of scrub pine and maple; she caught glimpses of a house or two nestled in among the trees and saw the end of the road coming into sight. On a low bluff above the circle that formed its end, she made out the tall, slim figure of her daughter-in-law standing at the top of a flight of stone steps and shading her eyes. Behind her a small windmill twirled busily in the wind. As Penny drew up, Sonya ran down the steps and opened the car door. "Oh, I am so happy to see you! I start to worry that something has happened. The traffic is dreadful, no? And father, he starts to fuss because it is the time he usually takes the children to Craigville for their presupper swim."

Penny was gazing dazedly at a slightly rusted gas pump. "Is that what I think it is?"

Sonya laughed. "Oh, yes. We are very self-contained here. The doctor who owns the house is a character. He has fought with all the local utility companies. The windmill gives us our own electricity and pumps up the water from our own well. This petrol pump he had put in during the gas shortage in the '70s—he said he had to have it to get to the hospital here. Very droll, eh?"

"Very," Penny agreed, as they hefted her bags and trudged up to the large, shingled frame house that stood facing the sea at the top of the bluff. "Quite a place by the looks of it! Where are the children?"

"It's huge—I show it all to you later," Sonya said. "And they are on the beach with Toby. This you have to see." She led Penny to an enormous living room whose huge windows looked out over the calm waters of Nantucket Sound, and beyond it to a study with a tiled floor and French windows opening out on to a wooden patio that led down to a small beach. She opened the door a crack and beckoned. "Come and look at this."

Penny peered out and took in the scene: her granddaughter sat enthroned on a miniature deck chair, serenely surveying the handiwork of her brother and grandfather. Clad in a frilly pink sunsuit, she was round, small and gorgeous, with golden curls that glittered in the sun and enormous blue eyes set in a miniature of her mother's finely chiseled face. Her twin, in marked contrast, was tall and thin as a string bean, with his grandfather's knoblike head, round face and button nose. His eyes were equally round and of an indeterminate hazel, and his hair was Penny's mouse brown. Marcus was a remarkably plain child. He and his grandfather, who, clad in a black and white striped terrycloth robe and a shapeless digging hat pulled down over his ears, looked like a very seedy Arab, were in the process of building a very elaborate sandcastle.

Toby's deep voice wafted to them on the breeze. "Having now completed William I's White Tower, we will now proceed to the outer fortifications."

"William I, 1066 and all that," Marcus chanted, with a triumphant glare at his sister.

"Precisely," Toby agreed. "The outer fortifications were mainly erected by Henry III, you may recall."

"Henry III," Marcus parroted, energetically shovelling wet sand into a plastic pail. "Dates?"

"Good God," Penny said faintly. "He's only two and a half! How long has this been going on?"

"Ever since father got here. Marcus, he do not forget anything he hears once. It is frightening, he is so precocious. What it will be like when he starts to read for himself I cannot imagine," his mother muttered.

Mala's eyes, along with her attention, had started to wander and she spotted Penny peering through the window; with a delighted grin she shot out of her chair, arms extended, and trotted toward the wooden steps. "Grandma!" she proclaimed, hurling herself at Penny's legs. "Grandma's here." Penny hefted her up for a hug and a kiss as Toby and Marcus turned toward them. Toby beamed benignly and advanced upon them. "Ah, there you are at last! We've been building the Tower of London while we waited, but we were just about to go to Craigville for a swim. Are you up to joining us after your trip?"

"What's wrong with one right here?" Penny demanded. "No crowds."

"The beach here shelves much too sharply; not suitable for the children," Toby said severely. "Craigville, being so flat, is perfect for them."

"That's only half the story," Sonya said, *sotto voce*, in Penny's ear. "You'll see."

Mala extended a gracious hand to Toby. "We go swim now, grandpa." she stated. Like the ballerina after whom she was named, she was a female of few words.

"Certainly. We will go right away," Toby said, taking her firmly out of Penny's arms.

"Aren't you going to say hello and give me a kiss?" Penny demanded of Marcus, who had been hanging back eyeing her uncertainly.

He nodded and in turn hurled himself at her and was lifted, his thin sand-covered arms hugging her fiercely around the neck as an equally sandy kiss was planted on her cheek. "If you go on growing at this rate you'll soon be lifting *me* up to give me a kiss," Penny said, kissing him back. If Toby had his preferences, so had she.

Marcus gave her a delighted grin and shot a triumphant glance at his unheeding sister. Over Penny's shoulder his mother wiped his runny nose absentmindedly with a tissue and said, "I don't think Marcus ought to go in, father. He seems to be starting a cold."

"Nonsense!" Toby trumpeted, leading the procession into the house. "Salt water is good for colds."

"I think I'll pass up the swim, too," Penny said firmly.

"Marcus and I will watch the rest of you."

"And I don't think I'll go in either," Sonya added. "Maybe we can go and do something else and come back later to pick you up."

There was a short period of hurly-burly while Mala was changed into a frilly blue swimsuit, while her grandfather donned his swimming trunks, and the children were installed in their safety seats in the back of the big station wagon. As Marcus was strapped into his he began to chant, "Charonea, 338. Try and remember that there date. At Issus in year 333, Alexander made the Persians flee." He kept up the chant all the way to the Craigville Beach parking lot—which, mercifully, was a very short distance.

"This performance you have to see," Sonya murmured as Toby and Mala were disgorged and wandered off onto the crowded beach. Penny watched with fascination. First Toby shrugged out of his decrepit robe, which he carefully spread out on the sand and placed Mala in the middle of while he piled towels around her. He buckled her into her swim-wings, removed both their shoes, pretended to put his digging hat on her golden curls, which sent her off into gales of laughter, then offered her his hand with a bow. The incongruous pair then sauntered off, hand in hand toward the water. Toby seemed oblivious to the heads that turned towards them—although Penny noted with amusement he had straightened up from his normal scholar's slouch—as Mala smiled and waved a regal hand at her audience, for all the world like royalty practising for an official parade.

"They go through this performance twice a day without fail," Sonya remarked. "I'm thinking of following them and passing the hat." She turned her attention to Marcus, who had fallen silent and was beginning to look a little sorry for himself. "Well, how about a little treat, eh? To make up for not being able to go swimming? What would you like to do? Shall we look for some little flags to put on your lovely sand castle?"

"The Tower of London," he corrected. His little round face screwed up in thought. "For a treat I would like to go to Ronald Mcdonald's and have a Coke, a Big Mac, and French fries— *two* lots of fries."

"But, darling, that will spoil your supper," his mother protested.

"That will *be* my supper," he said. "I'll have some ice cream with Mala later, if you like."

Penny heaved a vast sigh of relief. "The treat's on me," she said. "Thank God, he's a completely normal child after all! I was beginning to have my doubts."

Chapter 2

Penny was a strong believer in getting over jet lag fast, and to that end and against her usual no-pills-except-aspirin policy, had taken a couple of sleeping pills which had zonked her out so efficiently that she did not surface until after eleven o'clock the next morning. She awoke feeling completely revitalized, took a quick shower in the guest bathroom that stood between her room, overlooking the ocean, and Toby's, then dressed and descended to see what the family was up to. She found them at the table having an early lunch.

"Alex is coming in by plane from Newark at twelve-thirty," Sonya explained, "and we usually go out to the airport to meet him. Father wants to go to the beach, so we're having a snack now so that they all can digest it and still have time for a dip before Alex gets here. Would you care for some real breakfast or will soup and a sandwich do?"

"That'll do fine—with coffee, lots of coffee. How's Marcus?" Penny cast a critical eye at her grandson who was sniffing loudly between each bite of his sandwich.

"Still dripping," Sonya said. "And now Mala seems to be starting, but I don't suppose a quick dip will do her any harm.

We may as well all go to the beach and then go directly from there to Barnstable Airport."

"I could stay here and keep an eye on Marcus if you'd rather he didn't go out," Penny volunteered.

"I want to see the planes," Marcus said between sniffs. "And I want to tell Daddy about my Tower of London."

"And that, said Christopher Robin, is *that*," said Toby, suddenly surfacing from the local paper in which his nose had been buried. "Stop fussing about the boy. If there's anything wrong with him his father, presumably, will fix him up." He chuckled grimly. "Would you believe we've made the local social page?"

"*What*?" Penny gaped at him.

He referred back to the paper and read out, between chuckles, "'Doctor and Mrs. Alexander Spring and family are summering in the Hyannisport home of Dr. Clarkson, where they have been joined by Mrs. Spring's father, Sir Tobias Glendower, the famous English archaeologist and detective. The family party will soon be augmented by Dame Penelope Spring, Dr. Spring's mother, also noted for her activities in crime detection'—ooh, I like that 'also noted'!"

"How the hell did they get hold of that?" she gasped.

"Oh, dear! I'm afraid that's probably my fault," Sonya said, wiping away Mala's milk mustache. "Dr. Clarkson's daughter is a reporter on the local paper. She let me in when we first arrived and showed me around. When she asked me questions about our plans I did not think of this. I think she only is afraid we fill the house with noisy parties, so I tell her about you. Was that wrong?"

"Oh, no, it doesn't matter—I hope." Penny said uneasily. "Nobody reads that stuff anyway."

After the obligatory half-hour-after-eating wait, the usual changing and loading-up-the-car routine was gone through, although this time on the short ride to the beach they were spared Marcus' "date chant."

"Make it a quick one, father, we don't have much time," Sonya instructed, as they found an empty space and began to spread out their paraphernalia. "And I think the sun is about to go in—it looks as if we might be in for some rain." Indeed there were some dark-looking nimbus clouds starting to roll in from the east. Toby grunted and departed leisurely with Mala.

"How about building another castle here?" Penny said to Marcus, who had slumped down and was aimlessly digging his plastic spade into the sand.

He shook his head. "I don't feel like it." And when his mother had settled on her beach mat he nestled up to her and put his head in her lap. She stroked the mouse-colored hair that was standing up in spikes on his round head. "What is it?"

"I don't feel good," he muttered, wriggling frantically.

She felt his forehead. "He does seem a bit hot." She looked at Penny. "What do you think?" Penny felt it. "Yes, I'd say he does have a fever. Why are you wriggling so, dear? Do you want to go to the bathroom?"

"My back itches and I can't reach it to scratch," he complained.

His mother hoisted up his long-sleeved T-shirt and looked at his long pale back covered with freckles. "He is so fair skinned he just freckles up and never browns at all," she muttered. "Yes, there. It looks as if he's been bitten by something. Mosquitoes maybe?"

Penny peered at the spots Sonya's long slender finger was indicating and her heart sank. "Um, I could be wrong but that looks like chicken pox to me."

"Chicken pox? What is that?" Sonya said.

They were diverted by a piercing wail wafting over the sands and looked up to see Toby stumbling in frantic haste towards them, clutching Mala tightly; she was screaming her head off. As he came up to them his round blue eyes were panic-stricken. "Something is seriously wrong with Mala," he bellowed. "No sooner did we get into the water than she started to cry like this.

We must *do* something!" He dumped her in Sonya's lap and stood back. "She says her spot hurts."

Mala shut her mouth in mid-wail, looked up at her mother, teardrops as big as dimes clinging to her long golden lashes, and with a becoming pout pointed importantly to a single pink blotch marring her golden-brown thigh.

"Does it itch?" Penny demanded. Mala nodded solemnly. "Oh, dear, then they probably are both starting it. Toby, I think it's chicken pox. Sonya doesn't know the word in English. Can you tell her?"

He sought for it in Russian, but failing to come up with it switched to French, "La varicelle est la même que 'chicken pox,'" he informed his daughter.

"Oh, now I understand. Is that serious?" Sonya demanded.

"Not serious, but uncomfortable and very infectious," Penny replied. "Haven't you had it? Not when you were little?"

"Me—no I have nothing," Sonya said proudly. "I am always very healthy."

"Well, that's too bad. It hits grown-ups harder," Penny muttered. "How about you, Toby?"

"The only thing I ever had as a child was whooping cough—four times," he confided.

She was momentarily diverted. "That's impossible!"

"So I've been told. Nevertheless it's what *I* had," he returned. "The thing is what's to be done for the twins?"

"Well, first, you two better let me have both of them. I've had it, so they can't infect me. Haven't they had shots for it?"

"Alex, he give them shots for everything I think," Sonya said, stroking her son's head. "But is not serious so I don't mind if I get it from them."

"But with adults they often get herpes with it," Penny said. "And that's painful."

"*Herpes!*" Sonya looked at her in horror.

"Oh no, not *that* kind," Penny said hastily. "Herpes zoster. Quite different. Shingles is the common name." She looked at her watch. "Alex is due in half an hour, so I suggest we pack up here and get down to the airport and see what he thinks. I could be wrong."

At the airport she insisted they all stay in the car while she met the plane. "We don't want to start an epidemic. Just park over there where they can see the planes come in and I'll be back as soon as possible."

She watched impatiently as the small Continental Beechcraft touched down and rolled to a stop right beside the terminal and the tall figure of Alexander Spring emerged, almost bent double, from the tiny open hatch and its built-in steps. He spotted her, grinned and waved, then looked around for the rest of his family. "Don't tell me those lazy beggars have sent you all alone on airport pickup," he called as he collected his soft travel bag from the trolley beside the plane and loped toward her. As he kissed and hugged her, she said, "We've a bit of a crisis. Nothing serious, but I think the twins are coming down with chicken pox, and neither Sonya or Toby have had it. They're all waiting for you outside in the station wagon. Until they've been checked, they'd better stay apart from the rest of the world. Have the twins had the shot for chicken pox?"

He groaned softly. "Oh damn! No. It's the one shot they *didn't* have. I'm not all that keen on it because I'm not sure how good it is, so I didn't give it to them."

"Well, I could be wrong, but, remembering when you had it as a child, the spots on Marcus' back look remarkably the same to me."

They hurried out to the car; Sonya and Toby emerged to greet them and the twins strained at their seat belts and squealed with excitement. "Well, this is one for the books, my darling," Alex said, kissing his wife hungrily. "I'd better take a look at our bundles of joy." He groped in his pocket for a stethoscope and climbed in between the car seats, where the twins immediately clutched him in strangling embraces. "Whoa there, kids!

One at a time. Now let Daddy have a good look at you," he instructed.

"Mala's spot is on her right thigh," Toby said anxiously, peering in, as Penny and Sonya exchanged grins behind his back.

Alex studied the spot her chubby finger was indicating, tickled her in the ribs, sending her off into gales of laughter, and transferred his attention to Marcus. When he emerged with a "I'll be right back, so don't you two go anywhere," he closed the car door and said quietly, "It's chicken pox right enough and Marcus has already some rales in his chest and a fever. By tonight he'll be thoroughly miserable and Mala won't be far behind." He looked up at the sky as if seeking inspiration, then looked searchingly at Sonya. "Not pregnant, are you?"

She let out a gurgle of laughter. "Believe me, if I were you'd be the first to know. Why?"

"Because if you were I could not give you a shot and I think you should have one as soon as possible. Then, even if you caught it from them, the shot would cut down the risk of shingles. You know, I think the best thing to do is to go back to the house, pack whatever stuff you need, and we'll drive right back to New York. Then I can keep a close eye on things and the twins will be better off in their own rooms with their own things around them. They are going to be pretty miserable and hard to handle for the next few days, but by next weekend they should be just about through the worst of it and then I could drive you all back again. It beats sitting cooped up in that wretched little plane anyway where I can hardly sit up straight. And once in New York I can give you a shot immediately."

"You think this is all necessary?" Sonya asked. "So tiring for you after a hard week! You've only just got here and you haven't eaten. Though I could help you drive back," she added, hopefully.

"No, that's all right, darling, no need for that," Alex said, going a little pale. "I'm as fresh as a daisy, honest! The drive will be a breeze, and if we can get off in the next hour or so we can be back in New York by dark. The twins will flake out and sleep most of the way, like they always do, and we can get them treated and right into bed when we get home."

"But you haven't eaten!" she persisted.

"Ma can rustle me up something quickly, while you pack." He grinned meaningfully at Penny. "She and Toby will have to soldier on and hold the fort here until we get back. Part of the deal with Clarkson was that we never leave the house empty— not even overnight," he explained. "Something to do with their insurance. As you probably have noticed the house is stuffed with antiques and there's some clause that insists on a resident security guard if there is no one sleeping there."

Penny took the hint and forebore to volunteer to accompany them as she had been about to do. "Shouldn't Toby have a shot too? He hasn't had it either."

"I'm not having any damn shot," Toby growled. "Lot of rubbish at my age!" Which settled that, at least for the moment.

They piled back into the station wagon and Penny squeezed in between the twins in the back seat, leaving the front to the three tall family members. Marcus began an involved account of his Tower of London that lasted most of the way back to Hyannisport.

The next hour was sheer pandemonium, as Sonya rushed around, Marcus in tow, packing up, and Penny cooked a quick mushroom omelette and toast for her ravenous son. The only quiet members were Toby and Mala, who had settled by one of the windows looking out to sea. She had gone to sleep in his lap as he gazed lugubriously out at the sparkling ocean.

The station wagon was repacked, Sonya gabbling last-minute information about the house to Penny, the twins again strapped into their seats as the caravan prepared to depart. "You'll look after my tower till I'm back?" Marcus queried anxiously, his voice now hoarse.

"I'll guard it with my very life," his grandfather assured him.

"And the first thing we'll build when you get back will be the Bloody Tower."

"Ooh, good!" Marcus wriggled in ecstasy. "That's where everybody got murdered."

"Well, sorry about this turn-up, Ma," Alex said, firmly getting into the driver's seat and edging Sonya over. "But we'll keep in daily touch and, if all goes well, we'll be back next weekend. Hope you can amuse yourselves till then—maybe you'll find a nice mystery to solve!"

"God forbid!" she said. "Take care on the road now!" And waved them out of sight. As they disappeared around the curve of the dirt road, she said with a sigh, "Well, that was a very short family reunion. Not quite what I expected or hoped for."

"It won't be for long and everything has its compensations," Toby said to her surprise. He was busily stuffing and lighting up his pipe, so that he was soon enveloped in his familiar blue aura.

"Like what?" she demanded, as they trudged up the steps back to the house.

"Well, for one thing I don't have to sneak around corners to have a pipe, and I can get on with the notes for chapter six," he returned.

"Why should you have to sneak out to smoke? Surely Sonya is used to it and doesn't mind."

"It's the principle of the thing," he said stiffly. "Neither Sonya nor Alex smoke and now you've given it up again, so it's not for *me* to set a bad example for the children. I try to do it when they are not around."

She was amused. "I don't think either of them are quite at the age to rush out and buy a pack of cigarettes just because you light up, but I see your point. Very thoughtful of you."

He grunted and made for his room. "It's back to work for me. I'll knock off about six and then we can have a drink and go out to dinner somewhere. No sense in you slaving just for the two of us. What are you going to do?"

"I don't quite know, but thanks for asking," she said, trying not to sound sarcastic, as he disappeared from view. She packed the dishwasher and tidied the kitchen and then decided to go back to the beach. The earlier rain clouds had disappeared from view and again the sun shone serenely on the sparkling sea; it was too good a day to waste. She gathered her things into a large beach bag, selected a paperback from the bookcase in the study and called up the stairs, "I'm going back to Craigville Beach. I'll be back by six—see you then." There was a muffled shout of acknowledgement.

Thankful they had had the foresight to think of a second car, she drove the short distance to the beach, but this time decided on its far end toward Osterville, which she thought would be less crowded. It was, if marginally so, less full, so she found an empty spot, spread out her beach mat, applied suntan oil liberally all over her plump self and then, using the beach bag as a pillow, stretched out and basked, watching the wheeling gulls in the cloudless sky above. After a while she closed her eyes and savored the sounds of summer.

This was the unchanging Cape of her childhood summers, the Cape she loved: the gentle sound of the waves on the sandy shore, the muted murmur of voices and music around her, the cries of the shore birds, the drowsy throb of an airplane on its way to the outer islands. The rest of Cape Cod may have changed out of all recognition, but this had remained the same as it always had been, would always be, she hoped. Her mind drifted back to those childhood summers in Chatham, when she had so often lain like this. She was so transported in time that, if she opened her eyes, she felt she would see her adored, romantically minded father, after whom Marcus had been named, sitting by her on the sand, gazing dreamily out to sea, with her admirably practical mother sitting on the other side of him, endlessly busy with some handiwork. How her father would have adored the beautiful Mala, she thought wistfully, and so thinking drifted off into sleep.

When she awoke she was chilled, for a brisk onshore breeze had sprung up; the sun was perceptibly lower on the horizon and a thin haze of clouds scudded across its golden disk. She sat up and put on her beach robe, hugging it close and rubbing her chilled legs, as she looked around at the fast emptying beach. She was just about to start her own packing up when she saw something that transfixed her and started her heart pounding.

Coming toward her was Toby's unmistakable tall figure and he was flanked by two shorter, stockier figures in the dark blue uniform of the Barnstable police. Visions of a crashed station wagon and mangled bodies flashed out of her vivid imagination. "Oh God! There must have been a road accident," she muttered through chattering teeth. "They must be killed, injured. They're coming to break it to me."

Her knees were so weak with fear that when she got up she staggered and almost fell, but was amazed when Toby waved cheerfully at her and grinned. "Ah, there you are! We've had a devil of a time finding you, but I think you know both of these officers? Chief of Police Birnie and Detective-sergeant Robert Dyke? Amazing, what?—after all these years. They came to see me and when they heard you were here, naturally, they wanted you in on it too. So here we are."

She looked dazedly at the trio. "So it's not Alex? Not an accident?"

"An accident? Good heavens, no! It's a murder," Toby exclaimed, his blue eyes alight with interest. "Chief Birnie here is very keen for us to take a look at it—very odd, very."

"A murder?" She was still in a state of shock. "What's it got to do with us?"

The unfortunately named Ernie Birnie eyed her warily, for their former working relationship held few fond memories for him. "It's like this. We don't usually get a really weird kind of murder case around here. Last one I had a hand in was the body in the bog that you were mixed up with. Now we've got another weirdy."

"Another body in a cranberry bog?" she queried. "So?"

"No, no. Better let me," Toby said to the floundering chief. "There has been a murder at the local community college. One of the lecturers called. . . ?" He looked for help to Robert Dyke, who said promptly, "Clara Bacon, sir. A very longtime teacher there. She was found sitting at a desk in one of the classrooms this morning. She'd been shot in the back."

"And she wasn't there two days ago," Chief Birnie cut in.

Penny was getting her scattered wits together. "So she was shot sometime since then I suppose. I still don't see. . . ."

"But she's been dead for over a *month* and probably longer than that," Birnie persisted. "The doc says she's been like . . . well . . . preserved—a condition he calls *adipocere*," he pronounced all four syllables of the odd word gingerly.

"I've *read* about *adipocere* but I'd be most interested to see an actual example of it," Toby said quickly. "And, of course, that means that someone must have deliberately placed the body in the classroom."

"It's a real stumper," the chief said in deep gloom. "I just can't get over it."

"So I told the chief here we'd take a look at the body before it is moved and see if we can come up with any bright suggestions. Are you up to it? They'd like us to go right on up there."

"But . . . but . . . ," Penny stuttered, "We're just here for a family vacation."

"We're only going to take a *look*," he urged. "And the family won't be back for at least a week. What else did you have in mind to do?"

Robert Dyke looked at her in appeal, his snub-nosed face solemn. "It really would be a great favor, Dr. Spring—I mean it's the oddest thing *I've* ever seen and she was such a harmless, nice old girl. It sort of sticks in my craw what was done to her."

"She was a very nice *lady*," his chief reproved. "And a very good teacher, too. Took a course with her myself."

Looking at their resolute faces Penny gave in. "Oh, very well," she muttered, gathering up her belongings. "Just a look then. But hear me, Toby! If it goes beyond that, this was *your* idea not mine, and don't you forget it!"

Chapter 3

"How on earth did they know we were here?" Penny demanded of Toby as they rode in the back seat of the police chief's car with Robert Dyke at the wheel. Chief Birnie, sitting in the passenger seat in front, turned around, "I was just reading about you in the paper when the call from the college came in this morning," he informed her solemnly. "After I'd seen what we were up against here I took it for a real sign—an omen. Dr. Clarkson's my doctor, you see."

"Oh!" she said, somewhat baffled by this convoluted logic. She turned her attention to Robert Dyke. "I thought you were going to be an archaeologist," she said accusingly.

He grinned at her in the rearview mirror. "After all the trouble I got into in Israel I thought that was a bit too dangerous for me, so I became a policeman instead. So far not half as dangerous and uses the same deductive methods, right?" He chuckled at their bemused expressions and continued. "Actually, it's a lot simpler than that. Jobs in archaeology are few and far between, particularly around these parts, unless you are *real* good—and I knew I'd never be that. Then I married a local girl and we both wanted to stay on the Cape. So I took my associate's degree here at the community college, then finished off my B.A. in law enforcement and criminology at Boston University, put in a stint at the Police Academy, came back here, and am living happily ever after." He grinned sideways at Ernie Birnie who was looking equally bemused.

"What subjects did Clara Bacon teach?" Toby asked. "And was she a Miss or a Mrs.?"

"Mrs.—a widow," Birnie replied. "I believe she was a Crocker before she married, not a local Crocker though. She taught geology, genealogy, colonial architecture, Indians of the Northeastern U.S., and there was one other—do you recall it, Bob?"

The policemen searched their memories. "Massachusetts maritime history," Dyke finally came up with.

Toby was gaping at them. "How positively extraordinary! I mean, none of those has the faintest connection with any of the others!"

"She only taught two *credit* courses," the chief continued, "Introduction to Geology and the Indians course—the rest were community services courses and noncredit. All of them were in the continuing education section, not the regular day school. I took her colonial architecture course—got an old house, y'see. Very interesting it was, too. We went all over the Cape looking at old houses."

Never having emerged from the sheltered climes of Oxford, with its superspecialist teachers and one-on-one tutorial system, this was pure gibberish to Toby and he was totally at sea. He looked helplessly at Penny for a translation, but all she said was, "Later, I'll explain it all later. It would take too long now."

They had just turned off Route 132 and had entered the ring road circling the college. Robert Dyke slowed down to negotiate the speed bumps that straddled the tarmac at frequent intervals. "We're heading for the North building," he said. "This is the administration building we're passing now; next building up there is the library, then the South classrooms and after them the North." They looked to their left to see the uniform facades of the pleasantly mellowed brick buildings encircling the rocky knoll from which the college looked down upon the large parking lots that were on the opposite side of the ring road. "She was found in the dungeon on the ground floor of North."

This was too much for Toby. "This college has a *dungeon*! Whatever for?"

Birnie glared reprovingly at his young colleague. "No, no! That's just a nickname the students have for that classroom. Y'see, the architect who designed this place got a little carried away on looks and wasn't all that practical and, well, some of the classrooms aren't up to snuff. This particular one, NG10 I think it is, doesn't have any windows at all. The teachers and the students hate it because it's cold in the winter, hot in summer, and stuffy all the time—that's how it got its name. It's not often used—which may be why the body was put there."

They drew up before a long flight of concrete steps and got out. "Who found the body?" Penny asked as they toiled up the steep steps.

"Old Sam Nickerson," Birnie replied. "Used to be a Barnstable policeman but retired on a disability—his back went. Now he's a security guard here. Shook him up something fierce I can tell you. I left him on guard, so you'll see for yourself."

They went in through a double set of double doors that faced another flight of stairs leading upward; to their right were rest rooms and a long featureless corridor stretched to their left, its left-hand side studded at intervals with closed doors. A gray-haired man in uniform was leaning against the cream-colored concrete block wall of the corridor, beside a black metal ash can, its tray piled with butts. He was puffing hard on another cigarette and his long, hatchetlike face was as gray as the air surrounding him. He straightened up with a sigh of relief when he saw them. "Thought you were never going to get back, Ernie," he said as introductions were made. He looked meaningfully at the dark blue door on which NG10 had been scribbled lopsidedly in chalk. "I ain't going back in there—can't face it again. Can't I go home now? My back's killing me."

"Just hang on a bit longer, Sam, we won't be long, but Sir Tobias and Dr. Spring may have a few questions for you. Then you can go," Birnie said, as Robert opened the door, switched on the neon lights that flickered unwillingly and then glowed with a steady humming glare as he beckoned them in. Penny followed after Toby and recoiled as she saw what sat at the desk in the near corner—the effect was horrifyingly macabre. The small plump woman, her hair a sandy-gray, her bloated face a waxy-white, seemed to be leaning forward, peering out of clouded sightless eyes at the empty student chairs of the classroom. Her right hand rested on a small pile of books on the desk, its index finger pointed toward the blank blackboard on the corridor wall. The dark airless room stank of dank mold and the sickly sweet beginning of decaying flesh. "Oh my God!" she whispered.

The more resolute Toby was at the desk, where Robert was pointing out the entrance wound in the back and the exit wound in the murdered woman's chest. "Must have been a high-caliber bullet that went clean through," Dyke said with distaste. "To keep the body from slumping it was tied to the chair. It's really the *sickest* thing I've come across."

"The *adipocere* is certainly well-established all over the body by the looks of it," Toby muttered. "Quite remarkable."

"What exactly is *adipocere*?" Penny said in a strangled voice.

Toby looked back at her, his eyes steely. "According to Simpson's textbook on forensic medicine it is a stiffening and swelling of body fats which occurs occasionally when a body has been either buried in very moist soil or immersed in clear cold water—like a well, for instance—for a long time. In England it usually takes five or six months to develop. But there are circumstances like the sun's heat on the moist surface, or rain, that can speed the process up. Simpson had one case, I believe, where it occurred after only a month. I've no idea what the timetable might be in America."

"But surely she can't have been dead *that* long!" Penny protested. "I mean, five months or more? *Somebody* would have reported her missing before that, somebody would have raised the alarm!" She looked accusingly at Robert Dyke whose young face was furrowed with concern. "Nobody reported her missing to us," he said. "And, though we haven't as yet got too much in the way of facts from the college, we gathered that the last time she was seen here was in the third week of May, which was the final week of the spring semester. I gather she never applied to teach for the summer semester and someone said they thought she had gone to Florida. The chief may have more details on that. You see, she wasn't full-time faculty, just a part-time continuing ed teacher, and they sign contracts on a semester-to-semester basis. Once the semester is over their connection with the college is finished, unless they sign on for the next semester, and there would be no occasion for the college to check on them."

"Granted all that, but *someone* on Cape Cod—a friend, a tradesman, a business office—must have noticed her absence!" she cried.

He shrugged, "Well, all that we'll have to find out. I know it's odd. The whole damn business is odd."

"I think I'll go and try to find out some more details from Chief Birnie," she said. The room was getting to her and she was anxious to escape. She went out into the corridor where the chief and Sam Nickerson were in quiet conference with another uniformed policeman.

Left alone, Robert looked at Toby. "Got any ideas or suggestions?"

Toby filled and lit his pipe in bland defiance of the large NO SMOKING sign above the light switch. "A few, which I am sure must equally have occurred to you. I imagine it will be extremely difficult in these circumstances for whoever does the autopsy to establish an exact time of death, place of death, or even give you any idea about the weapon used, if the bullet is not lodged in the body—and I don't think it is. So that leaves you with only the 'why' to work with. Find that and it might conceivably indicate the 'who.' But you have a problem within a problem here. Who, so long after the actual murder, went to the trouble of resurrecting the body and bringing it to your notice in this bizarre fashion? My instinct is that it could *not* have been the murderer, unless he or she is a complete psychopath with a guilt complex who *wants* to be caught. But I don't think so. Whoever did this wanted the body to be found— though, by its situation, not *immediately*. I also think that where and how it was found was intended to convey some message— the 'teaching' image, the books, the finger pointing to the board. . . ."

"But there was nothing *on* the board," Robert broke in. "It's absolutely clean. Not even an erased mark on it."

"Umm, I wonder. All right to touch anything?"

"Yes. It's all been photographed and dusted for prints, for what *that* was worth," the detective said glumly. "There are thousands of them. It would take a lifetime to sort them all out and track them down."

"How about the light switch?"

"Just Sam Nickerson's on top of a lot of smudges."

"Hmm," Toby reached over and pulled on the metal ring of the rolled-up wall map above the board, which revealed itself as a large-scale map of Cape Cod. "What if she was meant to be pointing at something on this?" He whipped out his small steel pocket tape measure and gingerly extended it from the pointing finger until it touched the map. "Does that convey anything to you?"

The young policeman peered at it. "The town of Dennis— hard to say whether it's indicating land or sea. Let's see, what's on that bit of coast?" He pondered. "Only thing I can think of is a town beach called Crowe's Pasture. But the map wasn't down." Even as he spoke the spring roller let out a faint squeak and the map tidily rolled itself up again.

"Maybe it *was*," Toby said drily.

"Worth looking into," Robert said, busily scribbling in his notebook, as Toby went on. "Then there are the books, maybe they can tell us something." He cocked his head sideways and read off the titles: "Strahler's *Geologist's View of Cape Cod*, a genealogy of the Howes family, an atlas of the North American Indians, *Wrecks of Old Cape Cod*, and, good heavens, *Fell's Complete Guide to Buried Treasure on Land and Sea*. What an extraordinary collection! Convey anything to you?"

"Not a thing, other than, with the exception of colonial architecture, they represent every course she taught. I did take a look at them earlier and they're all her own copies and are not from the college library. She was a great one for bringing in books from her own library to her classes."

Toby straightened up. "Then that means whoever put her here must have had access to her house. Would it be possible for me to take these and examine them in detail? They may yield something."

"We'll have to clear it with the chief, but I guess so. You think whoever did this selected them with a purpose and just didn't grab a handful to prop up the hand?" Robert sounded doubtful.

"Either way it seems to underline the importance of the pointing finger," Toby retaliated. "And I doubt if you grab a handful of books from a bookcase that you'd come up with quite such a varied selection which apparently covers so many different subjects. Which brings me to another point. How did the person responsible get the body and the books here? Surely not up those steep steps we came in by. Is there another way into the building with a ramp or something similar? I can't imagine anyone—unless they are supernaturally strong—*carrying* the body for any great distance."

Robert's interest quickened. "Yes, there is. There's a driveway off the ring road that goes up the hill between the North and South buildings, and there's a handicap ramp built from it that leads to doors on the ground floor at the other end of this building. State law made them put in the ramps all over several years ago. Would you like to see?"

Toby's eyes had narrowed behind his round glasses. "Yes. Indeed that does give me an idea. In fact . . . have these floors been polished recently?"

Robert shook his head. "No. As a matter of fact that's how Sam happened to open this room up. The summer semester ended last week and after it they start cleaning the place up for the fall semester which begins in mid-September. Because of all the cutbacks in staff at the college, their cleaning crew has been cut to the bone and they've just been working their way gradually through the college, cleaning and polishing the floors of the corridors and classrooms. This building and this particular corridor are the very last to be done. That's why they were opening up the classrooms for it."

"Then we may not be too late," Toby said. "I think I may know how the body was brought here and we may still find some traces. Lead on! But step carefully and stop if I say so." They went out to see Penny in solemn conclave with the three uniformed men, but turned left along the corridor away from them.

Toby pointed at the two halves of a red door that had been flattened back against their respective corridor walls. "Are these kept open or shut?"

"Shut," Robert replied. "I imagine they're open now because of the imminent floor polishing. The doors cut down on the noise from the staircases and at this end, because that part of the passage and entranceway is the only area of the building where smoking is allowed, so it is packed with smokers during

41

the class breaks. It's another reason why NG10 was so hated by everybody—it's the only classroom beyond those doors and the noise level in that area is terrible. There's another set of doors like this at the other end of the corridor."

"I see," Toby mused, scanning the floor ahead of him. "So they would have presented two more obstacles for our person-with-the-body to negotiate." He froze and pointed, "Ah! Just as I had anticipated. You see those wheel marks?"

Robert followed his pointing finger and they both crouched down as Toby went on, "There are two sets—the first one more clearly defined than the second, which is very faint. The first set being the incoming one when the wheels were damper and dirtier and heavier than the outgoing. And, unless I am completely astray, these are the marks of a wheelchair—which would be the obvious answer to carting in a heavy, damp body. They run along this side of the corridor, so let's follow them on the other side and see if they end up where we hope."

Robert's face was aglow with excitement. "We'll have to check to see if there was a disabled person attending any of the classes down here, of course, but I think you're right. What a break!" They followed the almost invisible tracks to the second set of double doors and outside, but there on the concrete ramp the trail vanished. "Now if only someone spotted a car here either last night or the night before," he breathed, "we'll *really* be in business. Let's go tell the chief—we'll have to get these photographed right away."

As they came up to the group in the corridor Sam Nickerson was saying, his voice now almost a whine, "Can't I get out of here now?"

"Just a second, Mr. Nickerson," Robert burst out, "Were you on night duty here the last two nights?"

They all looked at him in surprise. "I don't do nights during vacation time," he answered. "Let's see, that'd be Ken Mayo. Why?"

"Because I think we have discovered how the body was

brought in," Robert announced and rattled off the explanation.

The scene dissolved into a flurry of activity, as the officer was sent to radio for the return of the photographic and fingerprint teams. "Send for the meat wagon too," Birnie called after him. "We've got to get the body out of here and up to Boston for the autopsy pronto. With the M.E. away on vacation I can't depend on his stand-in for an important job like this. Okay, Sam, you can go on home now, but try and get hold of Ken and have him here first thing tomorrow, eh? I want to see both of you. And if he saw a car up there any time during the past two nights have him call me right away at the station. But I want to talk to him anyway about the classroom doors. You say you found this one unlocked this morning," he nodded at NG10, "but I know they're all supposed to be kept locked in vacation time."

Sam looked uncomfortable. "Okay, soon as I get home and get me feet up I'll give Ken a shout." He shuffled away in the wake of the policeman.

Birnie turned his attention back to Toby. "That was very helpful of you, Sir Tobias." He sounded impressed. "But we're going to be tied up here in a lot of technical stuff for the next few hours and I don't want to keep you hanging around—unless you want to see how we operate. I was telling Dr. Spring, I'd have all the interviews with the continuing ed people she's asked for set up by tomorrow. Not that it will be that easy, because so many are off on vacation, but I'll do the best I can. There's nothing else for you to do here tonight so, for now, I thought I'd send you back home in my car with the other officer, if that's all right? I need Dyke here."

"Sir Tobias would like to take the books to examine them, if that's okay with you?" Robert spoke up, striking while the iron was hot.

Birnie pondered this. "I suppose so—though they *are* evidence, so you'll have to sign a receipt for them. You think they're important?"

"At this stage I have no idea." Toby was stiff. He looked over at Penny. "Do you want to go now?"

"Yes, I do," she said promptly. "I'd like to get out of here. Alex and the family should be in New York by now—they should be calling soon. I want to get back."

Toby turned back to Birnie. "One other thing. I'd very much like to see Mrs. Bacon's home. Have you examined that yet?"

"Haven't had time. We could fix that for tomorrow, after I'm through here," Birnie said with a resigned sigh. "I could have Bob Dyke pick you both up—say about nine?"

"No need, we have a car," Penny said. "I'll drive up and if Sir Tobias wants to go off with you, fine! It'll leave me free."

"Don't you want to see her house? I feel that may be very important." Toby was becoming querulous.

"We don't have much time before the family get back," she pointed out impatiently. "And if we continually go around in tandem we won't get half as much accomplished. No, you do your thing and I'll do mine. I cannot for the life of me understand why no one reported her missing all these months, and I damn well intend to find out. *That's* important also."

"Well, I don't want to rush you, but my technical team will be here any minute—they're just down the road—and I could use the officer, who'll be driving you back, here to help out."

She was momentarily diverted. "I thought your police station was down on North Street?"

"Oh, we moved out of that years ago," he said with some pride. "Got a brand new up-to-date facility just down here on Route 132. You'll have to see it for yourself when we get a breather. Real nice." He escorted them out and back to his car, as two squad cars and an ambulance drew up behind it. As they settled in the back of his car and took off, Toby looked inquiringly at her. "Shall we have him drop us off at a restaurant?"

"I don't know about you, but after all this I don't have much of an appetite. I need a drink, several drinks, and then I'll rustle

44

up something for us back at the house," she said. "Besides, I'm anxious to hear how things are in New York."

"Suits me," he rumbled. "We have a lot to talk over." They rode in silence for a while then he said softly, "Tell me, is it usual for a chief of police here to be so involved in a murder case? I don't recall last time even seeing the chief here."

She looked warningly at him and at the back of the driver's head. "I think it's a very personal matter," she murmured back. "He's very angry—he liked her. For that matter, so am I. According to everything I have heard so far she was a very nice woman and a dedicated teacher, whom everyone respected, and yet she's been dead for months and no one seems to have known or cared—except, perhaps, for whoever staged that ghastly spectacle back there. That really sticks in my craw, it *baffles* me!"

"Yes indeed," Toby said solemnly. "We are faced with a puzzle within a puzzle—we have here a classic conundrum."

Chapter 4

The New York call, when it came, brought confirmation and concern to Penny. Her son said tightly, "Well, we did the right thing. They're both in their beds and asleep now, but Marcus' fever was out of sight by the time we got in and Mala's spots fairly popped out on the way down and she was screaming her head off on arrival. We are in for a rough few days and I think I may have been overly optimistic about next weekend—we'll just have to see how it goes."

"Are you sure you don't need me to give Sonya a hand?" she queried.

"No, because if you come undoubtedly so will Toby, and he'd be at the greatest risk of getting and being hard hit by it *and* of being an infernal nuisance into the bargain. So, if you don't mind holding the fort at your end, that will be the greatest help to me."

"But once you go back to the office on Monday won't that be an awful lot for Sonya to cope with? Shouldn't you get in a nurse?" Penny fussed.

He snorted. "I don't think that will be necessary. I swear the entire Russian emigré colony in New York passes through this house, all willing and eager to babysit and sit at the feet of the divine Sonya. We have sad Slavic souls coming out of our ears—at this rate the kids will be bilingual by the age of four; as it is, even Mala knows more Russian than I do . . . ." There was a slight break and Penny could hear Sonya saying something in the background, then Alex went on, "Sonya says if any problems arise at the house you should get in touch with Dr. Clarkson's daughter at the *Cape Cod Times* and she will cope . . . ." A thin wail floated down the line. "Oops, there goes Mala again. I'd better go. Hope the weather stays good for you, and I'll keep you posted." The line went dead.

Wearily she hung up, and went off to relate the edited substance of the call to Toby, who was busily rooting through the medical books in Dr. Clarkson's study. He gave a distracted grunt, pronounced a perfunctory, "Poor little mites! I hope their father knows what he is doing," and added peevishly, "Can't find a damn thing about cases of *adipocere* in America. I wonder who the hell would know about it around here?"

"I'll leave you to it," she said with a yawn. "What with one thing and another it has been quite a day and my jet lag is back. Good night and happy hunting." She left him muttering to himself.

Another good night's sleep and a very substantial breakfast put her in a much better frame of mind and surcharged with new energy, so that she fairly pushed Toby—who had a tendency to morning dawdling—into the car and zigged in and out of the already thickening weekend traffic at a rate that elicited grumpy protest from her partner. A police car was already parked in the little bay off the college ring road in front of the administration building, that was separated from the road by an island sporting three tall flagpoles. The Stars and Stripes on the middle post, she noted, flew at half-mast. Chief Birnie and Robert Dyke were talking by the police car, and as she parked behind them Birnie came up, opened the door on her side, thrust a manilla folder into her hands, and declared, "I got the personnel file on

Clara Bacon out of the assistant dean—not easily. Here, you take a look at it for now, while we go off to the Bacon house. I'll get it back later, but there doesn't seem to be much in it. You'll find the dean in the continuing ed office up those steps. It's through that door and an inner door and straight ahead. She's a Miss Wanda Carlucci. We'll deliver Sir Tobias back to your place, right?

She tucked the folder into her capacious tote bag, nodded her thanks and assent, and puffed up the steep stone steps to the single glass door at the top, which gave upon a claustrophobically narrow passage with a solid metal door in its opposite wall. This, in turn, gave on to a slightly wider passage with a ladies' rest room on one side and a series of closed doors on the other. She persevered down it until she came to a high counter separating the business office from the passage. It was barren of life save for a small, dark-haired young woman who leaned against the inner side of the counter, worried apprehension evident on her thin, sharp-featured face, and before Penny could so much as get out a "How-do-you-do?" burst out, "I'm very sorry, Dr. Spring, but I'm afraid I can't be of any help to you at all. You see I've only been here three months. I never set eyes on the poor woman who was murdered. I tried to explain this to the police chief but he didn't seem to want to listen. The former assistant dean left at the end of the spring semester and is now in North Carolina, I believe. I could look in the files and give you her forwarding address, if that would be of any help."

Penny's heart sank. "How about the dean? Did he know Mrs. Bacon?"

"Well, yes, I expect so," Wanda Carlucci said reluctantly. "He's been here a very long time, but he's not here now, I'm afraid."

Penny fought down her impatience. "Then will you put me in touch with *him*; presumably he lives on the Cape?"

"Usually yes, of course, but not at the moment. He's on a camping vacation down in Mexico. Won't be back for three weeks. And I've no idea how to get in touch with him." The thin-faced woman looked down and plucked at a pile of folders with ill-disguised impatience, and it struck Penny that she was beginning to enjoy her unhelpful role and was eager to be rid of her.

"I'm afraid that just won't do," Penny stated, starting to bristle. "There has to be *someone* from the college who knew Mrs. Bacon and with whom you can put me in touch—*immediately*. Surely you must realize that the college is in for some very unpleasant publicity, so that the sooner this thing is cleared up the better? I think I had better talk directly to the president of the college. Would you get him for me, please?"

Wanda Carlucci recoiled, apprehension deepening into near panic. "Oh, I don't think that would help, the president has only been here six months himself, but . . ." she peered desperately down the corridor as if in search of inspiration. "There *is* someone who may be of help: our student guidance counselor, who has been here a long time. I *think* he is coming in this morning. You see on weekends there are very few people around here. . . ," she trailed off into a gasp of relief as a tall figure materialized at the other end of the long corridor and advanced toward them. "Why, here he is now! Washington, could you come here a second, please?" she called out.

The slim, elegantly dressed black man sauntered up to them, an expression of enquiry on his amiable face. "Washington, this is Dr. Penelope Spring," Wanda said, a pleading note in her shrill voice. "She is helping the Barnstable police with this awful murder of Mrs. Bacon. You knew her, didn't you? Anything you can tell Dr. Spring will be greatly appreciated. I have not been able to help her." She opened one of the files with finality and turned her back on them.

He looked steadily at Penny for a moment and then grinned widely as he held out a slim, long-fingered hand. "Why, of course, you're *the* Dr. Spring! I'm Washington Ford and very happy to meet you. I have heard so much about you. I'm a friend of the Dimolas, you see, and they sing your praises loud and clear."

Penny shook his hand with a little surge of relief. "Then I hope you can help me shed some light on this terrible affair."

"Anything I can. Why don't we go to my office?" He indicated a door in a raised area on the opposite side of the corridor from the main office and led the way up to his small sanctum, so packed with file cabinets that there was scarcely enough room for the desk and two chairs which stood on each side of it. He seated her politely in the visitor's chair and then took his own opposite her.

"Where would you like to start?" he asked.

"Anything and everything you can tell me," Penny said. "The circumstances are so bizarre it is hard to know where to begin. The thing that absolutely baffles and appalls me—apart from the fantastic depositing of her long-dead body in a college classroom—is how her absence was not reported or even noticed long before this."

He thought for a moment and then said reflectively, "So far as the college is concerned this is not as weird as it may seem. Perhaps my own relationship with Mrs. Bacon may give you an indication, and then I'll come back to this. She taught here in continuing education for nearly twenty years, I believe. I have been here for fifteen of them and yet all I saw of her, all I really *knew* of her were brief encounters on her teaching nights when I was the duty-officer on the desk out there, and those never went beyond polite chit-chat—the weather, the traffic, numbers in her classes, and so on. She was always perfectly pleasant, but also extremely impersonal; meticulous about checking her file for messages, getting her forms for materials to be copied and so on, but she never participated in any college affairs; never came to graduations, parties, or anything like that. That does not mean she was unfriendly, or even unusual. You see, most of the part-time lecturers do exactly the same thing: it is very rarely that we get to know them on a *personal* level. I did hear from the old assistant dean that Mrs. Bacon had not applied to teach in the summer—most unusual for her—and she had mentioned a possible move to Florida. And that was it. When she did not apply to teach in the fall semester—and those applications go in months in advance—we naturally assumed she had made the move and so no further inquiry was made."

"I can see how that applies to the administrative side of the college, but surely in all that time she must have made *some* friends on the faculty?" Penny broke in.

He shook his head slowly, "For someone who lived so much in the public eye she was a singularly private person."

Her interest quickened. "How do you mean 'the public eye'?"

He waved a hand, "Oh, she was in on just about anything you can name in Cape Cod affairs: the Historical Society, Indian affairs, land-development issues, the preservation of historic houses and landmarks, Cape genealogy—you name it and she was either in it or headed the committee."

"Then she *must* have had friends!" Penny protested. "Why haven't they been inquiring after her?"

This time he shrugged. "On that I have no idea. I could give you some names if that would help, and you could ask them."

Penny whipped out her notebook. "Great! Go ahead."

He steepled his long fingers and looked up at the ceiling in thought. "Well, there is Caleb Crowell from Dennis who is currently the head of the Historical Society. I don't know any of their addresses but you can easily get them from the phone book, or the police can help you there also. Then there's Calpurnia Howes, who heads up the Cape Preservation Society, Burrows Smith, chairman of the Mashpee Indian group for Indian rights, and, let me see now, Richard Fitzgerald, who is our local state senator for Barnstable and who has been backing Vincent Norman, a local boat owner involved in some kind of historical salvage work on the Mass. Bay side of the Cape. I know she was interested in that because she mentioned it a couple of times. He was after one of the old shipwrecks and that was one of her many fields of interest."

"And were any of these people connected with the college?" she demanded, scribbling busily away.

"Not directly, no, but now I think of it, one of our regular faculty was also involved in most of these things, too. Keith Corey, our head of the History Department—he has just retired. If he has not already left the Cape you may get some more insights from him . . . ." He pulled a Rolodex toward him and gave her a telephone number and a West Barnstable address.

"Oh, and that reminds me, there was another continuing ed. lecturer with whom she seemed to be friendly. Not that that is going to do you a whole heap of good, because she is no longer here either: an Englishwoman called Jocelyn Combe, who taught creative writing courses here over the last ten years. She wrote novels under a pen name as her main livelihood, but she enjoyed teaching and was also a keen amateur archaeologist and history buff. I used to see them together occasionally. She quit teaching last fall and I believe was planning to go back to England."

Penny sat back in her chair with an exasperated sigh and gazed at him. "Is it my imagination or aren't you having an abnormally high staff turnover rate at this college? Is this usual or is there something else behind it? I mean you have an almost new president, a new assistant dean, and three longtime faculty members all leaving within a few months of each other."

He smiled ruefully at her. "It is true we've been going through an unsettled period, but there is no sinister reason, I assure you, purely an economic one. The whole state has been in a miserable recession and the state colleges have all been pretty hard hit with cutbacks and layoffs. Morale has hit rock bottom. I've even been thinking of going myself. Added to that is the fact that many of our lecturers here came to the Cape, since it was such a nice place to live, after they had already retired from teaching jobs at larger universities, but were not ready for final retirement. Well, the Cape is no longer such a pleasant place to live, what with the many changes and the high taxes, so a lot of them have pulled out and gone off to seek fairer fields."

"So Clara Bacon was just following a trend and getting out?" Penny said thoughtfully. "Well, it is beginning to make a little more sense."

"Yes, it does look that way," he murmured. "Although I must say I was a bit surprised when Corey resigned. He was such an ardent Cape Codder."

Penny was following her own train of thought. "Could you get me the phone number and address of this Jocelyn Combe? And I'd also like a look at her personnel file if that's still around."

"I don't have that information, but the office should. I'll see what I can do." He got up. "You stay put and I'll be back." He added with a grin, "Wanda Carlucci is a bit overwhelmed with this new job and with the dean being away, so is inclined to be snappish, but I'll give it a try."

While he was gone Penny busied herself with the local telephone directory, adding numbers and addresses to the list of names he had given her. There was no listing for Burrows Smith and only an office number for State Senator Fitzgerald, so she added Vincent Norman's number and address for good measure. He, like Caleb Crowell, was an inhabitant of Dennis, she noted, whereas Calpurnia Howes lived in prestigious Osterville. When she had completed it, she gazed bleakly at the list. All of them, by the sound of it, were solid, sober, civically minded citizens of the Cape; the possibility of one of them being involved in this grotesque, senseless murder seemed incredible to her and she wondered if all this was a complete waste of time.

The door opened and Washington Ford came back in grimacing. "Not too much luck I'm sorry to say. Wanda got all official about the file, so unless the police impound it I'm afraid that's a no-go. I did get Mrs. Combe's address," he handed her a slip of paper. "But we have no telephone listed."

Penny looked at it and her eyebrows shot up. "Why, she's in Radley! That's just outside of Oxford. Thank you, that's very helpful. I'll be able to contact her easily enough."

"Glad to be of help," he said. "Is there anything else I can do?"

He was still standing and Penny realized she had already taken him away from whatever work had brought him back to the college on a weekend, so she hastily got up. "For the moment I can't think of a thing, but you've been very kind. May I get back to you if I think of anything else?"

"With pleasure," he said with relief, and took another leaf from his scratch pad and scribbled two numbers. "The first will get me here, the second is my home phone, and if you get my answering machine just leave your number and I'll get back to you."

"I hope I shan't have to bother you again, but who knows? Thanks again and my regards to the Dimolas when you see them."

"Why don't you give me your phone number also?" he queried, "I'm sure they would like to contact you."

"Oh dear! I'm afraid I don't know it," she confessed. "So much has been going on since I arrived that I never thought to look at it, but it's Dr. Clarkson's home in Hyannisport—you could tell them that. I'd love to hear from them."

The powerful Dimolas, she reflected, as she drove back down Route 132, might prove very useful allies if things got rough, and she had this sinking feeling that she was plunging into very deep and muddied waters. En route she stopped off at one of the mega-grocery stores that had sprouted along the big artery, to replenish their grocery supplies. Eating out on the Cape in high summer was not as easy as Toby so airily supposed, without careful advance planning, and she wasn't about to starve on the job as she had on previous occasions.

There was no sign of Toby back at the house and so, having stored away her purchases, she applied herself to her first objective. After consulting her watch and figuring out the time back in England, she called Ada Phipps' number in Oxford and hoped fervently that her Girl Friday was there. Ada's breathless voice came through after the sixth ring, "Oh, Dr. Spring!—Dame Penelope, I mean—it's *ever* so good to hear from you. Just came in the door, I did. Is everything all right? How's the family. . . ?"

Penny let the spate of questions run out before saying, "I'll fill you in later, Ada, but there's something I'd very much like you to find out for me. I need to get in touch with someone in Radley. Is that listed in your Oxford directory?"

"Half a sec. . . ." There was a rustling and heavy breathing at the other end, then a doleful, "Afraid not."

"No problem. This is what I'd like you to do. Find out from directory assistance the number for a Mrs. Jocelyn Combe, Briar Cottage, Fern Lane, Radley—got that? Call her and ask her to contact me at this number as soon as possible." She rattled off the numerals. "Tell her to charge it to my home phone at Littlemore or call collect. Okay? Tell her it's urgent."

Ada obediently repeated the instructions and the numbers and went on, "If I get her, shall I call you right back or wait until the rates go down at this end this evening?"

"Oh, don't worry about that," Penny said soothingly. "And when you do call, call collect—er, reverse charges, Ada, then we can have a nice chat."

"That would be ever so nice. What should I say to this lady if she asks what's so urgent?" Ada queried.

Penny hesitated. "Tell her it is concerning the murder of a Mrs. Clara Bacon. Sir Tobias and I have been asked to help the Barnstable police."

There was a startled silence at the other end, then Ada burst out, "Oh Lor' not *another* one! And you on your holiday, too! All Sir Tobias' doing, I'll be bound, getting you into these awful things. Well, *I* think it's a rotten shame, that I do! Never a moment's peace with that man around!" And on that aggrieved note she hung up.

Chapter 5

The police car turned off a side road lined with modest, new ranch houses on to a small, bumpy dirt road that ended in a barrier of trees, through which a circular graveled driveway branched off to the left. A two-storied wood-shingled house stood to the right of the driveway, and before it was a parked car. As Robert Dyke drew up behind it and cut the engine it was singularly silent in the little clearing. The encircling trees muffled all sound from the nearby road and only the chirp of an unseen bird and the light wind sighing in scrub maple and pine disturbed this sheltered oasis of quiet.

As Toby climbed out of the car and stared at the silent house, he was visited by a curious sense of dêja vu; he had seen this place, this house before—but where? Robert Dyke was already out of the car, trying all the doors of the car in front of them, but Chief Birnie lingered, noting Toby's puzzled round-eyed stare. "Something the matter, Sir Tobias?"

Toby shook himself out of his daze. "No, nothing really, just that I could have sworn I've seen this house before."

The chief glanced up at the deep-roofed front porch, supported by three substantial white-painted pillars, that ran along the entire breadth of the house, and then back at Toby. "Quite likely you have. A lot of this style house on the Cape, all built around the turn of the century. Old, but not old enough to be historical. Always remind me of barns with a porch tacked on."

"But the whole setting is the same," Toby murmured. "I just cannot bring it to mind."

Birnie chuckled suddenly. "Got it! This house is a dead ringer for Zeb Grange's place in Masuit. That's what you are remembering, *and* with good reason."

Toby's face cleared. "Of course! Stupid of me. Yes, that's it, same encircling trees, same type house. But Grange's place was remote, as I recall, yet this is slap in the middle of a built-up area, although you'd never know it."

"That secondary road we came down was only put in, oh, about ten years ago, I'd say. Fine old fight there was about that too—as usual! The Bacons must have hung on to a fair piece of land to keep themselves this removed from their new neighbors."

"The Bacons?" Toby queried. "I thought you said she was a longtime widow."

"So she was, but she lived here with her mother-in-law for quite a spell. The old lady was a semi-invalid for many years and died, oh, 'bout three or four years since."

Dyke rejoined them, his young face grim, "Locked up tight but evidently packed for a trip; lots of boxes in the back seat *and* a cat-carrier, but it appears to be empty."

Birnie seemed to gather himself together. He patted his breast pocket. "Well, we've got a general search warrant. Got the lockpick, Bob? After we've had a look at the house, you can have a go at the car." He led the way up the three shallow wooden steps with a chair ramp to one side of them, across the creaking boards of the porch, and opened the screen door. Dyke knelt at the main door and inserted the tines of the lockpick in the Yale lock. Birnie peered through the glass pane in the upper half of the door and grunted, "No sign of any kind of disturbance in there that I can see."

Robert straightened up, twisted the tarnished brass door knob and the door swung inward. A gush of musty air greeted them as they filed into a passage, with a staircase rising to the left and an open door to what was evidently a dining room at the opposite end. Birnie turned right through an archway separating the living room from the passage and stopped so suddenly that Toby, following closely on his heels, collided with his solid back. "Well, I'll be damned—look!" the chief exclaimed. Sitting in the middle of the room, which was overly cluttered with old-fashioned furniture, was a wheelchair.

"Better call in for more help, Bob," Birnie said gruffly. "A photographer and a uniform to help us go through the things in the car. Can you do the fingerprints?"

"Yes, I brought the kit with me," Dyke called back as he headed for the police cruiser.

Ernie Birnie sighed heavily. "Well, it looks as if you were right. The person who put her in the college must have had access to the house and must have used old Mrs. Bacon's wheelchair to cart the body. But why bring it back? Best not touch anything 'till Bob's done the dabs." This to Toby, who had drifted over to the tall, built-in bookcase that stood to the left of the open fireplace and was scanning the titles. "Let's check the rest of the house to see if there's been a break-in."

But a rapid search of the downstairs revealed all the windows shut and intact and both the inner and outer door of the kitchen, which opened off the dining room, locked and bolted. Birnie opened another narrow door next to the range and they went down the steep narrow stairs to a small, circular Cape-Cod-type cellar, but its windows and the door to the hatchway at the back told the same story. Looking around at the trunks piled in the gaps between the furnace and the hot-water heater, Birnie again sighed. "It's going to take weeks to go through all this stuff, and we're stretched thin as it is—it being high season and all."

"Didn't she have any relatives?" Toby asked.

"Not that I know of," the chief said. "I know her husband was an only child. As to her family, I just don't know. That folder Dr. Spring has may give us that later on." They remounted the staircase and took silent survey of the immaculately clean kitchen; the refrigerator stood open and darkly empty, but the small freezer beside it was still plugged in, although on inspection it was equally empty. "You don't suppose. . . ," Birnie mused.

"No, too small, and besides it would not account for the *adipocere*," Toby finished. He touched the chief's arm. "But we may have the date for the murder." He indicated a wall calendar from a local bank that was tacked on to the side of one of the blond wood cabinets: it was of the "one leaf to a day" kind and the last date revealed was Tuesday, May 26.

Birnie brightened up and started flipping through his notebook. "Jeez, that would make some sense. Let's see, she finished teaching on the 15th—that was a Friday—would have got her grades in probably on the following Monday or Tuesday, the 18th, started to pack and clean up, then waited for the Memorial Day weekend traffic to get done with over the next weekend and was set to go off the next day."

"But instead somebody shot her that day and deposited her body either in wet ground or water, where she remained until approximately three days ago when, amazingly, someone *else* disinterred her and then transported her, for reasons unknown, to the college."

"Why not the murderer?" Birnie demanded.

"What on earth for?" Toby said testily. "When you've successfully murdered and hidden the body so that no one has even suspected your victim's demise, why dig her up and put her in so public a place?"

"Maybe he's a loony. Plenty of those around on the Cape,"

Birnie retaliated. "Maybe he *wants* to be caught."

"I simply cannot accept that," Toby growled. "When you think of the planting of the body in that particular classroom and at that precise time, it indicates a detailed knowledge of the college and its workings, so unless you have your madman right on that campus *and* with easy access to and knowledge of this house, I feel that that is a highly improbable theory."

"Then maybe it's a question of thieves falling out and one of 'em out to get the other," Birnie said stubbornly.

"What's been taken?" Toby demanded. "What did she have worth stealing and worth killing for? There's no forced entry, no sign of any disturbance."

"We don't know that yet. Let's check upstairs." Birnie began to lead the way out of the dining room when he was temporarily halted by the arrival of the police photographer and a very young and anxious-looking constable, followed by Robert Dyke announcing, "I've got the car unlocked."

"You go ahead," the chief told Toby, "I'll be with you as soon as I've put these to work."

Toby took the short staircase two steps at a time, scanning the worn shag carpet as he went for any telltale traces, but there was nothing. On the narrow top landing only one door to his left stood open. He went in and looked quickly around. A handsome Victorian four-poster bed in blond maple dominated the room, and on its white coverlet a small overnight bag stood open. He went over and peered into its contents—a nightdress, a cosmetic kit, another plastic hold-all with a toothbrush sticking out of it, and a small, closed deedbox. His fingers itched to open it but he obediently kept his hands off and surveyed the rest of the room: the walk-in closet was almost full of winter clothes hanging in transparent plastic bags, so Clara Bacon evidently had intended to return. A tote bag of the kind so dear to the heart of his companion-in-crime stood on the dressing table and he peered longingly into it, wondering if this also was Clara Bacon's idea of a lady's purse.

With an impatient sigh he crossed the narrow hallway and flung open the door opposite that revealed a long room which spanned the whole front of the house. It had been fitted up as an office; a big desk with a word processor stood between the two windows, another table housing a small copier adjacent, and the rest of the walls were lined with overflowing bookcases and filing cabinets. Here again there was no sign of disturbance, no sign of violence done. Wrapping a handkerchief around his hand he tried one of the tall filing cabinets and the top drawer slid easily open, revealing its neatly filed contents: the other five cabinets also yielded to his touch. He felt a twinge of sympathy for the beleaguered Ernie Birnie—it would indeed take weeks to go through this mountain of material searching for some clue, some handle on the motive behind this bizarre affair.

Again he surveyed the large light-filled room and was struck by how impersonal it all was. There were no photographs, no personal knickknacks lying around; nothing to give him a clue as to what kind of woman Clara Bacon had been. "Damnation," he muttered and went out to continue his snooping.

The bathroom at the end of the passage was as clean and as sterile as the kitchen below, but the tiny room adjacent to it— evidently the guest room, but long disused judging by the piles of boxes on the narrow bed—at last yielded something positive. By the bed was another bookcase, which housed Mrs. Bacon's genealogical library, all neatly filed alphabetically. He hastily scanned the contents and let out a faint sigh of satisfaction—there was a gap in the Hs between a Harding and a Howland genealogy. So the books that had been found with the body had not been extracted from some bookcase at random, there *had* been method in that madness; that Howes genealogy had to have some significance . . . .

Heavy footsteps set the stairs creaking and Birnie called, "Where are you? Found anything?"

"Back here in the bedroom by the bathroom, and yes, I think so," he called back.

Birnie's burly figure appeared in the doorway. "Blood?" he asked hopefully.

Toby shook his head. "No, I'm willing to swear on oath that the murder was not committed anywhere inside this house, but . . . ," he pointed at the bookcase and rapidly explained his finding. Birnie slumped down on the edge of the bed, his massive head moving from side to side like a baited bull's. "Not a single damn break are we getting on this one," he complained. "Not a single damn clue. If she wasn't killed here she could have got it *anywhere*—anywhere on the goddamn Cape! I've never felt this baffled in my whole damn life and that's a fact."

"Oh, I don't think it's that bad," Toby soothed. "In fact it is highly probable that she *was* killed here—but not in the house. You'll find her overnight bag and handbag in her bedroom at the head of the stairs. Those narrow things down."

Birnie looked at him blankly. "How come?"

"Well, in the first place, when you've examined them I think you'll have to rule out a robbery as a motive. I didn't touch anything, but there's a bulky wallet sitting on top of the tote bag and you can see the dollars sticking out. In the second, it gives us a rough timetable of events. You see she had packed the car for the trip and was down to the last two items she intended to take with her, therefore she was murdered *before* she came back upstairs for those last two bags—not *in* the house, but almost certainly in the grounds. Since this place is so sound-proofed from its neighbors, chances are that a shot, even from a high-caliber gun, would not have been heard or noted."

"I don't see how that helps us much," Birnie grumbled. "If she was shot outside, as you say, we haven't a hope in hell of picking up traces this long after. It rained like crazy here most of June—hot as hell, too—so if you're right about that death date, and I think you are, any blood would have long since been washed away, and, in any case, the murderer could then have carted the body off to God-knows-where."

Toby again shook his head. "No, if you think about it, that's not likely. You are forgetting the other end of it—our mysterious Mr. X who disinterred her body—and, don't forget, that body was heavy. Is it likely that, if she had been buried at some far remove, he would have brought her *back* here just to use that wheelchair, which we assume was so used?"

"Oh, yes, no doubt that it was used," Birnie sighed. "We found some fibers from her clothes stuck to the seat. But it still don't make any sense. You say the body had to be buried in moist ground or water. Well, you won't find a bog, a marsh, or a pond within a mile of here, and that's a fact. So where does that leave your theory, eh?"

Toby was momentarily disconcerted. "There *has* to be something nearby," he muttered. "A spring in the woods or something like that."

"Not that I know of." Birnie got heavily to his feet. "Well, I'd better put Bob on dusting up here as soon as he's done in the kitchen and get photographs of the whole layout. You can browse around in the living room all you want now, they've finished with it."

"I think I'll go out for a bit and have a look around." Toby was longing for a smoke and felt constrained from lighting up in these pristine surroundings.

"Suit yourself," Birnie said and plodded away.

Once outside on the porch, Toby breathed a sigh of relief, filled and lit his pipe, and took in his surroundings. Clara Bacon's neatness had not extended to her garden: apart from the surrounding trees there were only a few scraggly shrubs, now almost obscured by the high grass, unmowed for three months. He peered into the car, now with all its doors open, and seeing a small cooler in the front seat, opened it up. It contained the moldering remains of two sandwiches, two cans of ginger ale, three hardboiled eggs, and a can of cat food. He looked somberly at this last item—what had become of the cat?

He continued around the house and on its sunny side was a row of overgrown rose bushes, a few live blooms still struggling amid a mass of dead ones. As he turned into the back yard the sun's rays were cut off abruptly by a huge maple that completely overshadowed the yard, so that here the grass was sparse and interspersed with clumps of bright green moss. A noise at the back door caused him to look up as Robert Dyke opened the screen door and came out. "Oh, it's you. Want to come in here? I've just finished."

"Anything on the chair?" Toby asked.

"Only smudges," Robert said. "Must have worn gloves."

Suddenly, across Toby's line of vision a gray shape shot out of the bushes and hurled itself at the screen door, letting out a blood-chilling wail. It was a very large, long-haired tabby—or rather, it *had* been large—for now, under its matted and burr-choked coat, its ribs stood out and what had been a considerable paunch hung in loose folds from its belly. "Good God, it must be the missing cat!" Toby exclaimed. "Let it in and see what it does."

Bob opened the door and it shot inside as they followed after. In the kitchen it leapt at the open refrigerator and again set up a piteous wailing.

"Dear God, it must be starving!" Robert said. "I saw some dry cat food in one of these cupboards. . . ." He opened a cupboard, got out a carton, and dumped the pellets into a plastic bowl in the sink. Before he could set it down the cat leapt for the sink and, growling, tore into the food, gulping it down feverishly as it watched them with malignant yellow eyes.

"Well, there I think we have our only eyewitness," Toby remarked, as the food disappeared. "What a pity it can't talk." Dyke lifted the carton to pour some more into the rapidly emptying bowl. "I don't know much about cats," Toby continued mildly. "But I don't think you'd better give it too much at one time—same principle as humans, its stomach has probably shrunk."

As if to confirm his opinion, the cat took a few more gulps of food, then jumped down and in the amazing way of cats started to clean its face and whiskers vigorously, its back turned to them in indifference. "What the hell was all that caterwauling out here?" the chief demanded, suddenly appearing in the doorway. The cat whirled around, arched and hissed, then hurled itself at the back door.

"I'll get it," Toby said quietly, and let the panicky animal out. It loped purposefully across the back yard and down a faintly discernible track leading off to the right. Toby followed after it, a whole new train of thought in his mind. The cat trotted steadily on through the deepening woods until it and its pursuer came to a tumbledown barn in the last stages of decay and, just beyond it, something that caused Toby's silvery eyebrows to shoot up and his hopes to soar: it was a built-up wellhead of brick, its wooden winding post and roof intact. Beside the well stood a galvanized bucket full of water towards which the cat headed and, with a paw on each side of the rim, began to lap eagerly at its contents.

Skirting the cat gingerly, Toby peered into the wide, dark opening of the well and dropped a pebble into it. A tiny splash rewarded his efforts. He stood back, fished in his sagging pocket for his pipe, and murmured to himself, "No water within a mile, eh? I would say that this would fit the bill very nicely. Five minutes ago I would have vowed that Chief Birnie would have been equally delighted with it. Now, I'm not so sure. . . ."

Chapter 6

Toby had hoped that Robert Dyke would be his chauffeur back to Hyannisport, for there were some burning questions he wanted to ask his young friend. But he was delegated instead to the anxious-looking young officer, who had been more of a hindrance than a help at the Bacon house and now proceeded to confide all his troubles to Toby's unheeding ears on the way home. He was an O'Malley of the Boston O'Malleys, he said—cops to a man for three generations, but he wasn't so sure he wanted to be one himself and had taken this summer job on the Cape to make up his mind. Now he was less sure than ever. "These Cape Codders aren't a friendly lot at all," he confided. "Don't give you any clear idea of what you're supposed to do and then, when you do do something on your own, get mad as hell. I'm real pissed off, I can tell you. If I make it through until after Labor Day it'll be a fucking miracle. That chief of theirs can be a real s.o.b."

The only response he got from Toby, who was listening with half an ear, was an assortment of grunts, for he himself was wrestling with a guilty conscience. He had said nothing to the police about his discovery in the woods, and this went against his law-abiding grain. On the other hand, he desperately needed to consult with Penny and to get her reaction before making up his mind on the matter, and was trying to console himself with the thought that another twenty-four hours wouldn't make that much difference one way or another.

O'Malley slowed the police cruiser to a stop at the bottom of the steps up to the Clarkson house, still talking. "So what do you think I should do?" he appealed as Toby got out.

"Many thanks for the lift. Best of luck on your new career—sounds splendid," Toby muttered, trudging off up the steps, leaving the dazed young man more confused than ever.

He found Penny sitting on a sofa by the phone in the huge living room. Her mouse-colored hair was standing up in spikes around her small head and she was gloomily consulting the manila folder on Clara Bacon. She looked up as he came in and said in an aggrieved voice, "About time you showed up! I hope this means you've been getting somewhere, because I sure as hell haven't. I suppose now you're here I better get dinner started."

She began to get up, but he held up a hand. "Sit! I've booked us in for dinner at the Daniel Webster in Sandwich for seven-thirty. What I need now is a long drink and a longer conference."

"The Daniel Webster, eh?" She brightened up at once. "Well, that's different—good thinking! And you can fix me one too, a bourbon and soda. What's up?"

"I'm not quite sure." He fixed her drink and made himself a brandy and soda before coming over and settling into an easy chair opposite to her. After a long and satisfied swig, he filled his pipe, lit it, and through the ensuing cloud of smoke glinted at her and demanded, "What do you know about cat behaviour?"

"*Cat* behaviour?" she echoed in astonishment. "Not a great deal, but what on earth has that got to do with anything?"

"I'm not sure," he repeated. "Do you want to go first or shall I?"

"Since I don't have all that much to tell, I may as well go first," she said and rapidly related the substance of her conference at the college and its aftermath. "I have been on the telephone the whole damn day—and to little effect," she complained. "Everyone seems to be out or on vacation. Ada hasn't been able to raise this Jocelyn Combe, who should be of some help if we can ever get to her. I can't find Burrows Smith. Keith Corey's phone is 'no longer in service.' State Senator Fitzgerald is out of town and unavailable, according to his office. Vincent Norman, ditto, according to his sad-sounding wife. Caleb Crowell said he had to go to Boston tomorrow, but would see me the day after, and Calpurnia Howes has consented to grant me an audience tomorrow morning, but was markedly unenthusiastic about the idea. In fact, neither of them seemed to give a damn about Clara Bacon's death. End of story."

"Grant you an audience?" Toby lifted an eyebrow.

"Oh, yes—very much the lofty lady! I had to be very insistent," Penny sniffed. "And *she* was very insistent that her name not be linked with the police or the inquiry."

"Indeed? Interesting!" he murmured. "Did you get anything out of that folder on Clara Bacon?"

"Damn little—list of her courses, dates, rates of pay, and so on. Precious little we didn't know already."

"Anything in it about next of kin?"

"Yes, I did see something." She opened the folder up again. "Yes, here it is. First there was a Mrs. Nicholas Bacon, then that was crossed out and there's a Mrs. Annabel Brown with 'sister' in brackets and a California address, then that's crossed out and dated eighteen months ago, and then a Stephen Brown, 'nephew' in brackets, but no address. That any help?"

"Not much. But she did have *a* relative, whereabouts unknown, who, presumably, if there is no will, would be sole heir to her estate," Toby murmured.

"Did she have much to leave?"

"Birnie carted off her deed box, so I don't know, but the house has a lot of land to it and that should be worth something," Toby mused, sucking on his pipe. "And money so often is the motive for murder, and motive in this case is about our only hope of getting a handle on it. The method and the means, even the where and when, we now know, but it doesn't get us very far."

"We do? For God's sake get on with it then and tell me," Penny exclaimed.

"Not before I've had another drink." He freshened their drinks and recapitulated the events of the day to his absorbed partner, who burst out at the end of his recital, "But that's great! What did Birnie say when you showed him the well?"

Toby shot a furtive glance at her. "I didn't tell him."

"Why ever not?" she cried.

He squirmed uneasily. "It's because of the cat, the way it behaved. The creature was starving; it wasn't afraid of Bob or me, yet the minute Birnie appeared it went berserk with panic, as if it had some reason to be afraid of *him*. I thought that very strange, so I kept that particular bit of information quiet. I'm not sure I altogether trust Birnie and his motive for keeping such a close personal eye on things."

"That's one hell of an assumption based solely on a cat's hissing and spitting!" Penny said vehemently. "I mean you and Bob had just let it in and fed it, so it had no cause to fear you. Birnie may just have startled it—it must be semiwild after all this time. Or it may have been his dark uniform."

"Bob was also in uniform," Toby pointed out.

"Well, maybe it was his loud voice, or because he was big and burly, unlike you two. . . ."

"It's not just the cat," Toby fretted. "It's a lot of little things. Birnie seems anxious to *mis*direct inquiries in a confused way. First he wanted to blame it on some madman, then on thieves, then to draw attention *away* from the house. As I told you yesterday I thought it odd he was so personally involved in the affair from the outset. And another thing—don't you think it is also odd, remembering your dealings with him over the Dimola affair, that he should have shot to the top so quickly?"

"Hmm, I see what you mean there," Penny mused, remembering her own past frustrations. "He does rather run to fixed ideas, but then strange things happen in small places. The main argument I have against your suspicions is that, of all the people we've talked to thus far, he's the only one who seems to have liked or given a damn about the corpse. I just can't picture him being involved in her murder. But, obviously, a quiet word with Robert Dyke is indicated. He may be able to give you some insight as to Birnie's rapid promotion."

"Er, I was hoping you'd do that," Toby mumbled. "It's a delicate subject, and you're so much better at getting people to open up than I am. Besides, I know I can trust Dyke and I don't want to jeopardize that relationship."

"Oh, thanks a bunch," Penny said drily. "But it strikes me we have a whole lot of other directions to look in first. Now that you have demonstrated that the books *do* seem to have a significance, we can start pointing fingers right and left. There was the Howes genealogy and we do have a Howes involved with Clara Bacon. There were books on shipwrecks and treasure hunting and we have Vincent Norman, who is a shipwreck hunter, and Fitzgerald, who is supporting him. There was a book on American Indians and we have the elusive Burrows Smith, local champion of Indian rights. The only odd book out is the one on geology. Maybe that'll point at Crowell, although the one subject that *wasn't* in the bunch—historic buildings— I would have thought would be more in his line. It is strange that all the *public* people who were involved with her to whom I have been directed seem to be indicated by those books. More than a coincidence, wouldn't you say? Come to think of it, the absence of a book on historic architecture might be a very subtle hint toward Caleb Crowell. What do you think?"

"Too early to tell." Toby was beginning to fidget; he looked at his watch and said, "We've got over an hour before dinner. I think I'll take a look through that Howes genealogy and see if I can pick up on anything."

"Then I may as well call the family in New York and see how things are down there. Then we won't have to rush over dinner," she said, and picked up the phone.

She reached Alex, who sounded somewhat worn. "Marcus' fever is down, Mala's is up and they are both so full of spots that they resemble steamed raisin puddings," he reported tersely. "Mala is also being a right royal pain. For a child who is normally so quiet, when not feeling well she becomes remarkably noisy."

"Poor little soul," her grandmother sympathized. She became aware of voices in the background and a curious melodic booming underlying the gabble. "What on earth's all that noise? It sounds as if you're having a party!"

A resigned sigh floated over the wire. "That's our babysitters gathered to help us in our hour of need—never a dull moment with our Sonya around. I would not be surprised if the balalaikas and a Cossack choir show up at any minute. They have all sworn to me that they've had chicken pox and I hope to God they're telling the truth, otherwise we'll be spreading an epidemic of gargantuan proportions throughout New York City."

Penny was amused. "And what's that odd booming I'm hearing?"

"Oh, that's our tame Russian basso from the Met, Boris Betski. He's singing Mala to sleep with Russian folksongs. She adores him—I think she thinks he's some sort of fuzzy animal because he's mostly black beard. Anyway, she hangs on to his beard, he sings and she goes to sleep. He's the only one who can shut her up at the moment."

Penny chuckled. "Well I think I'll leave you to it. It sounds as if you've got your hands more than full."

"Everything okay your end? Any reason for the early call?" Alex asked casually.

"Oh, it's just that we're going out to dinner at the Daniel Webster and might not be back until late. Everything's fine here," she assured him.

"Lucky you! I hope Toby is footing the bill and behaving himself. Have fun! And I'll call you tomorrow," her son said and hung up.

She was just about to get up and change into something a little more formal for the prestigious Daniel Webster Inn when the phone rang again. This time it was Ada Phipps' anxious voice on the line. "Just thought I'd call before I went to bed to tell you I've made a bit of progress on that Mrs. Combe. You see I've this friend who lives out in Radley. She's a hairdresser in Oxford and has lived out there ever so long . . . ." Ada proceeded to ramble on and Penny waited patiently for her to get to the point. ". . . so she found out from the postman that Mrs. C. is off visiting her daughter—somewhere in Devon it is, or maybe it was Somerset . . . anyway, *he* says she'll be coming back this coming Wednesday, so shall I wait and try her then?"

"Yes, do that, Ada. Just let me know when you've made contact."

"Anything else I can do to help?" Ada asked breathlessly.

"No, just that and thanks again. Until Wednesday then," Penny said, and hung up quickly before Ada could start in on one of her endless chats.

She went upstairs and changed her outfit. Noting from her ocean-view window that dark storm clouds were roiling seaward before a brisk offshore wind and that the sea was kicking up into whitecaps, and knowing the summer Cape and its sudden weather changes of old, she added a raincoat to her ensemble and had just reached the bottom of the stairs when the phone shrilled again. This time it was Ernie Birnie, who announced, "Thought I'd drop around and pick up the Bacon folder, if that's all right. In about twenty minutes?"

"We have a dinner reservation in Sandwich and were just about to leave," she said, with a quick glance at her watch. "Could you make it later, or is there something I can tell you over the phone? I've read the whole thing. Do you need her next of kin, by chance?"

He sounded mildly astonished at this apparent ESP. "Well, yes, that's just what I was after!"

"Up to eighteen months ago it was listed as a Mrs. Annabel Brown, her sister in California . . . ," and she rattled off the address in the folder. "But that was crossed out and Stephen Brown, her nephew, substituted, but there's no address given for him. That's all there is."

Birnie laboriously repeated the address and muttered, "Well I guess it's a start. Bob'll pick up the folder first thing tomorrow then, say about eight-thirty? You get anything out of the college?"

"Not much," she said hastily as Toby emerged from the study mumbling to himself. "I'll give my report to Robert at the same time, shall I? I'm seeing Calpurnia Howes at ten tomorrow morning."

"Okay," he grunted and hung up.

"Anything?" she demanded of her companion.

"Not very much, I'm afraid. We'd better get going. I'll tell you in the car," he growled, and as they sped towards Sandwich he complained, "That damn book only goes up to the turn of the century, so what good it is with our present cast of characters, God knows! There have been at least three, probably four or more, generations since then."

"So maybe it was just a general indication that there's a Howes involved—namely Calpurnia," she suggested.

"There was *one* thing . . . ," he went on, ignoring her. "Toward the end of the book there was an entry underlined in red: the marriage of a Mary Howes to a Joseph Dexter in 1901. Now Clara was not one to underline—I checked in all the other books, so it is *possible* that whoever put her body in the college did the underlining to draw attention to that particular marriage."

"Pretty thin!" she commented.

"I know," he said in deep gloom. "And where to go from there I've no idea."

"My mother went on a genealogy kick once," Penny reflected. "Did our entire family tree—Thayers and Snows, you know? Both old New England families, so I'm related to myself about fifty times over with all the intermarrying that went on. She got all her information from the New England Historic and Genealogical Society on Newbury Street in Boston, so you might get some help there."

"But that sort of research takes forever!" he grumbled. "I can't waste my time on that."

"I believe they'll do it for you, if you pay them—or, better still, if the police pay for it."

He snorted as they drew up in the parking lot of the Daniel Webster. "I can't see Ernie Birnie shelling out for something like that, can you?"

"Probably not, but if it's all you've got it's worth a try," she said, clambering out of the car and straightening herself out.

As they entered the deep-carpeted foyer of the inn, above the babble of voices from the dining rooms came the sound of live piano music. Toby flinched, "Good God! Don't tell me we've got to listen to that all through dinner!" He stalked up to a harassed-looking hostess at the reception desk and boomed. "Glendower. Table for two. Reservation made for seven-thirty."

Without looking at her list the hostess said, "I don't think there's anything at the moment. If you care to go to the bar for a predinner drink, we'll call you there when a table is available."

"I don't want a predinner drink, I want my dinner." Toby was definite. He looked pointedly at his watch. "And as it is now two minutes past seven-thirty I want it now."

The hostess was now scanning her list and her face changed as she got to his name, "Oh, *Sir* Tobias Glendower—well, er, I'll see what I can do, sir." She slipped from behind the desk and scurried toward the floor manager. "And as far away from that piano as possible!" Toby called after her and smirked at Penny.

In a few moments they were being led to a small table overlooking the garden in the farthest corner of the wood-panelled dining room, where the sound of the piano was reduced to an acceptably faint tinkle. Once installed, Penny cheered up at the sight of the menu and Toby at the sight of the wine list. After due consultation they both settled for little-necks on the half-shell, followed by lobster, hot rolls and Syrian bread, and a salad Niçoise, accompanied by a bottle of vintage chardonnay that brought a gleam to Toby's eyes.

By mutual agreement they did not talk of the murder as they browsed through the delectable meal. When the lobsters had been reduced to dismembered shells, Penny allowed herself to be tempted by a luscious Boston cream pie, while Toby settled for a Calvados and some Brie and French bread. By the time they were through the dining room was emptying out rapidly. Finally replete, Penny sank back in her seat and declared, "Well *some* things stay the same on the Cape, thank God! That was delicious—I feel like a new woman. Thank you, Toby. What made you think of it?"

"Oh, John Everett and I came here several times when we were trying to save you from *durance vile* on the Dimola case," he said. "I remembered what a good cellar they had."

"Maybe it would be a good idea to contact the Dimolas," Penny mused. "They may be able to help us on this genealogy business. After all, they are based in Boston and could surely spare a minion or two to do the legwork."

"It's an idea," Toby said, giving their waitress his gold American Express card with a charming smile and adding a hefty tip to the bill. "Let's get out of here, I'm dying for a smoke."

They ambled out to find a heavy rain had started, so scuttled to the car where Toby rolled down the windows and lit up. "Now what?" he demanded.

Penny was rummaging in the glove compartment and emerged with a crumpled road map. "Since it is on our way home I thought we might swing by and see if this Keith Corey is in his house. I know his phone is off but there's an off-chance he's still there, in the process of moving. Worth a try, and it's not much out of our way. High Popple Road, West Barnstable— see!" She indicated the route to Toby.

"Isn't it a bit late for an official visit?" he queried, starting up the car.

"In all probability he won't even be there, but we may get an idea if the house is still furnished or if he's gone for good."

"All right, but if he is there *you* can do the talking, I'll stay in the car," Toby said firmly and began to follow her directions. They turned off the Mid-Cape highway at the Route 149 exit and after following the winding road for almost a mile made a sharp right at the High Popple Road sign. Here the houses tended to be large and set well back on large lots, so they slowed to a crawl, reading the numbers on the mailboxes at the foot of each driveway. "Here it is!" she exclaimed suddenly, and Toby stopped the car before a smaller ranch house that sat much nearer to the road than did its neighbors. It was almost dark so he switched on the headlights and a realtor's metal sign sprang into view, a red and white banner across it announcing SOLD.

"Looks as if our bird has flown," Penny said, struggling into her raincoat. "But I'll just check anyway." She slipped out of the car and ran up to the house. Toby watched her resignedly as she peered into the glass panel of the front door and then into all the front windows. She ran back, shaking her head, "No, completely empty and cleaned out." She rummaged in her tote bag and brought forth a notebook.

"Now what are you doing?" Toby demanded, starting up the car.

"Taking down the realtor's name and number. He ought to know how to contact Corey and I won't be able to raise anyone at the college tomorrow to ask, it being Sunday. Let's see now—Paul D. Robideau, and that's another West Barnstable number and address. Corey is evidently one of the lucky ones."

"Lucky?" Toby was puzzled. "Why?"

"Because he's sold his house. Sonya was telling me what a ghastly real estate slump they've had on the Cape these past few years. Developers going down the tube by the dozen. They say the worst is over now, but there are still one hell of a lot of properties for sale. Haven't you noticed all the boards out?"

"Can't say that I have. Not that it's of the least importance," Toby said stuffily, and headed homewards.

Chapter 7

Penny's heart sank at her first sight of Calpurnia Howes, for before her was a woman of steel if ever she had seen one. Everything about her emphasized that fact; her hair was steel-gray and set in such rigid waves that it looked as if they would shatter rather than bend, if touched. Her eyes were the same steely-gray, hidden behind gray-rimmed glasses and set in a long unyielding New England face. To accentuate this aura, she was wearing a light gray linen suit and a blouse of darker gray, with stockings and "sensible" shoes to match. After a cool greeting, Calpurnia led the way into a living room sparsely furnished with Colonial antiques, all standing rigidly on a huge braided rug. There was an unused, museumlike stillness to it. The room's multipaned windows looked out over Nantucket Sound and in keeping with the mood, the sea, reflecting the cloud-covered sky, was the same steely gray.

Calpurnia waved Penny to a wing chair on one side of a fireplace that, by its pristine appearance, had never known a fire, and settled herself in a matching chair on the other side. By the chair was a small piecrust table on which reposed a white purse, a prayer book, and a pair of white gloves. She fired her opening salvo. "I know you did explain who you are and the object of this visit, but I must say that I find it quite extraordinary that the Barnstable police should call in summer *tourists* to help them in a murder case." She looked pointedly at the brass ship's clock in the middle of the mantlepiece. "I am afraid I can only spare you half an hour before going to church."

Penny decided not to take umbrage. "Sir Tobias and I were instrumental in helping the police solve an unusual murder some years ago, and since Clara Bacon's murder is also very out of the ordinary they believe we can again be of help to them. At this point we have had considerable experience in the field. Besides . . . ," she could not resist getting in a dig of her own, ". . . Chief Birnie thought it might be more agreeable for all the parties concerned to be interviewed in their own homes rather than be summoned to the police station."

This did not faze the Woman of Steel. "Parties concerned?" she echoed. "I fail to see how they can possibly imagine I was at all concerned with Clara Bacon. Ours was simply a business acquaintance, we did not mix socially."

Lucky Clara! Penny thought, as she continued, "But you served with her on many committees, I believe, and this is what I am trying to find out—had she had any serious disagreements with anyone? Was there some burning issue in which she was involved that could have been a sufficient motive for someone to want her removed from the scene? And, what to my mind is the most amazing aspect of the whole thing, why did no one on any of these committees apparently even *miss* her these past three months?"

"Clara was a woman of very definite opinions so, inevitably, from time to time, conflicts would arise, but nothing of any magnitude, and certainly nothing to warrant anyone wanting to murder her," Calpurnia said loftily. "I feel you are looking in entirely the wrong direction, if I may say so. Probably she was unlucky enough to run across some drug-crazed hoodlum who was looking for money for a quick fix. How was she killed, by the way? The paper did not specify."

"She was shot in the back—apparently at her home while loading her car for a trip," Penny said bluntly.

Calpurnia nodded her head triumphantly, "There you are then! Undoubtedly a random killing."

"I'm afraid it's not that simple." Penny was sharp. "I'm not sure what has been in the papers, but you must be forgetting that someone carefully took her long-dead body and placed it in the *college*, together with certain articles that clearly point to a very definite *local* motive."

"What articles?" Calpurnia demanded, suddenly attentive.

"I'm afraid I am not at liberty to say," Penny said primly. "And you have not answered my final question—why was she not missed?"

Calpurnia seemed to collect herself. "Because she had notified us that she was going down to Florida and move into her new condo."

"So did she resign from all these committees?" Penny queried.

For a second she caught a flicker in the pale gray eyes: for some reason this question had disconcerted her steely hostess. "Well, no, I gather she had not made a final decision about whether the move to Florida was to be year-round or not."

"Then surely there must have been some committee business that would have involved her?" Penny pressed. "If letters or phone calls went unanswered, surely someone would have remarked on her absence?"

"With so many people being away or extremely busy with personal affairs during the summer, many of the committees do not operate much during this period. You'd have to ask the chairpersons—*I* certainly did not need to contact her," Calpurnia murmured, but Penny scented evasion.

"Which brings me to another point, and I do hope you will be able to help me on this," Penny tried to keep a sarcastic edge off her voice. "I cannot locate either Burrows Smith or Keith Corey. Can you give me any idea how I can get in touch with them?"

"Professor Corey has retired and also gone to Florida. He has resigned from his various committees. I do not know his address there, but I suppose the college has it. As to Burrows Smith," she gave something between a sniff and a snort, "he is a very odd man. Lives in some kind of log cabin, I believe, out in the Mashpee woods—trying to recreate the habits of his ancestors, no doubt. The only way I know to get in contact with him is to leave a message at the Indian Museum in Mashpee. Sometimes, if he sees fit, he will get in touch; if he doesn't he won't." She again looked at the clock and started to fidget.

Penny took this as a sign that the audience was at an end. "One last question, Mrs. Howes. Do you know of any other friends or close acquaintances of Clara Bacon I should contact?" she asked, getting up.

Calpurnia was on her feet in an instant and gathering up her gloves and bag. "I'm afraid not. As I said, I knew nothing of Clara's personal life."

"Oh, well, maybe Mr. Crowell will know. I'm seeing him tomorrow," Penny said with a resigned sigh. "Thank you for seeing me."

"You are meeting with Caleb Crowell?" Calpurnia was sharp.

"Why yes, he was also much involved with Clara Bacon, I understand," Penny said blandly.

"Well, one word of warning then," Calpurnia said, as she ushered her to the door. "Caleb tends to exaggerate a great deal and I should not put too much stock in what he says."

"I'll bear that in mind," Penny said as the door shut upon her, but was interested to see through its glass side panel that, instead of following her out, Calpurnia had made a beeline for the phone in the hall. "And I'll be most interested to hear what he has to say about *you*, my fine lady," she muttered as she got back into the car and drove around the circular driveway. Just as she was passing the two-car garage attached to the house, its door slid upward and she caught a glimpse of the small car parked in it. Predictably, it was steel-gray.

She wound her way slowly back to Route 28, pondering her next move. Toby had gone off with Robert Dyke and was undoubtedly out for the day and, although the cloud cover was starting to break up and a watery sun peeking out, it certainly was no day for the beach. So what should she do? Coming to a sudden decision she swung her car toward Mashpee. "Burrows Smith, ready or not here I come," she announced and hoped the museum would be open on a Sunday.

It was, although she received a less than enthusiastic reception. A portly Indian woman who presided as ticket seller and souvenir-stand operator, received her request for Burrows Smith with a dark-eyed blank stare. "He's not here," she said in the wheezy voice of an asthmatic.

"I realize that, but I was told I could leave a message here for him to contact me. It *is* rather urgent." Her roving eye caught sight of a very dusty copy of an old book of hers, *The American Indian in the Twentieth Century*, in the bookstand behind the woman. She gestured at it. "My name is Dr. Penelope Spring and I see you have one of my books on display. I *need* to talk to Burrows Smith."

This only served to deepen the Indian's suspicion. "You're a journalist?" she wheezed. "He does not talk to newspeople anymore."

"No, I'm an anthropologist," Penny said, fighting down her impatience. "And a longtime champion of Indian rights. Look at the dust jacket of the book if you would, it has my picture on it."

The woman took down the book, studied the back cover and then Penny, and nodded slowly. "What message?"

Penny whipped out her notebook. "Ask him to contact me at this number or this address as soon as possible. I need to talk with him urgently."

"Why?" the woman said, accepting the proffered slip of paper.

"Er, it's a private matter."

"I'll see that he gets it. You want to see the museum now?"

"Thank you, but no. I did see it last time I was here." Penny started to leave but then a bright thought came to her and she turned back. "Is Eagle Smith related to Burrows Smith, by any chance?"

"Maybe," the woman said cautiously. "But Eagle Smith is not in Mashpee. He left."

"Then is his mother still here?"

"Yes, she lives in the old place."

"Then maybe you could tell me how to get there from here? It's been a number of years since I was there and I'd like to see her again," Penny urged.

The Indian provided directions. Penny thanked her profusely, put a ten-dollar bill in the donation box on the counter, and went out into the bright sunshine. The sky was now almost cloudless and her spirits began to rise.

She found the small, shabby house without any difficulty and knocked on the weathered door. It opened a crack and Mrs. Smith's dusky face peered out. "Mrs. Smith, you probably don't remember me, but I'm Penelope Spring—we met some years ago during the Dimola case?"

A faint smile appeared on the impassive face and the door opened wide. "Why of course I remember you! Eagle and I have often talked of you and that sad time. Come in, and welcome!"

"How is Eagle?" Penny said, as Mrs. Smith ushered her to an easy chair and hastened to put on a pot of coffee.

The faint smile turned into a happy grin. "Oh, he does fine now, just fine! After that trouble was over he went into the army for a while—a good thing for an Indian warrior, eh? Then, when he had earned some education benefits, he came out, trained as a medical assistant and went into Vista. He's out with the Dakota Sioux now, running a small clinic. He is very happy and soon to get married. I am very happy, too, for now I get grandchildren."

"I am so glad," Penny said, and meant it.

"Yes, you turned him around that time. I know that," Mrs. Smith nodded her head solemnly. "We owe you. So now what can I do for you?"

"Well, I was just wondering if you were related to or could put me in touch with Burrows Smith? I need to talk with him."

"My husband's brother," Mrs. Smith said. "You want to talk with him of this new murder? Do the police think Burrows kill Mrs. Bacon? Burrows would never kill like that—would never shoot a woman in the back."

Penny was astounded. "I do want to talk to him about the murder, but no, the police do not suspect anyone as yet," she gasped. "But . . . how on earth did you know how Mrs. Bacon was killed?"

Mrs. Smith brought in two steaming cups of coffee on a carved wooden tray and favored her with a smile. "Oh, news travels fast in Indian circles. But no magic involved, I have cousin in police here who keeps ears to ground. We have our coffee and then I take you to Burrows. He will see you that way. Without me he would not open his door to you."

"That's very good of you," Penny said, sipping the scalding strong brew. "It would be a great favor. I am trying to talk to everyone who had any contact with Clara Bacon to see if we can find a motive behind this very strange affair, and I understand the Northeastern Indian was one of her specialities.

Mrs. Smith snorted gently. "Oh, yes, much book learning but no understanding, so Mrs. Bacon know nothing of Indians. But come, we finish our coffee and we go."

They went out through the back door, which Mrs. Smith

carefully locked, and then directly into the woods that lay behind her tidy backyard. Mrs. Smith plunged into the trees apparently haphazardly for there was no sign of a path, but forged through the underbrush straight as a homing pigeon until they emerged into a small clearing in the middle of which stood an even smaller rough-hewn wooden cabin.

"You wait here," Mrs. Smith instructed. "I talk with him and he will speak with you outside. His cabin no place for visitors—always in a mess." As she went toward the cabin she called softly and then went in without knocking. She was gone for a good five minutes, while Penny took stock of her surroundings. She noted the huge stacked woodpile by the house, a hen house and a series of hutches containing very large and smug-looking rabbits. The door finally opened and Mrs. Smith came out, followed by a very tall man clad in blue jeans and a short-sleeved shirt; he was carrying three brightly striped plastic-webbed garden chairs, which he placed in the shade beneath a tall oak and silently gestured Penny to be seated in the middle chair.

As she sat she noted that, while he had the high cheekbones and aquiline nose of the Indian, his long jet-black hair, which he had tied back from his face with a leather thong, had a definite frizzy kink to it and that both his skin color and his full lips showed an admixture with the Cape Verde Islanders who, for the past century, had shared Mashpee with the Indians.

Before she could say anything, Burrows Smith said, "You wish to know if I had a motive for killing Clara Bacon. Some seventeen years ago the answer would have been yes, for she was one of those commissioners who decreed at that time that the Wampanoags were no longer a tribe with tribal rights because we lacked a full-time shaman." His deep voice trembled slightly. "This did us great harm at that time, but it is long past. And what is past is gone and cannot be recalled. I held no grudge against her for, unlike many, she was above all an honest woman who sincerely believed in what she did. Of recent years I have considered her an ally, for she fought the land developers and the despoilers of the land, as do I. To me her death is a loss, a great loss. I hope you find her killer." His dark eyes challenged her.

"At this point we are groping in the dark," Penny confessed. "Simply amassing information to get some idea as to *why* anyone would have felt threatened enough to want to kill her. So anything you can tell me of her and her private life would be of help."

"Of her private life I know nothing," he said. "But if you ask me where to look I would say, look to the developers. She had battled them many times. Sometimes she won and sometimes she lost, but she, above all, kept a vigilant eye on them."

"But I understand that, since this recent recession, all that sort of thing is at a standstill on the Cape," Penny protested.

A curious gleam came into his dark eyes. "There are many ways of skinning a deer. No one seems to have realized what a ripe plum for the plucking the Cape is, just now. There are thousands of properties for sale at bargain prices. Anyone with the money to do so could be quietly buying them up piecemeal, and when the tide turns again, as it most surely will, they will be in a very powerful position here. Money is the key, you will find, and the fact that Mrs. Bacon was an honest woman." Mrs. Smith, sitting silent on the other side of Penny, nodded solemn agreement.

"Do you know of any such buying operations?" Penny queried. "Can you give me any names?"

He shook his head, "No, but Clara Bacon was an efficient woman—you may find it in her papers."

"Was Calpurnia Howes also involved in these fights with developers, or, for that matter, with Indian affairs?" she asked.

He snorted. "Ever since the first Thomas Dexter arrived here, none of the Dexters has looked on the Indians as anything other than an inferior race to be swindled and exploited. He did it, and they have continued to do so ever since."

"I don't understand—what has that to do with Mrs. Howes?"

"She is a Dexter by birth, a Howes by marriage," he rumbled. "I thought you would have discovered that by now. As to fights with the land developers, I do not think that is of any interest to her except when some historic building is involved. I believe she did fight to save the Freeman place in Sandwich."

"I see." Penny was still grappling with the amazing Dexter/Howes revelation that again seemed to support Toby's tenuous find. She sat in silence for a minute, as the two Indians watched her, and another idea struck her: Burrows Smith may have had no motive to kill Clara, but an excellent one for seeing her body found and the murder brought to light. How could she put that to him? Finally, as the silence lengthened uncomfortably, she said with some desperation, "I realize that you had no reason for wishing Clara Bacon dead and that her death is a blow to you, so please do not be offended by my next question—where were you between last Wednesday and Friday?"

A faint smile touched his full lips, the dark eyes knowing. "You think *I* put the body in the college?" The smile became a chuckle. "No, I'm afraid there you are again mistaken. All last week I was at a conference of Northeastern Indians in Vermont. I only returned yesterday and the news of her death was as much of a surprise to me as it was to everyone else on the Cape. I did not know she was dead, I did not kill her, nor did I find her. But I am glad that someone did and wished to see justice done." He uncoiled himself from his chair and towered over her. "I wish you well in your quest, and if there is any help we can give, it shall be given."

"And I thank you, Mr. Smith." She clasped his proffered hand and got up. "You have given me much food for thought. I will certainly avail myself of your kind offer if the occasion arises, but I hope I won't be bothering you again."

As her silent guide led the way back into the bushes, Penny looked back at her host to see him standing immobile beneath the mighty oak, his long arms clasped across his chest and his head bowed, deep in thought. Well, she thought, as they emerged in Mrs. Smith's backyard, that's one suspect I think I can cross off the list. Now for the others!

As she thanked Eagle Smith's mother profusely and got back into the car, her mind was already on her next project. Would Birnie let her into Mrs. Bacon's files? Her small face tightened, for, if he refused, it would mean that Toby was indeed on to something and that Birnie was not what he seemed.

Chapter 8

Robert Dyke was so full of news and so eager to impart it that Toby, still struggling with his conscience, sank thankfully into the role of attentive listener. "Well, that deed box sure gave us a better handle on her personal affairs," Dyke enthused as they settled down in Dr. Clarkson's study. "She had raised a home equity loan from a local bank on the Bacon place and had bought the Florida condo outright. It's in a small place just outside of Orlando—Clear Springs—so we're contacting the police on that end to see what's been going on there. There was also a will, updated about a year ago: some fairly sizable bequests, ten thousand to the Indian Rights movement, ten to the Historical Preservation Society and ten to an ecology group that's been active here on the Cape, a thousand to the local Animal Shelter and the residue to nephew Stephen Brown 'if he can be located,' it said. That did nothing to cheer Ernie up, I can tell you. There were deeds to the two properties and a few stock certificates and CDs and some annuity and health insurance papers. In total I figure she'd have had an income of about twelve thousand dollars a year, which is no great fortune but enough for a single lady, I guess. She only had the monthly loan payment to pay and the general upkeep on the two houses and the car. She had also just become due for her Social Security—pretty meager, too, so it must have been based on her late husband's contributions—but it would have made up for what she lost by not teaching at the college anymore."

"So what was her total estate worth?" Toby asked.

Robert shrugged. "Hard to say since the bulk of the value would be in the Bacon place. There's seven acres of it and before the crash that would have been worth a bundle: quarter of a million at least, I'd say. But now . . . ," he shrugged again, "I've no idea. Depends on how much of a hurry this Stephen Brown is in to sell it—*if* he can be found."

"It really does not help us a great deal in establishing a motive," Toby rumbled. "For it is evident that whoever killed her in the first place did *not* intend the body to be found, and that seems to rule out the missing nephew, who is the only one who stood to gain anything substantial from her; without the body he would have had to wait at least seven years to collect."

"Yes, but it's possible he is our mysterious Mr. X who *found* the body," Robert pointed out. "That would make sense, for then he could show up out of the blue now and get the money pronto."

"I'm afraid that just does not hold up," Toby said, a mite testily. "Presuming he was, like his mother Annabel Brown, also California-based, how would he come by the intimate knowledge of the college and its workings? And how do you explain those books?"

"Well, maybe he knew more about his aunt's affairs than we do and that whole scenario is a red herring to point the finger away from him—he'd be our most likely suspect if he was here." Robert warmed to this idea. "After all, he *could* be the murderer. How about this—he shows up in May, say to put the arm on Mrs. B for some money, just as she's taking off. She won't part with any, so he kills her and hides the body, then waits for someone to raise the hue and cry that she's missing.

When no one does, he realizes he'll have this long wait to collect, and so comes back and digs her up, and then plants her in the college along with some phony evidence to point us in the wrong direction."

Toby sniffed. "A highly farfetched theory, if I may say so, without a shred of evidence to back it up. She did not even know his whereabouts, which does not support your basic thesis that he knew about her life here, because they were not even in contact."

"Not when she *made* the will," the policeman said stubbornly. "But they could have been in contact since. Maybe we'll turn up an address on him and letters in her files. Anyway, we have so few facts that theories are about all we have to work on at the moment. Even the autopsy raised more questions than it answered." He heaved a deep sigh.

"It's in then? What did it say?"

"Nothing really helpful. The ME first of all wanted to put her death in late April, for God's sake! When we told him she was known to be alive in the third week of May he got all bent out of shape and said, according to all his books on *adipocere*, that just wasn't possible! And, as we feared, there was no bullet in the body, so we haven't a clue about that or the gun used. About the only useful thing he did come up with—not that it helps us much—was that there was so little earth on the body or clothing that he favored her being in water—fresh, not salt—rather than being buried, unless she was buried *in* something like a coffin. But the lab boys came up with something that seems to make nonsense of that also, for they found traces of moss on her clothes, and moss does not grow in water. Anyway there *is* no water on the Bacon place, so we are worse off than ever."

Toby squirmed uneasily, and then his guilt feelings got the better of him and he burst out, "I think I can explain that. Are you off duty today? Would it be possible for you to take me to the house? Dr. Spring has our only car."

Bob looked inquiringly at him. "I probably won't be off duty until this damn thing is settled, and I was going by the house anyway to put some food out for the cat. What's this all about?"

"I'd rather not explain until we are there and you can see for yourself. Shall we go?" Toby said and retreated into a forbidding silence until their short trip was completed and the cat, who was hanging hopefully around the back door, fed.

"Well?" Bob challenged.

Still silent, Toby retraced his path of the day before and led the way to the well. "I think you'll find this is where she was," he muttered. Dyke looked at him and then at the well and exploded, "Why the hell didn't you tell us about this *yester-day*?"

Toby swung around, leaned on the coping of the well, and proceeded to light up his pipe. "Because . . . ," he said between puffs, "I was trying to sort some things out in my mind and I wanted to talk to you alone before announcing this particular discovery. I know I can trust you."

"And what the hell is that supposed to mean? I don't get you!" Bob said heatedly.

"It's like this . . . ," Toby said, and went over point by point his doubts about Birnie. "Frankly," he concluded, "remembering him from the Dimola affair, I was astounded to find him now in his present position. I was hoping you could explain all this."

To his surprise Robert started to roar with laughter, and when his paroxysm of mirth had subsided, gasped out, "Oh, boy! Are you ever barking up the wrong tree! Suspecting *Ernie*? That's the funniest thing I've heard in years. But . . . ," he sobered himself with an effort, "I can see your point, so I'd better explain. Ernie is where he is not because he is *dis*honest but because he is so damned *honest*—Mr. Incorruptible himself. We all know and *he* knows he is no great brain, and he was terrified when this was first thrust upon him by the powers-that-be. He tried to refuse but they decreed it because the prestige and morale of our police department had to be restored.

"There was a very nasty scandal here a couple of years ago, right at the time when things on the Cape were at their worst," he went on. "I won't bother you with details but it involved drugs the police department had confiscated and which had been sold off on the local market, and both the state police and the FBI got into the act. Our Chief at the time was heavily involved and got the axe, and so, as it turned out, were a lot of officers, all of whom were forced to resign and some of whom have been indicted but not tried as yet. The only knight in shining armor that emerged squeaky clean was honest Ernie. Hence the rapid promotion. And I must say that, on an everyday level of operation, he's done wonders. Morale is back up and routinely we are doing a pretty good job. It's just that anything at all out of the ordinary throws him for a loop—why do you think he flew to you and Dr. Spring so fast? He's out of his depth and he knows it. Added to that he is desperate that this should not reflect badly on any of the *locals*—hence all this waffling about druggies and thieves. God knows we've had too much local scandal already. But to suspect him of complicity . . . well, I'd sooner suspect my own mother!"

Toby knocked his pipe out on the heel of his shoe and straightened up. "I'm prepared to take your word for it," he said quietly, "and so suggest that this discovery was made jointly by us this morning. Tomorrow you can get someone down the well and, if I'm not mistaken, will find that the moss on Mrs. Bacon's clothes matches that on the sides of the well. Her 'rescuer' probably scraped the walls when he was getting the body out."

"It must have been one hell of a job—how do you suppose he managed it?" Dyke said, peering in fascination into the depths of the well.

Toby indicated the stout winding post with his pipe. "It would not be too difficult. I imagine something like a block and tackle around that and a grappling iron at the other end of the rope and up she would come. Dump the body into the wheel-chair from the house and the rest would be easy enough."

"But if he *wasn't* the murderer, how do you suppose he ever tumbled to the fact her body was in the well?" Dyke muttered.

Toby shrugged, "We won't know that until we find him, but maybe he did what I did—followed the cat." He looked thoughtfully at the bucket beside the well. "Maybe he was going to give it a drink, wound the bucket down and hit the body instead, and was either too scared or too intimidated just to do the obvious and report it. But who knows? It's just another theory to add to our endless supply of them."

"All things considered, we haven't been doing too badly," the policeman reproved. "In three days we've more or less pinned down the how, when, and where—which is pretty good going, I'd say."

"But *not* the all-important why," Toby retaliated. "Or rather the double why—the why of her killing and the why of her resurrection. Until we've got those we have nothing. Since we're here, what about having a quiet browse through her files? That may give us some further pointers. We may be able to locate significant gaps or even a lead to that missing nephew."

Robert looked uncomfortable. "I don't think we can do that. Birnie made a great point of saying that the files should not be touched until we've heard from the Florida and California police. He wants a one-time and all-out effort on them with a squad of men, and we can't afford the manpower at the moment. He thought maybe in the middle of this coming week."

Toby regarded him with raised eyebrows. "I should think that a squad of policemen all pawing through them at once would be the very worst way to go about it. Two men who know what they are doing and what the background is would be far more effective. Surely you can see that?"

Robert looked away from him. "Sorry. His orders were definite. No can do."

Toby frowned, his suspicions reviving. "Then there is one thing I think you should make very clear to Chief Birnie. Dr. Spring and I agreed to help on this but our first priority is what we came here for initially: a family vacation. In all probability our family will be back next weekend. After that we will no longer be available, so speed is of the utmost importance if he is seriously interested in our input."

"You mean you'd just drop it?"

"Precisely," Toby said loftily. "After all, this is basically none of our business, is it?"

Robert gulped. "Look, tell you what I can do. Gaps in the main files wouldn't tell us all that much, because she had a lot of files with her in those boxes in the car. Ernie didn't say anything about those, so what I *could* do would be to let you look through those and, if you would make a list of them for me, that would speed things up when we do get to the other files. How would that suit you?"

"Better than nothing," Toby growled. "Where are they?"

"Still in the car. We just locked it up again. We found her keys in that tote bag." He slapped his pockets frantically. "I think I've still got them—yes, here they are. We could take them back to your place and I'd pick them up tomorrow. Okay?"

Toby nodded, and as they walked back through the wood Dyke asked, "Did you get anything out of those books?"

"I haven't had time to study them in depth, as yet, but as Dr. Spring pointed out in that report she gave you, they do seem to indicate the various projects in which she was involved when she was killed. And I did come across an interesting thing in the Howes genealogy . . . ," and he went on to explain that.

Robert's comment was identical to Penny's. "Pretty thin! After all, you said it was an old book. That mark could have been put in it any time between when it was published and now."

"The mark appeared to be fresh to me," Toby insisted. "So

I think it's worth a follow-up. I wish I knew someone who was into genealogy. I haven't the time to do it myself."

Robert perked up. "My wife is crazy about that kind of stuff—she's a Bourne, you see. She'd do it like a shot, if you'll tell me what you want done."

Toby looked at him in surprise. "But I thought you said you had children?"

"So we have. Two. But Linda could dump them on her mother for a few days. She does it all the time anyway, and would just love a genuine excuse to get into Boston. *That's* her idea of fun."

"In that case," Toby said, as they unloaded the boxes from the car and transfered them to the cruiser, "I'll give you the details of this Dexter-Howes marriage back at the house. And I would be delighted to pay all expenses involved."

"What I would like her to do," he continued, as they headed back to Hyannisport, "is to try and trace the descendants of that particular family and see if they link up with any of the people Clara was intimately connected with here. Those would be, according to our information thus far, Fitzgerald, Norman, Crowell, Corey, Smith, and Mrs. Howes."

The policeman whistled softly. "Some mighty big Cape names in that lot! Somehow I don't think Ernie is going to be very happy when he sees Dr. Spring's report. If any of them are personally involved in this, we're in for some fine old fireworks, but I'm still backing an outsider myself—namely, Stephen Brown."

They unloaded the boxes into Clarkson's study and Toby provided the names and marriage date before Dyke took his speedy departure. With the young policeman's farewell warning that he would have to pick them up again early on the morrow, Toby got right to work. The list of the files was quickly made in his small, neat handwriting, but then he went back through them and abstracted several that had caught his eye and began to study them in detail, with growing and absorbed interest. He was so intent that he became belatedly aware that someone was moving around in the house and, tearing himself reluctantly away, opened the study door and peered out.

"Oh, there you are!" Penny said. "Come on, I was just fixing soup and a sandwich—let's eat. I have lots to tell you."

"I'm very busy," he muttered. "Can't it wait? I think I'm really on to something."

"No it can't. You had no breakfast after I left, by the looks of it, and it'll be hours until dinner. And I think I'm on to something too," she said, bustling about the kitchen. "Oh, and by the way, this should cheer you up. I've got a Dexter-Howes link for you. . . ." She proceeded to enlarge on her morning's work, as she heated soup and slapped together two enormous sandwiches.

Toby listened to her in round-eyed fascination, as the food appeared before him at a speed that would have brought a gasp from a short-order cook. Penny sat down opposite him and started in on her soup, saying, "I've simply *got* to get hold of Keith Corey. I've set up an appointment with Robideau, or rather his assistant, for this afternoon. Don't want to wait until tomorrow for the college to open to get Corey's address. Since he is no longer on the Cape, it strikes me that he'll be more of a disinterested party and more likely to open up about what's been happening here. What Burrows Smith said makes a heap of sense to me, so I think I may be on to the motive."

"Oh?" Toby murmured, "And what is that, pray tell?"

"Something to do with land developers—Clara Bacon was a constant thorn in their side and there's big money in land development. Don't you agree?"

"No, not unless you can come up with something a lot more concrete than you have now. All you have is a vague theory. You see I've just come up with an even stronger motive," Toby said, and dropped his bombshell. "Treasure trove—buried treasure, and Clara was right in the thick of it."

Chapter 9

When Penny pointed out that Toby's theory was every bit as devoid of facts as hers, a lively argument developed until, almost simultaneously, they realized the futility of their sparring. Toby was the first to sue for peace; he broke off in the middle of an acid riposte and chuckled, "This is senseless. We *both* may be on to something, but it's far too early to say what is meaningful and what isn't, so let's get back to work. You do your thing and I'll do mine."

The wind completely taken out of her bellicose sails, Penny gobbled for a second and then grinned back at him. "Fair enough. We really do seem to be improving with age, time was when we'd have kept this going for hours." There was a wistful note in her voice.

He got up and smiled ruefully down at her, "Well I'm glad that age is improving *something*. I'd hate to think it was all downhill. And we haven't much time left to waste." He ambled back to the study.

As she drove toward her rendezvous with the realtor, she thought about his "treasure" theory. In essence it was based on a scholarly row that had grown between Vincent Norman, the boat builder turned marine archaeologist, and Clara Bacon, and was based on a file of newspaper clippings heavily annotated by the murdered woman. The clippings, all from local papers, spread over a two-year period and commenced with a short news brief: "Vincent Norman of Dennis claims to have come upon the wreck of the steamer *Portland* which foundered November 26, 1898, in 162 feet of water, two miles off Provincetown. Norman states he is going after the fortune in bullion on board." This was followed by a long letter from Clara to the same paper, stating that first of all she doubted whether he had found the *Portland* in the position given, and second, that the "treasure" involved was of no great magnitude since it was known that the ship carried a mere $220,000 worth of gold and silver and a further $18,000 in uncut diamonds.

An exchange of increasingly acidulous letters had taken place between Norman and Mrs. Bacon, culminating in Vincent's assertion that he was continuing the hunt. Then there was a six-month interval followed by a full-page article from which Clara had underlined, "Dramatic find by Norman. Sunken U-boat found near wreck of Portland. Gold ingots recovered. Heavy security being clamped on all further diving in area. Local fishermen angered. U-boat believed to be the World War I submarine U156 that attacked barges off Orleans in July, 1918."

This had been followed by a positively querulous letter from Clara stating that this also was an impossible claim, since the U156 was known to have hit a mine on returning to its base in Germany and had sunk with all hands in the North Sea. Norman had then countered by withdrawing his first identification and stating that the U-boat was more probably from World War II, but that it definitely had carried bullion and had been destroyed by a huge internal explosion that had scattered it in fragments all over the seabed in the vicinity of two other wrecks, the purported *Portland* and the schooner *Addie E. Snow*. He also went on to claim that he had recovered approximately two million dollars in gold and silver ingots, with a lot more to come.

Public interest and support, including State Senator Fitzgerald's, had swung over to Norman at this point. The only subsequent item from Clara had been a challenge to identify this purported World War II U-boat, although she had filed the subsequent reports on Norman's continuing success. "It all sounds very fishy to me," Toby had commented. "The man changes his story three times after being prodded by Clara."

"But he has produced the treasure and so it must have come from a wreck. So what does it matter?" she had pointed out.

"At this stage I just don't know. But Clara thought there was something phony about it and I do too," Toby had stated firmly, and it was at this point they had called it a day.

She came to with a start to find in her ponderings she had missed her turn in West Barnstable and had now emerged on Route 6A on the opposite side of the Cape. Vexed, she drew the car over, groped for a map, and drove down the old King's Highway until she could turn back toward Route 28 and rectify her error. She groped her way back slowly and finally came upon her goal a good fifteen minutes late for her appointment.

The realtor's office stood in a mini-mall that, judging by its scarcely weathered shingles, was only a few years old. It spread in a semi-circle off the road, an almost-empty parking lot in front of it. It also, very evidently, was a mini-mall that had never got off the ground for, apart from the realtor's office that occupied its central store, only two of the other stores were occupied, one a hairdresser's and the other a small gift shop of the type omnipresent on the Cape, that announced on its front window ALL MERCHANDISE 50% OFF. The rest bore FOR RENT signs under the Robideau logo in their dusty, blank windows.

She parked in front of the realtor's office and hurried inside. "So sorry I'm late," she apologized to its sole occupant, a young red-headed girl. "We talked earlier, I believe? I'm Penelope Spring—it's Miss Duncan, isn't it?"

The girl got up and showed her to a chair. "Yes, I'm sorry Dr. Spring, but I did try and call you to cancel but you'd already left. I'm afraid I haven't anything for you. Mr. Corey's file isn't here—Mr. Robideau must have taken it for some reason, and I'm not sure where he is at the moment. He's off-Cape. He should be back in the next day or so."

"Oh, dear, what a disappointment! All I wanted was Mr. Corey's new address in Florida." Penny looked pointedly at the computer on the girl's desk. "Wouldn't you have that in your computer?"

"I'm afraid not, I did check. All we have in there is the address of the house we sold for him, the date of transfer of ownership, the price and so on."

"What a pity!" Penny bounced up from her chair. "Well, I won't take up your time, and I'm sorry to have put you to so much trouble for nothing."

"No trouble," the girl murmured. "There's not much doing at the moment. Things are still very slow."

"So I gather. Mr. Corey was very lucky to sell, I believe."

"*And* at a good price!" Miss Duncan seemed thankful to have someone to talk to. "The only really good sale we've had in a while."

"Oh?" She was mildly curious.

"Yes, $225,000 he got for it," the girl prattled on.

Penny was startled. "*That* much! Who bought it?"

"Some corporation in New York—a summer home for one of their top executives I expect," Miss Duncan confided. "I could give you their name and address, if you like."

"No, it's not important—but thanks anyway." Penny headed for the door.

"Shall I have Mr. Robideau contact you when he gets back?"

"No, that's not necessary either, I can get Mr. Corey's address and phone from the college tomorrow." Then another thought struck her and she turned back. "Oh, just one other thing. How would I go about finding out information on housing developments on Cape Cod, say in the last ten years? Would you have that sort of data here?"

The girl looked at her curiously. "No, only our own holdings. Your best bet would be the Registry of Deeds. That's in Barnstable Courthouse on 6A. What developments did you have in mind?"

"Oh, just in general," Penny said vaguely. "I'll have to do some map searching first. Thanks again," and went out.

The sun was still shining so she decided that she had done all she could for the day and would get in some beach time. She returned to the house, changed, told Toby of her plans, eliciting a preoccupied grunt in response, and drove to Craigville. Finding a spot for herself at the far end, she repeated her performance of two days before by falling asleep almost immediately and waking hours later, chilled to the bone by the sea breeze. As she rubbed herself briskly, she looked down the rapidly emptying beach and did a double take. Striding purposefully towards her was Toby's tall figure flanked by two blue uniforms, and for a second she thought she was experiencing *déjà vu*. Then Toby waved and boomed out, "A remarkable development. Thought you'd want to be in on it. The Florida police report that Mrs. Bacon's condo has been burglarized and searched!"

She sprang to her feet. "What was taken?"

"Nothing, apparently." As they came up to her, Toby was the only one of the trio who looked at all happy about this new turn of events; Robert Dyke wore an anxious frown and Ernie Birnie appeared to be in deep gloom.

"One interesting thing the police there spotted. There were masses of mail piled up, most of it junk mail, a number of bills, bank statements, and so forth—but not one solitary piece of personal mail. One bright lad down there suggested that maybe that's what the burglar was after and that he made off with all the personal stuff."

"Any idea when it happened?" she queried.

"Nothing conclusive, but we may have a pointer." He nodded at Dyke. "You tell her."

Robert looked even more anxious as he took up the narrative. "Well, the cop who had the idea about the mail checked back as a matter of routine with the local post office—it's a substation and not all that busy except in their winter season. A mail clerk there came up with an interesting bit of info. About a month ago someone came in with one of those slips to claim an undelivered registered letter. The clerk happened to remember the name on the slip as Bacon, because *his* name was Egg and this struck him as funny. And he remembers the first name was a woman's name so he would not surrender it to the man who was trying to pick it up. He insisted the addressee come in herself. The man did not put up an argument—he just went away."

"Could he describe the man?" she asked eagerly.

Robert sighed and shook his head. "No, that's as far as his memory went—couldn't say if he was tall, short, old, young: nothing but male."

"What happened to the letter then?"

"That's what we're trying to find out." Birnie broke his glum silence. "It's no longer there. But we believe there's some sort of regulation that says if a registered letter isn't delivered within a certain length of time, it is then returned to the sender. So it could be anywhere."

She and Toby eyed each other. "Or, if Mrs. Bacon had sent that letter to *herself*, it most probably would have come back here to the old address," Toby murmured. "And if *that* address were no longer operative, what would happen to it then? A continuous cycle, or would the post office here keep it?"

"If, if, if . . . ," Birnie snarled suddenly. "Nothing but fucking ifs! Why the hell should she send a letter to herself? Just another cockamamy theory, that's all." He turned on his heel and stamped off down the beach.

"It's worth a try. I'll check the main PO here tomorrow,"

Robert said apologetically. "And the Florida police are sending the rest of the stuff—junk mail excepted—by Federal Express, so we should have that tomorrow. I'll let you know if we come up with anything. Now I'd better get after him. He's real upset." And he followed after the chief.

Penny gathered up her things, and Toby and she trudged after them. "Getting interesting, isn't it?" he murmured. "Whoever tried to pick up that letter knew a month ago that Clara would never be around to pick it up herself—ergo, it was either the murderer or her resurrector. But, if the latter, why did he wait another month before acting?" Then he proceeded to answer his own question. "Most likely because he *couldn't* do it earlier for some reason. Perhaps that letter had something to do with him and he had to get his hands on it before he could reveal the body."

Penny was busy with her own train of thought and did not pay much mind to his musings. "You know there's another oddity we haven't considered up to now," she volunteered. "Why would Clara head down to Florida just in time for its most unpleasant season? Granted the end of May and June aren't too bad, but July and August are awful, a regular steambath! Could she have been getting out because she knew someone was after her? Did she leave then because she was afraid for her life?"

Toby grunted. "It could equally well be that she only planned to stay down there a short while and then return to the Cape when it got hot. Or maybe she and this Corey fellow were planning a romantic rendezvous down there. Who knows? Seeing the reflective gleam appear in Penny's mild hazel eyes, he added hastily. "For Heaven's sake, I wasn't serious! Just pointing out this endless speculation isn't getting us anywhere."

"Nevertheless it's an idea," she mused. "I just can't believe that anyone could be as friendless as Clara Bacon seemed to be—she *had* to have had some intimate contact, someone who cared."

They had regained the shelter of the car, and while Toby lit up his pipe she gazed absently at the beach. Its character had changed with the dimming of the light and the stiff breeze that had driven the basking family groups homeward. Now all that remained were a few elderly people armed with metal detectors, who were pursuing with grim determination solitary paths that crisscrossed the empty beach with the deliberation of some strange formalized dance. She watched them in growing astonishment. Directly in front of her was an old woman so armed, clad unsuitably in faded pastel shorts and a shabby tank top. A shapeless linen hat was crammed down over her forehead from which tendrils of wild gray hair writhed in the wind. Her bare legs were bluish with the cold and the darker blue of ropelike varicose veins wound up her legs like ivy around a tree trunk. Her rival for this portion of the beach was an elderly pot-bellied man, whose bald head shone pallid in the waning gleams of the sunset and whose withered arms and hands were mottled with the liver spots of age. They did not speak, nor did they recognize the presence of the other, but when the woman's metal detector pinged, the man stopped and watched anxiously as she burrowed like an eager dog in the sand. When she emerged with a metal beer cap which she threw with disgust on to the tarmac of the parking lot, a faint smile touched his lips and he went back to his work. When his pinged the same scene was reenacted. The woman froze and watched intently as he burrowed, emerging triumphantly with a sand-covered dime, which he carefully brushed off and then pocketed before moving on. The woman's lips thinned with determination and, slit-eyed, she headed for that portion of the beach.

"Extraordinary!" Toby murmured, "Never seen anything like it. What on earth do you suppose they hope to find?"

Penny looked at him bleakly. "Their treasure trove—spare change, a dropped watch, a piece of jewelry. It all adds up if you're old and poor and on Social Security. Besides, it's cheap entertainment." She sighed. "Let's get out of here, I find this profoundly depressing. We'll eat at the house. I don't feel like going out tonight."

On the short drive back Toby broke the silence. "Since I really do think I'm on to something with this bullion salvage angle, do you mind if I check up on Fitzgerald and Norman? I'd like to sound them out first hand."

She roused herself. "Go ahead, be my guest, and I hope you'll have better luck in tracking them down than I've had. Pity marine archaeology isn't your field; it would give you an in with Norman."

"Perhaps, and then again, perhaps not—if he *is* up to something fishy," he murmured. "But just being an archaeologist should make my enquiry a legitimate one that he can't easily ignore."

"Once everything opens up again tomorrow I'm going to be very busy anyway." She was regaining her briskness. "To the college for Corey's address, then to Barnstable to snoop into their Registry of Deeds on the land-development angle."

"I thought you were interviewing Caleb Crowell," he said, as they made their way up to the house.

"So I am." She headed for the kitchen and peered thoughtfully into the refrigerator.

Toby strolled after her. "I came across something in Clara's files that makes me think you should handle him with due caution. In fact I should tell him as little as possible about what we've been up to."

"I wasn't about to give him a blow by blow, but why the sudden concern?" She extracted a bag of frozen shrimp and a packet of frozen peas and two eggs, and then foraged in the cupboard for noodles and a can of mushroom soup.

"Because the original name of the widespread Cape Crowell family was Crowe," he rumbled.

She deposited the makings of their dinner on the counter by

107

the sink and looked at him. "So? What's that got to do with anything?"

"Your memory is definitely not what it used to be," he reproved. "Don't you recall that I told you about my little experiment with the map in the classroom? Clara Bacon's dead finger was arranged to point at something on that map, and the only place young Bob could come up with was a beach called *Crowe's* pasture. Get it?"

"Got it," she said. "We're having shrimp casserole and salad. Okay?"

Chapter 10

The nightly bulletin from New York had had its pluses and its minuses: Marcus' fever had spiked again, Mala's had come down a little, so now they were a matched pair of miserable tots. All the Russian babysitters, save the melodious and indispensable Boris, had been banished for the moment by Sonya, to be resummoned on an individual basis in case of dire need. She herself was looking somewhat wan, Alex had reported anxiously, so he did not think they would be up by the coming weekend. Penny, as she drove to her Crowell appointment, felt a guilty twinge of relief—this would give them a breathing space to go on with their investigation, another whole week in fact, for Toby and she had agreed that as soon as the family was together again they would drop the investigation, hand over whatever information they had acquired to the police, and get on with their interrupted vacation. Having stated this firm and worthy intent, she was certain that Toby was just as reluctant to let go of this fascinating conundrum of a case as she was.

In spite of Toby's cautious admonitions she had high hopes for her coming interview, for the wary Calpurnia had been so negative about it that she felt this was a sure sign that Crowell must have valuable information to impart, and she edged impatiently along in the bumper to bumper traffic that moved sluggishly toward Dennis on Route 28. The Crowell house was right on Route 28 in West Dennis and she located it without difficulty, turning thankfully out of the continuous stream of traffic. She drew up to a ramshackle barn at the rear of the house, which was a pleasantly unpretentious, rambling mid-Victorian building. As she climbed out of the car, its back door opened and two very large cats emerged, one black, one white, followed by the burly figure of a man. He was of middle height, but his burliness made him appear short, his black hair thinning over a round skull, his face equally round and high-colored, with small, dark sparkling eyes and a very large nose. He grinned cheerfully at her.

"Welcome to the old homestead, Dr. Spring! No architectural gem, as you can see, but built by my great-grandfather Ebenezer with his own hands in 1854 to house his family of eight. Since I am a bachelor I rattle around in it a bit, but, what the heck, it's home! Want a tour before we get down to business?"

"Maybe later," she smiled back at him. "I'm on a rather tight schedule today."

"Well then, come on in and let's get to it." He took her by the elbow and steered her through the back door, which gave on to a small, neat kitchen, and then into a large, green-carpeted living room with pleasantly shabby furniture mixed in with genuine colonial antiques. He seated her in a chintz-covered overstuffed chair that engulfed her and sat down opposite her. "Anything I can get you before we start?" he enquired. "Coffee, tea, a drink?"

"No, nothing thanks." Despite his genial air there was something about him that rankled. She felt an almost immediate antipathy that made her wary.

"So what can I do for you? Or am I being grilled as a suspect?" His grin seemed a permanent fixture.

She ignored the second question. "I'd just like you to tell me everything you know about Clara Bacon—what she was like, who her friends were, whom she quarreled with, and, if you have any ideas on who would want her dead and why, I'd like to hear those too."

He puffed out his cheeks in mock alarm. "That's a large order! I knew her for a very long time, and her husband before that—played football against him in high school. He was Barnstable and I was in Dennis-Yarmouth of course. Regular Mama's boy he was, an only child and all . . . ," he rambled on. She did not interrupt so that eventually and somewhat grudgingly he returned to the point.

"Didn't really get to know Clara until she came back to the Cape as a middle-aged widow twenty-odd years ago. She was a regular joiner—joined everything in sight, and very keen. Always worked hard to be in with the 'in' group, though not being a Cape Codder, I think she found it hard sledding. Lived with her mother-in-law, who was, and that helped a bit, I guess. They got along all right. Then about, oh, five or six years ago, the old lady started to fail and Clara had to spend a lot of her time looking after her. Resigned from a lot of things then and rarely showed up at the others. When the old lady passed away it must have been a relief. Anyway Clara came roaring back, trying to make up for lost time—she'd lost a lot of ground and clout and so got pugnacious about pushing her way back in."

"Did she quarrel with a lot of people?" Penny interjected.

He pursed his full lips. "Quarrel is too strong a word, but she crossed swords with most of us at one time or another. If Clara had one outstanding characteristic I'd say it was obstinacy. She was as stubborn as hell if she thought she was in the right. A regular bulldog—she'd clamp on and hang on until her opponent dropped from sheer exhaustion. Even our Iron Maiden couldn't down her when she was in that mode."

"Iron Maiden?" Penny queried innocently, knowing full well.

"You had your Iron Maiden in Maggie Thatcher, we have our Cape Cod version in Calpurnia Howes," he grinned at her. "I know you've met Calpurnia, so you must know what I mean."

"Not *my* Maggie Thatcher," Penny corrected. "I'm an American."

"Yeah, but you've been in England so long that you must be more of a limey than a Yank by this time," he scoffed. "You see I've been checking up on you, just as you've been checking up on me. I know all about you and your highfalutin sidekick and your globe-trotting sleuthing. You must really get a kick out of it!" It was almost a sneer.

"Not really, let's just say I have an aptitude for it. And I'm not here to talk about me," she said severely. "So let's get back to Clara Bacon."

But he appeared to have worked himself up into a state of excitement. "So what did Calpurnia have to say about me?" he challenged. "I bet she gave you a lot of guff about me being the black sheep, do-nothing of the Crowells, living it up on what remains of the Crowell patrimony. Calpurnia can be a real bitch when she chooses and she's never been overly fond of me and my doings. Not that she hasn't plenty of skeletons in her own cupboard to rattle!"

"Was she also on bad terms with Clara Bacon?" Penny demanded.

This seemed to deflate him. "Bad terms? No, I wouldn't say so," he muttered. "Certainly not bad enough to want her dead. That's something that puzzles the hell out of me. I can't think of *anyone* who disliked Clara enough to want her dead. Basically she wasn't an *un*pleasant person—certainly not in the way that Calpurnia is most of the time. She wasn't overly aggressive or opinionated, and she *could* be very reasonable. We got on famously on the whole."

"Who were her closest friends, would you say?"

His heavy brows knitted. "Friends? There you have me. She

wasn't an unfriendly person, but then again she wasn't all that friendly either—sort of standoffish, if you know what I mean?"

"How about Keith Corey?" she prompted.

He snorted. "*That* old woman! Always was a bit of a fussbudget and a nickel squeezer, but he's got a lot worse since his wife died a couple of years back. I, for one, was glad to hear he was taking himself off to sunny Florida—good riddance!"

"You don't know of any, say, romantic attachment he may have had with Clara Bacon?" she said tentatively.

He gazed at her in utter astonishment. "Romance! He and Clara! You're off your rocker. Clara was about as romantic as an old boot. As for him, if he hadn't been so mean I think he'd have gone after the young chicks; he was that sort."

"Then how about Clara's feud with your Dennis neighbor, Vincent Norman?"

His face closed up. "He's no neighbor of mine. He lives on the other side of the Cape in Dennisport. We don't move in the same circles and whatever Norman is up to he does not confide in me. He's a close one, and close-fisted into the bargain. Very tight-lipped about what's going on in those wrecks of his. Not like Barry Clifford and his *Whidah* finds . . . ," and he went rambling off on a long digression about the spectacular finding and salvaging of the pirate ship *Whidah* during the 1980s, concluding with, ". . . now Clifford had his share of controversies, but you always knew where you stood with him. With Norman no one seems to know what's going on or where all that bullion is coming from. I've heard tell he's up to ten million . . . ." There was a note of yearning in his voice. "Not that the Cape will get any benefit from it, I'll be bound—after the government has taken its cut it'll all go to him and his mysterious backers."

She was interested. "I thought Senator Fitzgerald was backing him."

Crowell snorted again in outrage. "That lace-curtain Irishman! Didn't have two nickels to rub together when he came down here from Boston to set up his law practice. He's done all right since, but hasn't got the kind of money to back Norman's operation. No, I've no idea who's in back of it. Maybe it's drug money."

She brought him back to the point. "So you would not say Norman was upset by Clara's challenges?"

He chuckled suddenly. "Oh, she was a thorn in his side right enough! I've seen him mighty red-faced at meetings when she calmly shot down his fanciful theories. But nothing succeeds like success, and once the public was on his side he just ignored her."

"So did she give up on it?"

"Oh, Clara never gave up on anything. As I said, she was as stubborn as hell." He stirred restlessly in his chair.

"I believe she also had some fights with land developers. Do you know anything about those—who they were and so on?"

"Not in detail, no. One of the big fights she lost was the one near her own property. Very bitter about that she was. Hated Robideau's guts after that."

"Robideau!" She was electrified. "The man who sold Keith Corey's house?"

"Did he?" Crowell sounded indifferent, his gaze now fixed longingly on a whisky decanter on a small square table across the room by the large window overlooking Route 28. "Sure I can't get a drink for you now? I'm going to have one." He sprang up and headed for it.

"Not for me, thanks," she called after him, and waited patiently while he poured himself a large whisky on the rocks, returned to his chair, and downed it in three huge swallows. "So what can you tell me about Robideau?" she prodded.

He looked startled, as if he had forgotten she was there. "Him? Oh, a French Canadian—relative newcomer to the Cape. Came down some ten or eleven years ago when things were still on the upswing here. From the Montreal region, I believe. Did well enough at the start, but got hit like everyone else when the bottom fell out of the real estate market. Always been a bit of a wheeler-dealer, I understand. Clara was convinced he was a crook, but then she was biased. Hated to lose a fight, did Clara." He sprang up again and loped across the room to replenish his glass as Penny, her thoughts in a whirl from all this information, groped around for unexplored avenues.

When he was once again seated and working happily on his second large drink, she said, "Do you know anything of Jocelyn Combe?"

"The mystery writer? Heard her speak a couple of times—bit of an old frump, but writes a rattling good mystery story, I must admit. I like mysteries," he confided with all the gravity of a small boy. His eyes were already slightly unfocused and she wondered if she was witnessing part of his usual daily routine or if something she had asked had plunged him into this sudden drinking bout. "I understand that she and Clara were friendly," she prompted.

"Were they?" He looked at her blearily. "Anyway, what odds? She couldn't have done it. She left the Cape and went back to England—saw that in the paper months ago." Again he returned to the decanter.

Penny felt it was time to go before he passed out on her. She made one last try. "So have you any ideas of your own about who might have killed Clara Bacon?"

He slumped down in the chair, his eyes dull, and wagged his head emphatically from side to side. "None." He leaned his head back, closed his eyes and sighed, "Poor old Clara! I'll miss her. Yes, I'll miss her." To Penny's dismay two large tears rolled down his rosy cheeks from beneath his closed eyelids: a crying drunk she could live without.

"I must go now," she said hastily, "I have another appointment, but thank you Mr. Crowell for all your information. You've been most helpful."

His eyes opened. "Have I?" he queried. "Good! Well,

anytime, dear lady, anytime at all. Come back anytime . . . ." He struggled to get up.

"Don't get up, I can see myself out," she said, "Thanks again." And she hurried back to the car.

Not wanting to face the congestion of Route 28 again, she consulted the map and then headed for the Mid-Cape highway, zooming down it until she came to the Route 132 exit and the community college sign. As she gained the ring road of the college and drew up before the administration building, she saw Sam Nickerson come out of the office door and head purposefully for the flagpoles on the cement island beside her. She rolled down her window and called out, "Is it all right if I leave my car here for a bit while I go to the continuing education office, Mr. Nickerson?"

He jerked his chin toward the 15 MINUTES ONLY parking sign in the bay and said, "If you're going to be any length of time, you'd be best off in faculty parking over there." Again he jerked his chin at the lot opposite.

She quickly rounded the island and parked in a lot opposite the flagpoles, and as she crossed the road was interested to see that Sam was busy lowering the Stars and Stripes to half-mast. As she came up to him she queried in surprise, "Is that still for Clara Bacon?"

The security guard looked gloomily at her. "No, another faculty member went over the weekend. This is for him."

"Oh, I'm sorry to hear that." She went to move on.

"Yes," Sam continued. "Just retired too. Didn't get to enjoy much of it—stupid hit and run accident."

Penny turned back slowly, a cold feeling growing inside her. "Who was it?"

"Professor Corey. Used to teach history here. Just went down to his new home in Florida, then whammo! Cut down in the street by some drunk driver. Saturday night they say it happened." Sam said with gloomy relish. "Makes you think, don't it?"

The cold enveloped her. "It certainly does, it most certainly does," she muttered, and made her way slowly up the steps.

Chapter 11

Sir Tobias Glendower was feeling very pleased with himself, positively smug in fact. Not only had he tracked down Fitzgerald and Norman, but had made an immediate appointment with the former and had received a pledge from the lugubrious Mrs. Norman—having established he was *not* a journalist—that her husband would contact him for a meeting on the morrow. Added to this double coup, he had decided it was high time he had wheels of his own, so he had Robert Dyke, who had come by on his way to work to fill him in on the latest news, drop him off at the nearest car rental agency. His delight in his new liberty, however, had been somewhat dampened by the fact that all he could hire was a bright green compact with automatic drive—which he despised.

In spite of this he had taken it, for what he had in mind required him to distance himself as far as possible from his connections with the official police. Despite all the other developments he was still very unsure of Birnie, and a nugget of news that Dyke had just confided had reawakened his doubts. The packet from the Florida police had duly arrived and Birnie had immediately taken sole charge of it. On top of this, he had ordained that all the files in the Bacon house be removed to the police station unexamined "for safekeeping."

"But that's absurd!" Toby had protested. "Since we know both the murderer and the resurrector had access to the house and therefore could have removed any documents at any time they pleased, the only value in those files would have been to examine them for *gaps* in her system—for we know she was a very systematic woman—to give us at least some indication of the areas of the murderer's interest. Once a bunch of you have bundled them all willy-nilly into boxes, that particular line of evidence will be hopelessly destroyed. It's as bad as unsystematic excavation. A classic example of shutting the stable door after the horse is gone!"

"Well, that's what's being done." Robert, himself, did not look too happy about it. "Though personally I think the vital stuff must have been in that registered letter, but there's no sign of that, either in West Barnstable or Hyannis. I'm going to try at the main clearing center at Buzzards Bay next—but it's a faint hope, I'm afraid. God knows where it is by now. It's proving as elusive as Stephen Brown."

"Nothing on him then?"

"The California police are working on it, but so far not a trace, although he *was* in their computer. Arrested three years ago for drunk driving. Got off with a fine. He was living with his mother at the time, so that's no help."

They had parted with a mutual pledge to meet at the Bacon house that afternoon, for Toby had decided he needed more of Mrs. Bacon's genealogy books for consultation and Robert was still on the cat-feeding detail. "It's a nice cat and I'd take it like a shot but my wife, Linda, is allergic to cats," he confided. "I'm trying to find a home for it. After all it has been through I'd hate to take it to the animal shelter, at least not until it's back in shape. Oh, and Linda will be off to Boston tomorrow to start on your genealogical queries." And on that promising note they had parted.

Toby cruised along North Street in Hyannis until he located the building housing Fitzgerald's local office, then turned into the public parking lot on the opposite side of the road, already crowded with morning shoppers. He crossed the road and entered the square redbrick building which, he noted with passing interest, also housed the local FBI office. In Fitzgerald's outer office he was greeted by a somewhat haggard-faced, smartly dressed woman, just on the wrong side of forty. "Oh yes, Sir Tobias, you do have an appointment, but I'm afraid the senator is still occupied, so if you'd kindly take a seat until he's free?" Her voice was a flat, nasal monotone.

Toby obediently sat down, then reached in his pocket and started to fill his pipe. "No smoking in here!" the flat voice snapped. "You'll have to put that away."

His silvery eyebrows rose a fraction and he surged to his feet. He was unaccustomed to being snapped at and, furthermore, had never appreciated the current American fanaticism about smoking. "In that case I think I'll just wander along to the FBI upstairs," he said stiffly. "Perhaps when Fitzgerald is free you could call up there and let me know?"

He started for the outer door, but before he reached it the door to the inner office swung open and Fitzgerald came bursting out, hand outstretched and a falsely bright smile fixed on his lean, young-looking, yet obviously middle-aged face. "So sorry to keep you waiting, Sir Tobias—an important phone call. Please do come in. I'm Tom Fitzgerald." He positively bustled Toby through the inner door and into a blue leather wing chair by a handsome cherry desk. Sitting down on the other side of the desk, he said brightly, "Now what can I do to assist you?"

Toby launched into his carefully planned scenario. "As I explained on the phone, I'm an archaeologist, summering here with my family, and have become most interested in a project in which I believe you are involved, namely, Vincent Norman's marine archaeological excavation. I wondered if you could give me some insight on the economics involved in such an enterprise? I am thinking of backing one myself—off Scotland—and would like to know about approximate costs, number of backers required, how the salvage shares are allotted, all that sort of thing."

Fitzgerald was staring at him in blank surprise. "What's that got to do with Clara Bacon? I thought that's what you were here about," he blurted out. "Aren't you assisting the police with her murder?"

Damn it to hell, Toby thought, as his beautiful scenario went up in smoke. How the devil did he know that! Some loose lips at the police station for certain. He tried to salvage what he could from the wreck. "Oh that," he managed to look puzzled. "Well, yes, they have asked my advice on a couple of things— but that's not what I came here for. Why? Was Clara Bacon connected in any way with Norman's enterprise?" He went on the attack. "If so, I'd be most interested to know about that."

Fitzgerald was visibly disconcerted. "Well, no, not really, Not at all in the *active* sense. Any more than I am. I think you have been misinformed."

Toby stared fixedly at him. "I understood you were Norman's principal backer for this enterprise."

"No! That's not right," the senator exploded, then collected himself with an effort. "As state senator for this area I am interested in anything that brings favorable attention and people to the Cape, which, as you may have heard, has been going through some hard times. So, naturally, I have supported such a newsworthy achievement as Norman's all I can, helping him with legal angles, bureaucratic red tape, and so on, to the best of my ability, but I have not the means to back him financially."

"But if you are acting as his lawyer on this then you must know who his backers are," Toby pressed. "And if you don't know the answers to my questions perhaps you could put me in touch with them and I could contact them directly."

Fitzgerald was flustered. "I'm not sure it would be my place to do such a thing," he stuttered. "Salvage is an expensive undertaking and there are multiple backers. I do know some of them but, since it is always such a speculative business, many businessmen involved prefer to remain anonymous. I'm afraid I can't help you. You'll have to get this from Norman himself, or at least get his approval for me to tell you anything."

Toby's round blue eyes widened innocently, "I had no idea there was so much secrecy involved in underwater salvage. But then, when the yields are this great, I can appreciate the need for it. I understand he has found a lot of gold and silver bullion."

"Ten million to date and more to come," Fitzgerald said gleefully, and then looked as if he wished he hadn't said it.

"Of course mine would be a much smaller operation," Toby said smoothly. "A sunken Armada galleon off the coast of Mull."

The senator greeted this with a gasp of relief. "Oh yes, *your* proposed excavation! Well, I'm sorry I can't be of more help, but you'd best talk to Norman himself. He'll be back from Florida soon, I believe."

Toby's scalp prickled. "So that's where he's been! I thought he was on the salvage ship directing operations from there."

On what he thought was safe ground at last Fitzgerald became expansive. "Oh, no, he often has to pop down there on business. That's become the center for treasure-salvage work and equipment now, with all the finds off the coast they have made." He positively brightened. "Actually, if you could face a trip down there at this time of year, I'm sure you'd get all the information you could possibly want from the experts. They know all about Spanish galleons. Vincent wouldn't be of much help to you on that; this is his first venture into this kind of thing."

"I might just do that," Toby said, "Thanks for the suggestion."

The senator got up and extended his hand. "I'm afraid I have to rush off now to address a meeting—it's why I'm down on the Cape today. It has been a pleasure meeting you, Sir Tobias, and I hope you enjoy your stay on our beautiful Cape. Sorry I could not be of more help to you."

Toby shook the extended hand and regarded him blandly. "Oh, but you *have* been of great help, Senator Fitzgerald. You've given me all sorts of ideas," he murmured. On that ominous note, he left Fitzgerald sunk in an uneasy reverie.

Emerging into the sunlight he stood on the stone steps of the building, lit up his pipe with a sigh of satisfaction, then took out his black leather notebook and began to make notes to himself in his minute handwriting. "Florida, eh? Bob should be able to get a line through official channels on where and when Norman went. Things really seem to be developing," he muttered to himself. "I wonder if Fitzgerald is really as stupid as he appears to be—but then I suppose intelligence has never been a prerequisite for politicians." Fortified by this great thought he ambled back to his car.

It was still too early to set off for his rendezvous at the Bacon house so he dithered about having a bite of lunch somewhere downtown. One look at the seething crowds on Main Street, however, put him off that idea and he headed for the calmer climes of Hyannisport, armed with the worthy purpose of fixing his own lunch and repairing Marcus' sand castle before his next assault on the conundrum. When he saw Penny's car parked in the circle before the beach house, his first chauvinistic thought was that at least he would not have to bother about fending for himself, but one look at her grimly set little face as he came into the enormous living room banished it. She was pacing up and down, arms crossed over her plump chest, head bent. "What's up?" he said.

She looked up, uncrossed her arms and waved him to a couch, heaved a sigh and said, "There's been a development. Sit down and I'll tell you all about it. We've lost one of our suspects, but *I* think we've another murder on our hands." She settled beside him on the couch and looked at him defiantly. "I know you think I let my imagination run riot at times, but this new death is just too damn pat to be a coincidence, so hear me out.

"Keith Corey was killed on Saturday night—or rather very early Sunday morning—just outside his new home in Naples. I spoke with Washington at the college and he did not have much in the way of details—I'm hoping you can get more out of Bob later. But, in short, he was knocked down and run over by a car—*twice*. It happened between two and three in the morning. The Naples police are listing it as a hit and run accident—probably by a drunk driver.

"He was found by a young yuppie couple, who live in the same complex, when they returned from a party: their head-lights caught something huddled in the gutter. They thought it was a dog that had been run over so got out to investigate, otherwise in that quiet residential neighborhood he would not have been found until morning. He was not there *before* two A.M., because that's when another couple in the complex came back from another party and parked at the next house to his. There was nothing in the gutter at that time. No witnesses to the event itself, but one insomniac in the complex watching a late, late movie reported to the police later that he thought he heard a loud thump out in the road around 2:15, but did not bother to investigate further."

"So, with no witnesses, no description of the car and nothing to proceed on, the Naples police have understandably shoved it under the rug as an accident, even though there is one point that perplexed them—Keith Corey was fully clothed, probably dressed for an evening out, and yet his own car was locked in his garage and had evidently not been used that night. I should add it's a very posh complex, town houses with attached garages. Also, since he is a newcomer and has only been there a couple of days, he knew none of his neighbors, so was not visiting anyone within the condo—the police did check that out." Toby gave an encouraging grunt, got up, fixed them both a drink in silence, handed her her glass and urged, "Go on."

She sprang up and resumed her pacing. "Well, it seems to me that a very good case could be made for Keith Corey being the answer to the *second* half of our puzzle: the man who put her in the college. Who would know better the workings of the college than a longtime professor? Who was closely connected to her by all those committees, which we think hold the key to Clara's murder? Who was also a resident of West Barnstable? Who left the Cape just before the finding of the body?"

"All very well and good," Toby rumbled, "But there's still no vestige of a clue as to *why* he should have done such an extraordinary thing."

She stopped her pacing and swung around to face him. "What if Corey had been mixed up in something illegal that Clara had found out about and was about to blow the whistle on. What if he was the man in Florida who tried to get that registered letter back and, having failed, went into a panic because, although he did not kill her, he knew that someone else had and so literally wanted to point a finger at them? Don't you see it fits? You asked why the man who knew she was dead had waited another month before doing anything about it. The answer is that Keith Corey *had* to wait because he was still teaching until a few days ago, and he wanted to be off the scene before the body was found and inquiries made."

She paused for breath and then went on. "The picture of Corey I got from Caleb Crowell—who seems to be a drunk, by the way—was of a fussy old-womanish type of man who was very money hungry: just the type to be lured into something that promised him easy money, but also the type to panic if anything untoward happened—like Clara Bacon's murder. What if that very large price for a very small house was some kind of payoff? And that would bring in the elusive Mr. Robideau and the land-development angle again. Corey cannot come into the open and accuse the real murderer; he is chained here until he collects the money and can officially retire from the college. But, before he goes, something sparks him into further panic and he rescues the body from its watery grave and leaves the bizarre setup we came in on, hoping to point the way to the murderer and get *himself* off the hook if push came to shove. It did not work: once the body was found and before we could get around to him, he had to be silenced. Hence this so-called accident. Have I made my case?"

Toby uncoiled himself from the couch and began pacing in his turn. "It's not that I disagree with you, but you do have one hell of a lot of 'what ifs' in there. Also, may I point out that, unless Corey has obligingly left a letter confessing to his involvement, we haven't a hope in hell of *proving* any of this. We have to keep our sights on Clara Bacon and the all-important 'why' of her killing." He stopped, looked at his watch and let out an exasperated sigh. "Look, I have to meet Bob in an hour and I'm starving. How about some lunch? Over it you can tell me about Crowell and I'll tell you about Fitzgerald and Norman."

"Right! You open and heat a can of soup and I'll fix the sandwiches," she ordained. "And there's cheese and biscuits if you want more than that."

After a diligent swapping of notes as they ate, Toby inquired, "Did you get anywhere at the Registry of Deeds?"

"Haven't had time to go there yet," Penny said, dumping their dishes in the dishwasher. "I was so staggered by this Corey development that I had to come home and think things out. I'll go to the registry this afternoon. Is Bob picking you up or shall I drop you on the way?"

"No need, I hired another car," he admitted. "The way things are going I don't even want Bob to know all of my movements. The police station is obviously a sieve when it comes to leaks."

As they emerged from the house, Penny exclaimed, "Heavens! What a ghastly color!"

"Isn't it? It was all I could get," he agreed, and on that note of amiable agreement they went their separate ways.

He arrived at the Bacon house a few minutes before Bob showed up, and sat smoking and pondering until the police car pulled in behind him. The young detective seemed preoccupied as he opened the door and they made their way upstairs. Toby extracted a Crowell and a Dexter genealogy from the back bedroom bookcase, silently handed Dyke a receipt for the books, and then asked, "Is it all right if I look through the front room?"

"There's nothing left there. All the files are gone," Robert said tersely. "Just some odds and end left in the desk, that's all—nothing of importance. But look if you want. I thought I'd take another turn out by the well to see if there are any other pathways leading from it to someone else's property, so I'll leave you to it, but I can't hang around more than half an hour."

Toby entered the large front room and looked around at the file cabinets, all gaping open and empty. He made purposefully for the desk and began a rapid and systematic search. The right-hand side contained bank books and checks in the top drawer, and bank and dividend statements in the bottom file drawer. Putting everything back, he turned his attention to the top left-hand drawer, emptying its contents on to the desk before him. Its front section contained Clara's paid and receipted bills, the back a miscellaneous collection of committee meeting notices and minutes. Right at the back edge his questing fingers found a folded single sheet of paper wedged in the crack. He pulled it out and opened it up.

It was a photostat of a newspaper item culled from the *Cape Cod Times* and bearing an October date of two years previous. BRINK'S JET HEIST NETS $13.7 MILLION the headline read and went on to report a predawn robbery, at Dorval International Airport outside of Montreal. The robbery had been carried out with commandolike precision by four men, who were heard speaking both French and English. They had got clean away with their booty.

Toby's eyes fixed somberly on the last paragraph against which a large inked query mark stood: "The men took gold and silver ingots, bonds, securities, and jewelry. However, they left behind an unspecified amount of cash. Police said no one was injured and no shots fired." He quietly pocketed the item and started to return methodically everything else to its proper place and carefully closed the drawer. He leaned back in his chair and gazed up at the ceiling. "I wonder," he murmured, "Could this be it?"

Chapter 12

The Cape crouched under a sudden and savage summer storm whose torrential rain and high winds sent vacationers and locals alike scurrying for the nearest shelter. Even the large Clarkson living room was shrouded in greenish gloom as Toby came in, dripping and swearing softly under his breath. Penny was there ahead of him, staring moodily out of the streaming windows at the angry white-capped waters of the Sound. She turned her head as he came in. "You too? I got soaked just getting from the Barnstable courthouse to the parking lot and then up to the house here. You'd better change."

"Yes, be with you in a minute," he growled and dripped upstairs, reappearing in a few minutes in a fisherman's sweater and dry slacks and vigorously toweling his silvery thatch of hair. "Well, I hope you got further than I did this afternoon," he observed, making for the brandy decanter. "I got absolutely nowhere—such a promising idea I had, too."

She joined him at the drinks tray and pointed at the gin bottle. "A 'g and t' for me—very strong. And ditto ditto. I'm so frustrated I could scream. It's not that they were unhelpful at the registry, it's just that without any specific names or places to give them, and not being able to explain why I wanted the damned info, they could not even point me in the right direction. I floundered about by myself for a bit, then a title-deed searcher took pity on me and tried to show me the ropes, but with my lack of expertise it would take *weeks* to ferret it out. There's only one thing for it. I've got to get in touch with the Dimolas and see if they can help. After all they are in the construction business so they ought to know how to go about it. I tried their Masuit number but no one is in residence there, so tomorrow I'll have a go at their central office in Boston. From previous experience though, I know that getting through to a Dimola is about as easy as getting in touch with God." They had wandered back to a couch with their drinks and were sitting side by side gazing out over the turbulent seascape. "So what problem did you run into?"

"One partly of my own making," he said gloomily. "I had to check the back files of the *Cape Cod Times*, but was terrified that if I gave my own name I'd be pounced on by that Clarkson woman for some ghastly interview so, like a fool, I gave false name and reason for research. I found the initial item easily enough but I couldn't find a single damn follow-up on the story, and then I couldn't very well ask anyone if and when Clara Bacon had ever asked for that particular item. Chances are no one would have known anyway, because they have a machine there that you pop in a quarter and get a printout on any page you are studying. So, I'm not one bit further on."

"Whoa there!" she exclaimed. "You're starting in the middle. What item? And what's so important about it anyway?"

"Because it was obviously important to Clara Bacon—I found it in her desk. And it started me thinking along the lines *she* must have been thinking . . . ," and he proceeded to expound at length on his newly formed theory.

Penny listened in growing amazement until she could contain herself no longer. "Talk about *me* being overly imaginative! Why on earth would professional thieves do something as crazy as dumping millions of dollars worth of gold and silver bars into the deep ocean and then have to go through all the hassle of hauling them up again? It's wild, completely wild!"

"On the contrary," Toby said severely, "It makes very good sense indeed. To fence that enormous amount of bullion would take a lot of doing and would increase the chances of leakages and therefore of getting caught immeasurably. Dump it all in the ocean and then 'discover' it during a legitimate marine salvage operation and they'd be home free. True they'd have to give the government its cut on the treasure trove, but they'd get to keep the rest and would make one hell of a lot more out of it than they would if they had to sell it off through fences. Inspector Gray and I have had many discussions on this type of robbery and it is remarkable how little the actual perpetrators get from such heists. They are lucky if they get, in your terms, thirty cents on the dollar."

She was momentarily diverted. "You've been seeing Gray of Scotland Yard? When? I thought he couldn't stand either of us."

Toby gazed down his button nose at her. "That's all long forgotten. When I'm in London we often have dinner together at the Athenaeum. Damned interesting chap and full of useful information."

Penny was already off on another line of thought. "Of course there could be something in what you say. Robideau was from Montreal originally."

"Oh, for Heaven's sake! So are a million other people." Toby was testy. "There's not a smidgeon of evidence to link *him* with this. It's Norman I'm talking about: Norman *has* to be in on it. Norman who changes his story of the find three times under Clara's relentless prodding; Norman who has been down in Florida and so could well be Corey's executioner; Norman with a thirteen million dollar motive for murder—and that's one hell of a motive."

"By that newspaper account this was a French-Canadian

crime with a lot of local know-how," she fired back. "And Robideau is a French-Canadian. And *he* has been off Cape too, so equally well could have been in Florida. Not that that means anything, since you can buy a clean hit on someone as easy as Corey—I believe the going price is around two thousand dollars these days. And don't forget it was Robideau who arranged the sale of Corey's house at that inflated price. Besides, apart from that scholarly row with Norman, Clara had nothing particularly against him, whereas—according to Caleb Crowell—she hated Robideau and was actively out to get him. That's also a good motive for wanting her out of the way."

"You can't have it both ways!" Toby roared. "First you are saying Robideau is in on the robbery, then that he is acting independently. For the first to be true there would have to be a linkage between him and Norman—and there is no such link."

Their mounting argument was cut short by the shrilling of the phone and Toby stalked over to answer it. "Clarkson residence, Glendower here." He listened, his face growing more thunderous by the second. "I see. Well that is most unfortunate. Please have him contact me the minute he returns. It *is* of some urgency." He slammed the phone down and stalked back. "Damnation! Another delay. That was Mrs. Norman. Because of the storm Norman is concerned about the salvage operation, so has taken off to supervise. She doesn't know when he'll be back."

"And another thing," Penny went on as if there had been no interruption. "Aren't you trying to have it both ways? You said yourself that the murderer had ample time to remove anything incriminating in the files, so if Norman is the culprit why should he leave behind all those clippings? I haven't heard a word about any *Robideau* files, and there must have been some on that land dispute."

"Which may well be sitting in the hodgepodge of files at the police station. Even if they aren't there we'll never know it now because of the mess-up Birnie has made," he snorted.

Again they were interrupted, this time by the front door chimes. "Who the hell . . . ?" Toby muttered and mooched off to answer it. There was a murmur of male voices and he returned shortly followed by a wet and grim-faced Robert Dyke, who gratefully accepted a drink and sat down in a chair facing them.

"There's been a development that I thought you should know about right away," he announced, and then seemed at a loss as to what to say next. He cleared his throat nervously and began again. "I've been over in Buzzards Bay trying to find that damned letter. I checked back at the police station before going home. Birnie was all fired up—he believes he has the motive and the culprit. On going through Mrs. Bacon's personal papers he came across a codicil to her will, duly signed and attested and executed at the beginning of May—just three weeks before she was murdered. He thinks it throws a very different light on the case." He pulled a slip of paper from his pocket and read, "In the event that my nephew Stephen Brown cannot be located after due advertisement within a period of six months I direct that, in addition to my original bequest, the residue of my estate be given to the Cape Cod chapter of the Wampanoags for Indian Rights to improve the lot of the Cape Cod Indians."

He looked up at them. "We haven't paid much attention to Burrows Smith up to this point, because the amount she left in the main will seemed too insignificant to constitute a motive. This changes the whole picture. A quarter of a million dollars in land and securities would make one heck of a lot of difference to the Indians, so Birnie is hauling Burrows Smith in for questioning."

"But that's absurd! There is no evidence that the nephew is dead!" Penny gasped. "Even if he were, how could Smith possibly have known about that codicil?"

"Wait, there's more," Robert said unhappily. "When I was out at the house this afternoon it occurred to me that he had not

133

done anything about trying to find traces of Mrs. Bacon's clothing from the well, to make it definite that that was her last resting place, you know? When I went by the station on the way to Buzzard's Bay I also fixed up with a cop friend of mine—who is a Vietnam vet and an ex-Navy SEAL—to investigate the well. He's all gung ho about that kind of thing; has his own scuba equipment and so on. So off he went, complete with grappling equipment and a noncop buddy of his to help him in and out of the well." He paused and sighed heavily. "Not only did he find the fibers from her clothing on the side of the well, but in grappling the bottom he came up with a gun. He recognized it at once as a revolver most commonly used as a side arm by officers in 'Nam: large caliber, and very probably the weapon that could have blown that large hole in Mrs. Bacon."

Toby sat up straighter. "So?" he prompted.

Robert looked miserably at him. "So Burrows Smith was in 'Nam for three years, an infantry lieutenant. And a lot of guys brought their side arms back as souvenirs, you know. Anyway, Birnie has convinced himself that he has found the motive, the means—and the man."

"But surely there must be dozens of Vietnam vets on the Cape?" Penny protested. "Why should Burrows Smith be singled out as owner? And the gun could have changed hands a dozen times in the last twenty years!"

"Doesn't the army have records of issue?" Toby rumbled in counterpoint. "Those guns have serial numbers, don't they? Original ownership could be established."

"The serial number had been filed off—and recently too. That clinched it so far as Birnie is concerned. To quote him, "Burrows has always been a cunning, devious bastard; trust him to think of everything." And once the chief has made up his mind on something you can't budge him. In fact," he paused again and looked uncomfortably at them, "that's another reason why I'm here: he sent you a message. He said to tell you that you needn't bother yourselves further on this case and that the police will take it from here on. And to thank you for your help. He's very grateful." A small silence fell, then he went on. "I take it you'll not want Linda to go on with that genealogy in Boston, Sir Tobias?"

Penny and Toby exchanged a long look and she nodded slightly. Toby cleared his throat. "Bob, do you trust me?"

The young detective was puzzled. "Well of course I trust you—whyever not? We went through a lot together in Israel."

Toby shook his head impatiently. "No, I mean *really* trust me and my judgement. Be honest about this, for if your answer is still yes, it could lead you into a lot of difficulty for yourself. If the answer is no, I'll say no more."

Dyke flushed. "I guess the answer is still yes. You're the most formidable pair I've ever met. But I don't understand what all this is about."

"You will shortly," Toby rumbled. "In the first place I think Chief Birnie's case against Burrows Smith is so flimsy that it will never stand up. He has either been got at by someone *with* a lot of clout or he is so anxious to get this thing over and done with that he has grabbed at the first likely suspect *without* a lot of clout. I have had my reservations about him from the outset. In the second place, Dr. Spring and I have been very actively carrying out investigations which, while we differ on their respective significance, lead us to believe that there is a lot more to this case than the worth of Mrs. Bacon's modest estate. Ideally, I would have liked more time to substantiate some of the things we have uncovered before I confided them to you, but a crisis point has been reached now, and we are still going to need your help in getting information that can only come from official sources. However discreet we are about this, it could lead to official trouble for you, you could even lose your job, so I think the only fair thing to do is this. Tonight I will write a summary of all we have discovered thus far, a lot of which we have not confided to anyone. I suggest that you come here tomorrow morning before you go to work, read it, and if you do not think we have anything or if, on sober reflection, you decide you don't want to stick your neck out—which we would well understand—well, that would be that. I think you should know, however, that we fully intend to continue, with or without official sanction. So please ask your wife to go on with her research," he added blandly.

Dyke stood up. "Sounds fair to me. See you tomorrow then. And one thing I will promise ahead of time, whether I go in with you or not, is that I will keep you posted on developments on our end. If Stephen Brown shows up, for instance, in which case the chief is going to have egg all over his face." Toby escorted him out, and when he ambled back in Penny said drily, "Whatever happened to 'as soon as the family gets back we drop the case'?"

He stared down at her in shocked surprise, "Good Lord! I thought with this new development that you'd be one hundred percent in favor, considering your feelings about the Indians! Aren't you with me on this? If not I'll carry on by myself, the family will understand. Anyway they *aren't* back, nor likely to be just yet."

She held up a placating hand. "No need to get riled up. Of course I'm with you. And we do need Bob's help. You couldn't have said anything else to keep him hooked."

He gobbled a little at that, then said stiffly, "Well I'll get right on with that report. It should help to clarify both our minds—I hope! I take it we're eating in tonight?"

"In this weather," she looked out at the storm, "You'd better believe it! You go on with your business and I'll get dinner. There's a couple of T-bone steaks in the freezer and I can do mashed potatoes and a salad. Okay?"

"Sounds fine to me," he said, retreating to the study.

She was in the middle of her preparations when the phone rang: "Probably Alex with the daily dole of woe," she called out, "I'll get it!" But when she lifted the receiver the crackling static and tinny echo on the line signaled an overseas call, and a woman's voice said tentatively, "Am I speaking with Dr. Penelope Spring of Oxford University?"

"Yes, Dame Penelope here," Penny said grandly.

"Oh, good! This is Jocelyn Combe. I received a call from your secretary, Miss Phipps, and was appalled to hear of Clara Bacon's murder. Miss Phipps asked me to call you immediately, so here I am."

Penny was puzzled, for the voice on the phone was a high, young voice that scarcely fitted in with Caleb Crowell's "old frump" description or her own preconception of a woman of Clara Bacon's age group. "You're the Jocelyn Combe who formerly taught at the Cape Cod Community College?" she queried.

"That's right, the very same," It was Jocelyn Combe's turn to sound puzzled. "You did want to speak with me, didn't you?"

"Oh, very much so," Penny assured her. "We are involved in the investigation of Mrs. Bacon's death and understand that you were a close friend of hers, so I'm hoping you can give us some valuable insights and information."

There was a momentary hesitation at the other end, then, "In so far as friendship goes, I suppose I *am* the closest to a friend Clara had—but actually that's not saying a great deal. It's hard to explain over the phone, and I'm not even going to try. I need to talk to you face to face and I *know* I can help. Look, the reason I'm calling now is that I'm coming over. I'm booked on the first flight out of Heathrow to Boston tomorrow, and I was wondering if you would do me a favor. I know the Cape is full to bursting this time of year, so could you phone around the local motels and B & B's to see if any of them can fit me in somewhere? Then I could rent a car in Boston, drive directly down to you—I know where Dr. Clarkson's place is—and you could tell me where to go from there. I should get down to the

Cape between five and six, traffic permitting. Would you do that?"

Penny thought quickly. "To start with you could stay right here, there's plenty of room. My son and his family are temporarily back in New York because of illness, but until they return—which will be at least another week, I believe—you'd be very welcome to stay here."

Jocelyn Combe was also evidently a woman of quick decision. "If you're sure that's all right, that would be fine—at least for a day or two until I get my bearings. Once I find which of my friends are still on the Cape this time of year and available, I'll probably move in on one of them. You are doubtless thinking all this is a bit weird and I'll explain it all when I get there, but, among other things, even though I've been a mystery writer for twenty years now, this is the first real-life murder I've ever been involved in. I can hardly wait! See you tomorrow then!" And on that alarming note the line went dead.

Chapter 13

Guilt had kept Penny unnaturally silent for an entire day. Her first thought after Jocelyn Combe had hung up was, "What have I done? I've invited a complete stranger into the house and she may be cracked!" Her second was, "How am I going to break this to Toby," for she knew full well that he would not take kindly to the prospect of a strange female under the same roof. Initially she found a simple solution—she just did not tell him, and was helped in this by his own preoccupation with his report, so that he did not even inquire about the call.

She realized her craven reaction was only a very short-term solution, but continued to procrastinate, hoping that some bit of good news would lighten his present mood. She waited in vain, for nothing of the sort happened. Toby, as it turned out, did not remark on her lack of conversation, for he also was struggling with guilt feelings—his thoughts being centered on the young detective whose career he would be putting in jeopardy. So, in the large, storm-battered house, they avoided one another, each waiting for the storm to blow itself out and a new avenue of inspiration to open up.

The nightly phone call from Alex had brought little in the

way of cheer: the children were on the mend and consequently a lot more energetic and harder to handle. Sonya was definitely sickening and was exhibiting telltale signs that she was coming down with chicken pox herself. An actress friend, currently "resting" and also chicken pox proof, had been added to their entourage along with the faithful Boris, so all the invalids were being cossetted. "But the bottom line is—God knows when we'll be back on the Cape," Alex had ended wearily.

It was at this juncture that Penny had broken their solemn resolve and told him about the murder and their involvement. He had been grimly amused. "Incredible, absolutely incredible! Well, at least it'll save you from going out of your skulls with boredom and from getting on each other's nerves too much. I think I shall suppress this news from Sonya. Knowing her propensities she'd probably rush up to join the fray, spots and all."

The morning had brought the serious-faced Robert Dyke with his daily dole of news. "Before we get down to cases," he said, "I thought I'd fill you in on the fruits of a colleague's labors yesterday. Birnie gave him the Florida mail file and had him check with all the Cape bill senders as to why they had not made any moves about Mrs. Bacon's three months silence. He checked the utility companies, the telephone company and so on, and they all came up with variations on the same theme— Mrs. Bacon was such a good 'payer' that they did not want to hassle her, and they expected her to pay up 'as soon as she got back.'"

"So they expected her back?" Penny was interested.

"Yes, apparently she told them all that she was going to settle in down there and then would be back for a while to close up the house here. They thought she was waiting until after Labor Day and for the usual calm to return to the Cape."

"What about her Florida bills?" Toby put in. "After all, she was known here, but was a newcomer there. Didn't they start any inquiries?"

Dyke shook his head. "Again she was a victim of her own efficiency: there *were* no Florida bills. Apparently she had paid her condo dues three months in advance; the phone company was waiting to hear from her and had not turned it on yet, and so no one down there was alarmed or even interested."

"What's happened about Burrows Smith?" Penny demanded.

"He is still being held for questioning. He denies ownership of the gun, but he can't give a satisfactory account of where he was during the vital period in May."

"Oh, really, how ridiculous! Who can remember offhand where they were and what they were doing three months before?" she snorted.

Toby gazed up at the ceiling. "On May 25th I gave a talk to the Society of Antiquaries in Burlington House. Stayed overnight at the club. Had dinner there on May 26th with Inspector Gray. On May 27th left London and went to visit that LBA farmhouse site they were excavating near Brighton and on the 28th I returned to Oxford."

"Oh, we all know about your photographic memory, Toby," she said crossly. "Do shut up. We're talking about *normal* people. Do you remember what *you* were doing over that period?" she challenged Dyke.

"Haven't a clue," he said amiably. "Although the station records should show what I was doing."

"Too bad Burrows Smith doesn't have that advantage. By the way, what does he do for a living?" she asked.

"On that plot of land of his he is largely self-sufficient. Technically he is one of our great mass of unemployed; in actuality he acts as shaman to the Wampanoags. I thought you'd have tumbled to that." He looked at her quizzically.

A bolt of enlightenment struck her. "Well I'll be . . . ! No, I didn't tumble to it. But they keep it very quiet because he is not a full-blooded Indian? That explains one hell of a lot."

"That I wouldn't know," Bob said and looked at Toby. "I can't stay too long, so may I see that summary?"

"By all means," Toby rumbled. "But you can't take it with you, it stays here and is for your eyes only." He led him away to the study.

Penny seized the opportunity to make up surreptitiously the bed in the guest room, which was as far removed from Toby's room as possible, and to ferret out a supply of towels. That done, she applied herself to the phone, her sights set on Alexander Dimola.

As anticipated, it proved very difficult; she was bounced from person to person until finally she was in contact with his private secretary, who informed her gleefully that he was out of town and would not be back until Thursday. "Then please make an appointment for me to see him as early as possible on that day," Penny said, reining in her impatience. "This is a matter of urgency and I am a personal friend of Mr. Dimola. The name is Dame Penelope Spring of Oxford University."

Still the secretary—a man—hemmed and hawed. What was the nature of her business? Mr. Dimola was a very busy man.

"Of that I am well aware," she said icily. "I repeat—I'm a personal friend and the business is also personal. Tell him it is another Cape murder. He'll know what I mean."

The secretary grudgingly allowed that he could fit her in for a few minutes around two P.M. on Thursday, but would she please confirm the appointment that morning.

She felt, storm or no storm, she had to get out of the house for a while, and decided to go grocery shopping to restock their dwindling larder. Suitably rainproofed, she emerged to find that, while the rain was still coming down in a steady torrent, the wind had died. But as she drove through the near-empty streets, she could see the damage it had wrought, with cascades of leaves flowing down the streaming gutters and limbs and branches of battered trees lying on lawns and sidewalks. There were few cars in evidence and fewer pedestrians as she headed for the Super Stop and Shop on Route 132 and did a leisurely shop. On emerging with her piled-high shopping cart, she saw that the rain was beginning to slacken and the rain clouds rolling out to sea were visibly brightening as the strong August sun struggled to break through.

When she returned to the house she was relieved to see that Toby's car had gone, and she quickly stashed away her purchases in the kitchen before making herself a pot of coffee. As she sipped the strong hot brew another thought came to her and she took it and her coffee mug into the living room and dialed the number of Robideau's office. The redhead's voice came breathlessly over the phone, "Robideau real estate. This is Diane. May I help you?"

"Yes, This is Dr. Spring again—we talked the other day? I was wondering if I could change my mind? You kindly offered to give me the name of the New York company that bought Professor Corey's house? I would be obliged if you could let me have it now."

"Why, yes," the voice was puzzled. "I'm sure that's okay. Half a sec . . . ." There was a pause and the clatter of computer keys. "That would be the Amdex Corporation," and she gave a Manhattan address.

"Thank you very much," Penny gushed and then added, "Is Mr. Robideau back from Florida yet?"

"Why yes, he got in last night. Would you like to speak with him? He's on another line at the moment."

"No, that's all right. Maybe later. Thanks again," Penny said gleefully and rang off. She could hardly wait to pass this choice item on to Toby.

She was on her third mug of coffee when he finally mooched in looking none too cheerful. She waved her mug at him, "Coffee?"

"Not just now thanks. I have some phoning to do." He stalked over to the windows, now heavily rimed with salt-spray and stood gazing out. "For what it is worth, Bob was very impressed by my summary and will give us all the help he can. He was none too happy about my making off with that newspaper item on the robbery. I had to go to the house and show him where I found it—I left him clearing out all the rest of the stuff, although I'm sure that's a waste of time. However, he *is* going to have a quiet go at tracing Norman's activities in and trips to Florida, as well as Keith Corey's bank accounts."

"While he's at it he might look into Robideau's trips also," Penny said. "I learned from his secretary that he just got back from there, and I also got the name of the corporation that bought Corey's house."

Toby looked down at her, his round face inscrutable. "Indeed! I'll pass that on. I have a couple of other news items, one of which should bring a gleam to your eye, although it's too soon to tell if it'll get Burrows Smith off the hook. The Los Angeles police got nowhere on Stephen Brown so passed the all-points bulletin on him to other Pacific Coast states: they got a nibble from Oregon. They had Stephen in their computer, arrested on a drunk and disorderly charge and spent a week in jail because he couldn't raise the fine. Some small place outside of Portland. They've been asked to follow up on that. Unfortunately, it was over six months ago he was jailed, so Birnie's attitude is that until he is found alive and kicking Smith remains a viable suspect. I was interested to learn from Bob that Birnie's wife serves on a couple of committees with Calpurnia Howes— it seems to be a major Cape Cod pastime—and that she is very much in awe of her."

"Which may well be the source of the pressure on Birnie. Calpurnia struck me as pretty anti-Smith," Penny commented.

"One last thing before I get back to work, I think I'm getting the runaround from Norman. His wife called again with a message from him. The gist was that he had talked with Fitzgerald, understood I was interested in Spanish galleons and suggested I contact a Walter Prescott who lives in Provincetown. Prescott was involved with the *Whidah* operation and knows something of the Florida marine excavations. Also that the storm has caused problems out at his wreck and so he doesn't know when he'll be back." He sighed. "So, I'll have to go through the motions I suppose, since this is such an interconnected society. I'll call Prescott and try and set up a meeting for tomorrow. Feel like a trip into Boston? I am going to check the *Boston Globe* and the *Herald* files in the public library there this afternoon. It occurred to me that, since they are both major papers, they'd be more likely to have a follow-up on the Montreal robbery than the *Cape Cod Times*."

"Thanks, but I think I'll have another bash at the registry, now I have this Amdex corporation name to check," she said hastily, thankful for another reprieve. "Why don't you treat yourself to dinner in there? Lots of good restaurants around the area by the public library."

"I might just do that," he grunted and headed for the phone.

As she threw together a hasty lunch, she hugged herself with silent glee. By the time Toby got back from Boston, Jocelyn Combe would have arrived and settled in and, faced with a *fait accompli*, he would be forced to accept it—with good grace, she hoped. In any case it would give her a breathing space to size up this new player in their weird game and to take steps to rectify the situation if it turned out she had made a ghastly mistake. She almost pushed Toby out the door and on his way, and felt vast relief as the bright green car bumped off down the unpaved road and out of sight. Instead of going to the registry she called up her friendly title-deed searcher, and after agreeing on a search fee, gave her the particulars on the Amdex Corporation and asked her to check on any other Cape purchases by them. Feeling extremely pleased with herself, she went upstairs and took a long and tranquil nap from which she awoke recharged with energy.

To keep herself occupied as the designated hour of arrival approached, she prepared an elaborate chicken casserole, an even more elaborate salad, and was even contemplating a fancy dessert when the door chimes summoned her. She deep-sixed the fancy dessert idea, rushed to the door and flung it wide. A tall, scrawny woman stood on the threshold, her wiry salt-and-pepper hair standing up around her thin, weatherbeaten face. She fairly bristled with energy: her brown eyes sparkled with it, her whole body radiated it—but her clothes were a walking disaster. At one time they had obviously been expensive and well tailored, now they sagged and bagged around her spare frame, the pockets of the jacket bulging, the hemline drooping on one side and riding high on the other; she looked for all the world like a high-class bag lady. She thrust forward a lean brown hand and smiled, revealing a mouthful of large and very white teeth.

"Hi! I'm Jocelyn Combe. Penny Spring I presume? God, how I *hate* airplanes, they are so *boring* and I swear our pilot hit every air pocket over the Atlantic just to keep us on our toes!" The voice was the girlish voice of the telephone, emerging oddly from the elderly face.

Penny took the proffered hand, grinned, and drew her inside. "Glad you got here in one piece. I expect you could use a good stiff drink after all that. We'll get to your bags later." Her spirits were rising by the second: offbeat their house guest might be, but the dancing brown eyes were sane and alive with intelligence, and she felt an immediate empathy and liking for the gawky woman.

While Penny prepared gin and tonics for both of them, Jocelyn darted around the large living room, avidly examining the Clarkson's extensive scrimshaw collection and the antique bric-a-brac and chattering away brightly. "I've been here before. The Clarkson girl fancied herself a budding novelist at one stage and belonged to a Cape writer's group I was in. She entertained the group here a couple of times. Never *finished* the novel, of course." It was only when Penny had dug out some cheese and crackers and settled them down with their drinks that Jocelyn sobered.

"Sorry about all this chatter. I always babble when I'm nervous and I've been feeling horrible ever since I hung up on you yesterday. You must think I'm an unfeeling monster or as batty as hell. Either way, not the first impression I wanted to make. I tend to blurt out whatever is passing through my increasingly addled mind, but I hope it did not put you off. I was just terrified you'd say no, don't come, or 'I won't see you' or something dreadful like that. I really *am* deeply upset and concerned about Clara's death and want to see justice done. Although we weren't close friends—there was no getting close to Clara—I think I was really all she had, so that's why I'm here." Her dark eyes begged understanding. "I was so stupefied by your secretary's message that I hardly took in what little she did tell me, so if you'll assume I know nothing and take it from square one, I think I'll be able to see in which areas I can help. Am I dreaming or did she say Clara had been murdered in May but only found last week?"

"Yes, that's right. We think she was killed on May 26th, or possibly the 27th, then her body was dumped into an old well on her property, where it was well-preserved by a freak of nature. Then it was taken out of the well and placed in a classroom in the college, where it was discovered last Friday, although it may have been placed there a day or two prior to that. But before I go into this whole weird setup, I'd like to hear from *you* exactly what kind of a person Clara was. It has stuck in my gullet right from the start how *anyone*, let alone a person as much in the public eye as she was, could disappear for three months and not be missed by a single soul! So, please, start from there."

Jocelyn groped in a sagging pocket, emerged with a crumpled packet of cigarettes and waved them at Penny, "Do you mind?" and as Penny shook her head lit up and took a deep, satisfied drag. "Helps me to think," she confided. "This isn't easy but I'll try. We knew each other for almost twenty years. Did a lot of things together—movies, the Cape Cod symphony, the occasional shopping orgy in Boston—had a lot of similar interests, talked endlessly, and never had a cross word. And yet, in all that time I don't think we ever had what you'd call a heart-to-heart on anything; at least, not anything personal to *her*. She never talked about her dead husband, her family, her old bag of a mother-in-law . . . . I've no idea whether her marriage or her life in general was happy or unhappy."

She sprang up and began to pace restlessly. "Oh, I'm doing this very badly. But—well—I have this close friend from college days at Oxford; sometimes we haven't seen each other for years on end, and yet the minute we're together again we are chattering away just like we did as eighteen-year-olds and as if we hadn't lost a minute in between. With Clara, if you hadn't seen her for a couple of days, it was like meeting her for the first time all over again; you were constantly breaking the ice with a stranger. The odd thing was that I don't think she *wanted* to be that way. I always had the feeling that she *wanted* to be close to someone, that she wanted friends, but she simply didn't know how. She either couldn't or wouldn't care enough about people as people for them to care a hoot about her. So that's one part of it, and I think therein lies clue number one. No one would have *hated* her enough to kill her for a personal reason— it had to have been something else. Something she knew or something she was going to do that threatened somebody to the point that they killed her.

"That's one part of it. The other part is the Cape. . . ." She stopped pacing and sat down again. "There are so many elderly people on the Cape now; people who have outlived their families, their friends; who live alone in isolated houses. . . . Ask the Visiting Nurses or the Elderly Affairs people—they could tell you countless horror stories of people lying dead for days, even weeks, before anyone notices or finds them. It has become a very isolated society."

"But we're talking about months," Penny interjected.

"Ah yes, and there I think you have your second definite clue," Jocelyn sat up excitedly. "The person who murdered her knew just *when* to do it so that there *would* be an unusually long delay before she was missed. The people here knew she planned to go to Florida, the people there thought she was still here."

"So *you* knew she was going to Florida?" Penny prompted.

"Oh, yes, and fool that I was I didn't realize the significance of that at the time. Clara was not much of a correspondent. After I left here for England in January all I had from her was one postcard, then this one letter written at the end of April and telling of her plans to go to Florida as soon as the spring semester ended. And I quote her, 'But first I have to take care of a very important bit of business here; something I should have dealt with long since. And then I am getting out of here— fast. Say a prayer for me that all goes well. I'll need it.'" Jocelyn looked significantly at her absorbed hostess. "I didn't pick up on it then—too busy with my own affairs—but Clara *never* asked for help in any shape or form. That last line should have told me something was very wrong. Clara was frightened. Even then I think she was frightened for her life . . . ."

Chapter 14

Toby was feeling aggrieved and much put upon, the tenor of his thoughts heavy with his natural misogyny. Women! he thought to himself, unconsciously echoing Shaw's Henry Higgins—why are they so illogical, irrational, and constantly incomprehensible? What could have possessed Penny to invite a total stranger into the house and, to compound her error, become as thick as thieves with the weird woman in no time flat? Since his late return from Boston yesterday he had not managed to have a single quiet word with her to find out what the hell was going on. The two women were inseparable, heads together and chattering the whole damn time. He had done the only thing possible in the circumstances: withdrawn into his shell, like the tortoise which unfriendly critics had often said he resembled, and further withdrawn physically in a dignified huff into the study, where he would not be distracted by their endless chatter.

Not that this Jocelyn Combe was entirely without merit, he reflected, flipping through his notebook: she had offered some interesting insights and background on some of the principals in the case and had assured them she could get more from her network of friends still on the Cape. He had also been impressed by the rapt attention she had given to his own exposition of events, with none of the irritating interjections or wandering of attention into other avenues to which he was so inured from his partner. No, he had to give her that, she was a good listener—a rare quality in a woman. Unfortunately, from his point of view there were two strikes against her: the first that she knew virtually nothing about the man in whom he was most interested, Vincent Norman; the second, and more important, that she was here under the same roof and for God knows how long!

With a sigh he pulled himself together and began to translate the notes he had made into more readable form. *"Calpurnia Howes.* Married to a stockbroker. No children. Howes died fifteen years ago of a stroke, aged 50. Estate left comfortable, but rising costs and heavy upkeep of Osterville home, plus moneyed set she runs with, are eating up capital. Rumored for some time that she would like to unload house and move to less costly quarters, but times against her. *More important*—belongs to 'old guard' on Cape and has always been 'big frog in small puddle.' This position threatened by new elements on Cape, and has lost ground and power in some areas. Needs money to reestablish clout and former dominance.

"Caleb Crowell. Unmarried. JC confirms drinking problem, but affirms CC much smarter than he appears. Never has 'worked' in accepted sense. Income derives mainly from Crowell properties widespread on Cape, so also hurt from real estate decline. Needs money. JC thinks would be prepared to bend principles to get it, but very much on the quiet. Even more prickly about 'status' than CH."

At Keith Corey, Toby paused and lit up his pipe. Jocelyn Combe had known him well and had been very interesting about his relationship with Clara. To his surprise and in answer to one of Penny's queries about some sort of "attachment," Jocelyn had answered, "You know I think you're right! I believe she may have had a 'thing' about him. He was quite good looking in a seedy sort of way and Clara had a weakness for a handsome face. Oh, nothing overt, you understand, but I noticed—particularly since his wife died—Clara always sat up and took notice when he was around; she was positively skittish at times. I know she was very hurt when he backed Norman up over the validity of his finds. She was just plain mad at Calpurnia for doing the same, but really upset by him." And on further probing, she admitted, "Well, if she were that smitten, she *may* have gone so far as to cover up for him, but she was so damned honest and obstinate I'm not sure how far she'd have gone." *That* Toby had found most interesting. He carried on with his notes.

"*Keith Corey.* Notorious for his miserliness, loved money and was always moaning about how hard up he would be when he *had* to retire. Interesting that recent retirement his own idea not college's. One son, killed in Vietnam. No near kin. From Rhode Island. Not a Cape Codder or Cape Cod family.

"*Burrows Smith. . . .*" Again he paused. Jocelyn had been interesting on him also. On being informed of the codicil to Clara's will she had been as startled as they had been, but had gone on, "Come to think of it I'm not all that surprised. Clara had some heavy guilt feelings about what she had been instrumental in doing to the Wampanoags. Went back years to some committee she had been on. I remember her telling me once that she'd been misinformed and that it was partly their own fault, but she still felt badly. Of recent years she's bent over backwards to support them, and was pretty thick with Smith, though, personally, I've never met him."

She equally had no firsthand knowledge of Paul Robideau and could only confirm by hearsay his reputation as a "sharp" business man, but—to Penny's dismay—had no knowledge, other than the earlier property fight, that Clara had ever had any direct dealings with him. "I know she'd go red in the face if his name ever cropped up in conversation and would always change the subject," she had volunteered.

On Norman she had virtually nothing to say other than, "I know he's not a native Cape Codder but is a longtime resident. I think his wife is though. In fact I think she's a distant relative of Caleb Crowell." *Check that out*, Toby advised himself, and shut his notebook with a snap.

He stood up, stretched, and looked at his watch. He still had an hour to kill before he set out for Provincetown. What to do? He brightened: he would repair Marcus' sand castle, which had been all but demolished by the storm. Arming himself with several plastic pails and a spade, he stalked with dignity through the living room where the women were still chattering, and out the French doors to the patio and the battered beach beyond.

Jocelyn stopped in midsentence and craned around to gaze out of the window. "What's he up to now?" she demanded, and got up for a closer look.

Penny joined her at the window and peered out to see Toby solemnly spading sand into the buckets. "Oh, he recreating the Tower of London for our grandson. Promised to look after it until Marcus is over his chicken pox."

Jocelyn watched in fascination as the White Tower once more began to take shape. "How sweet! Isn't he a perfect *poppet*!" she cried.

Penny chuckled, "Well, I've heard him called a lot of things but never that. Actually he's a very disgruntled poppet at the moment, but pay him no mind, he'll get over it. It's nothing personal, he just has a lot of trouble adjusting to the female of the species or, for that matter, to anyone who diverts my attention away from him for any length of time. Thank God he's got an appointment in P Town this afternoon, so he'll be out of our hair for a while, and it'll give him something else to think about. These moods of his don't last half as long as they used to—he really is improving with age."

"Has he been to Provincetown before?" Jocelyn asked.

"No, and don't you tell him what it's like either, or he'll probably panic and not go," Penny said drily. "Doesn't take at all kindly to that sort of ambiance, does Toby."

"Then he *is* in for some surprises," Jocelyn said. They both chuckled happily and returned to their heart-to-heart conversation.

The sand castle restored to his satisfaction, Toby cleaned his tools, returned to the house and washed up, armed himself with a map of Provincetown, and announced his departure to the unheeding women.

"Want a bite of lunch before you go?" Penny asked.

"No, I'll get lunch there if I feel like any," he said, peering disapprovingly down at them. "And I don't know when I'll be back."

"Not to worry. Jocelyn is taking us out to dinner tonight at The Roadhouse in Hyannis. The reservation is for eight, I expect you'll be back by then. If not, no problem," Penny said comfortably.

"Oh, very well," he huffed, "Then I'll be off."

"Good hunting!" she called after him and grinned at Jocelyn.

The heavy traffic on the Mid-Cape demanded his full attention so he had no time to brood on his grievances; beyond Orleans, where the divided highway ended, the traffic heading for Provincetown was bumper to bumper and he had to slow to a crawl that continued on to the narrow streets of the town itself and left him fuming with impatience. He had carefully marked the downtown street where Prescott lived, but when he got there he could not find a single parking space open. He combed the whole downtown area to no avail; all the parking lots were full and his search took him further and further from the heart of town, heading, as the signs told him, toward Race Point. Finally an empty space at the curb appeared and he pulled into it with the speed of light, then groped for the map to see where he was and how far he would have to walk back. There came a tapping at the window and he looked up to see a strangely attired woman, sporting a large picture hat, bobbing up and down outside and grinning in at him. Cautiously he rolled down the window and peered out, "May I help you, madam?"

The strange figure started back from the window, then, with a tentative smile, held up a brown bag from which the neck of a port bottle protruded and gestured towards the unseen beach. Puzzled, Toby shrugged and the woman again approached the window and peered in. Toby took a closer look then recoiled in dismay: under the garish makeup was the unmistakable blue shadow of a beard. Shaken, he hastily rolled up the window again, shook his head vigorously, then gripped the steering-wheel and stared fixedly ahead. The transvestite hovered uncertainly for a moment, then shrugged in turn and went wandering somewhat unsteadily off towards the shore. Toby waited until he was at a safe distance, then got out and locked the car. "Extraordinary!" he muttered to himself and started walking briskly back towards the center of town.

As he walked, his confusion and unease intensified as he passed countless couples who strolled hand in hand or closely intertwined. They were dressed in the whole gamut of fashion, from punk to yuppie, but they shared one thing in common: they were all of the same sex as their companions. His puzzlement grew with every step he took.

When he reached the first bar, he dived into it in search of a much needed drink, but it merely furthered his growing panic. He was the only male in the place and was met by the steady, mostly hostile, stares of a sea of female couples. He backed gingerly out, muttering incoherently, and took flight.

What *is* this place? he thought, Sodom and Gomorrah, American-style? Was Prescott of this ilk and had Norman sent him here as some kind of bizarre joke? He was almost on the point of giving up on the whole thing when he regained the center of town, ajostle with family groups and tourists, and in this familiar ambience managed to get a hold on himself. He marched up to the white, wood-shingled Prescott residence grimly prepared for the worst as he rang the bell, and was vastly relieved when it was opened by a man of his own age, with a thatch of white hair and a seafarer's nut-brown face with penetrating periwinkle blue eyes, and puffing on a yellowed meerschaum pipe. He almost fell across the threshold in his relief. "Walter Prescott? Tobias Glendower. So sorry I'm late. Couldn't find a parking place."

"No matter. Terrible this time of year, isn't it?" Walter Prescott held out a hard, calloused hand. "Been here before?"

"Never," Toby said fervently. "And I don't think I'll be back either."

A twinkle appeared in the blue eyes. "You look as if you could use a drink. Provincetown isn't what it was. Takes a bit of getting used to nowadays. Used to be an old-fashioned fishing town, then we got the artists, and now we've come to this gay heaven—in the summertime especially." He led Toby into a pleasantly cool living room, where rustic antiques mixed in with comfortable, out-of-date furniture, got Toby settled into a rocker and produced some excellent dark rum. "Straight or with lime?" he asked.

"Straight, please," Toby muttered, mopping his sweating face.

Prescott nodded his approval. "Right choice! Now, what can I do for you? Spanish galleons, is it?"

Toby took a grateful sip of the excellent rum and appraised his host over the rim of his glass. "Not really," he murmured. "Although it was the excuse I gave Senator Fitzgerald to get information from and about Vincent Norman. Is Norman a friend of yours?"

The blue eyes narrowed. "Can't stand the crooked bastard. What are you after? You a journalist?"

Toby took the plunge. "No, I am an archaeologist, but that's not my primary interest in this. I think there is something very strange about that salvage operation of Norman's, and I'm trying to find a link between it and the murder of Mrs. Clara Bacon. I think one exists. So, whatever you can tell me either about the operation or Norman himself will be deeply appreciated."

Prescott pursed his lips in a silent whistle, "So that's the way the wind blows, is it? Well I'll be damned! Wish I did know more, but I'll tell you what I can. Not that I'm a pro at this sort of thing, but I was with Barry Clifford on the *Whidah* operation long enough to know that there is something very odd about Norman's whole setup. Item one—Norman's no salvager or archaeologist. Never done anything like this before and, so far as efficiency goes, has gone about it in a half-assed way right from the start. Item two—when he started, long before he made his first 'find,' he was so secretive and so security-minded that none of the local experts, like Clifford, was consulted, nor did he employ any *local* divers. Some tried, but he wouldn't look at them. All his are from out of state, some out of country, I'm told, and he's got a bunch of really mean thugs as security guards. They had nasty run-ins with some of our local fishermen as well as journalists and the usual thrill-seekers. It's all been hushed up, so he's got a lot of clout operating somewhere, but seamen around here are as mad as hell, I can tell you! Item three—when he was blown out of the water initially about the *Portland*, he changed his story in a hurry, and twice. And I don't think story number three is one bit more believable than the other two: it just don't add up."

"Why?" Toby interjected.

"Because, according to him, this supposed U-boat blew up and scattered itself and all this bullion over the seabed—okay so far, *if* it ever existed. Now here's where it gets interesting. . . ." Walter Prescott straightened up, his eyes alive with enthusiasm. "There's a guy who dives for Norman who really loves his booze when he's on shore. We got hold of him on one of his binges, oh, 'bout a month or so back. Treated him royal with the hollow leg technique? Well, he talked all right, even showed us some underwater pictures he'd taken and very interesting they were. You could see the bars sitting scattered *on* the bottom right enough, and the bottom there is *sand*." He stopped and looked significantly at Toby.

"So?" Toby was puzzled.

"So like, when we excavated the *Whidah*, the bulk of our finds and all the heavy stuff was buried under twelve *feet* of sand. Real murder it was to get out, I can tell you. One of those Cousteau pressure hoses to blow the sand away, and then you'd have two or three minutes to work in before it all settled down again! Granted the *Whidah* went down over two hundred years ago and Norman's U-boat less than fifty, but, even so, heavy stuff like gold and silver bars would tend to get covered up quick just from tidal action—I'd say at least a foot or more—and these were sitting *on* the surface."

"So you think they were dumped recently—the site salted, in fact?" Toby queried.

"That I do," Prescott said earnestly. "Though where the hell Norman got the bullion from or why he should is beyond me." He sighed in exasperation.

"But surely your government people must have investigated all this? Wouldn't they pick up on that? I know you can never tell about gold because it doesn't corrode, but how about the silver? That corrodes quickly in salt water."

"Oh, they've had a treasury agent keeping a careful check on what's been brought up—but he stays topside. The only government diver that's been down is a young coastguardsman from the station here. I've had a word with him and what he had to say makes me certain that the whole operation is crooked. When he went down—with Norman, by the way—he was led to a spot where the bars *were* about a foot down in the sand and had to be dug out, along with bits of the so-called sub."

"Were the bits verified?" Toby interrupted.

"As bits of a submarine? Yes, but that don't mean much either. I can name you at least three marine salvage outfits in

Florida alone that could sell you relics like that. Same with the silver bars. Yes, they were corroded and consistent with a fifty year submersion, but that don't mean a damn thing. In Florida they have outfits that can make genuine 'fake' relics for any age you please just by dumping new silver pieces in an acid bath— Revolutionary War, Spanish, French, you name it, they can make it. The tourists gobble them up at five times the making price. And you don't have to be no Einstein to do it neither— *I* could do it, come to that."

"Do you know what has been happening to the salvaged bullion?"

"All crated up in wooden boxes sealed with a government seal and carted off to some safe-deposit storage in New York. Norman can't get it out of state fast enough—not like Clifford, who had to keep all the stuff right here on Cape until the *Whidah* was finished. Norman's coming down to the wire now himself, his permit is up in two months I'm told, and after that the final accounting will have to be made. The government and the state will take their cut and he and his backers will get the rest." Prescott added with grim relish, "I bet this storm gave him conniption fits. Must have stirred up the bottom something cruel, and we're only just coming into hurricane season, so he may be in for more unpleasant surprises."

Toby was following his own line of thought. "Any jewelry or precious stones been found, do you know?"

Prescott shook his head and frowned. "Not so far as I know. Why?"

"Just wondering," Toby was vague. "And do you know if the government has taken any steps to verify this bullion-loaded U-boat story?"

Prescott shrugged. "The way I heard it some professor over at the college came up with some story about a U-boat sent out from Germany in the final days of World War II with funds for the high-ranking Nazis who had fled to Argentina, and Norman claims this is it. Though why the hell a U-boat bound for Argentina should founder off Cape Cod is beyond me."

"Was the professor's name Corey?" Toby asked, his heart stepping up a beat.

"Sorry, no idea. But what beats me is where all that bullion came from," Prescott muttered. "It makes no sense, no sense at all—and yet it's there."

Toby debated with himself for a moment and then said cautiously, "I have a theory about that, unprovable at present, but it would provide an answer. I'd like for you to keep what I'm going to tell you to yourself for at least three more days. By then I hope to have more answers to some vital questions. After that, since you obviously have expert knowledge of the local scene which I so sadly lack, I would like you to drop the theory in such a way that it gradually percolates back to Norman. Just the fact that an investigation is under way about the bullion possibly coming from a land-based *robbery*. I am hoping that may spook him sufficiently to make some overt moves that may lead us to his partners in all this. Will you go along with me?"

Looking startled, Prescott nodded, "You bet!" And Toby expounded his theory.

"Well I'll be double-damned!" the old seaman gasped. "It's off the wall, but it does make sense. And you think it is tied in with this murder? But how the hell are you ever going to prove it?"

"Indeed I do, I am certain of it," Toby sighed. "But you have asked the vital question—how to prove it? At the moment I haven't the faintest idea. . . ."

Chapter 15

Having hit pay dirt in the person of Walter Prescott beyond his most sanguine expectations, Toby had thrown off dull care and had become sunnily cheerful. Some of the cheer had come from the bottle of rum he and his good friend Walter had killed before parting with warm and somewhat maudlin protestations of eternal friendship, but the glow continued well after he had departed from the unbeckoning charms of Provincetown. He was in no hurry to get home, so meandered slowly back up the Cape, lunching well and at length at the Wayside Inn in Chatham and then wandering back to scenic Route 6A, where he explored the delights of the Brewster Natural History Museum, went on one of their conducted nature walks, took in a couple of historic houses that were open to the public en route and arrived back in Hyannisport in time for a drink before their dinner appointment. Beyond blandly assuring the two avidly interested women he had had a positively splendid day, he continued to be cheerful, charming, amusing, and totally uncommunicative, knowing full well how much that would irritate Penny.

It did, but, constrained by Jocelyn's presence, she was

helpless to do anything about it until after breakfast the next day, when she managed to corner him alone, while Jocelyn was upstairs "getting ready for Boston." "What's with you?" she hissed. "Why all the mystery? What did you find out in Provincetown?"

He managed to look surprised. "It was extremely informative from my point of view, but of no interest to your own line of investigation. I thought we had agreed that you go your way on this and I'll go mine. Also. . . ," he unleashed his big guns, "I have no intention of putting all my cards on the table in the presence of a third party, particularly since I find it passing strange that someone who was not even supposed to be back from an English vacation until yesterday has not only been *here* for two days but is also avid to know what we are up to. You may have perfect confidence in your guest but, since we know practically nothing about her, I do not share it. Have you considered that she may be involved in this thing also?" And he added a parting shot as Jocelyn could be heard on the staircase: "However, since I doubt whether your Robideau investigation has really any bearing on the matter, I see no harm in letting her in on that."

"Well, we'll just see about that," Penny muttered crossly as Jocelyn appeared in the dining room. Her "going-to-Boston" outfit consisted of a drooping two-piece silk dress and jacket, where large red poppies rioted on a background of black and white zigzags, a hat that looked as if it had been translated directly out of a 1950s Doris Day movie, and a pair of yellowing white kid gloves. "Are we ready?" she said brightly. "Why don't we take my car? I know this route and my way about Boston with my eyes shut."

Penny forbore to point out that she herself had been born and raised in Boston, but was more than willing to let someone else deal with summer traffic, so agreed amiably, and off they set. "Oh, and don't worry about dinner," Toby called, waving them off. "I'll book us into the Daniel Webster—my treat!"

By the time they reached the Mid-Cape highway Penny was already regretting her decision. Jocelyn was a demon driver of the first water, weaving in and out of the lanes at a speed that had Penny grasping the edge of her seat white-knuckled, expecting every moment to be her last. It was not until they had reached Plymouth that Jocelyn's undoubted expertise at the wheel convinced her that they might survive after all and she calmed down enough to think coherently. Toby's barb had sunk deep and she decided to tackle the issue head on. "What happened to your summer vacation? I understood from Ada Phipps that you were not expected back in Radley until yester-day, so it was a pleasant surprise to have you get over here so speedily."

Jocelyn gave a nervous titter and shot a sideways glance at her. "Yes, I imagine that does look a bit odd, considering everything else that's been going on, but the simple truth is that I was escaping from the fond embrace of my family. My daughter in Devon has three children, all under the age of six—a boy and two girls, and my grandson is a holy terror. While I love them all to distraction individually, collectively and for more than a few days at a time I find them too much for me. I think I'm just too used to the peace and quiet of a writer's life to cope with the endless noise and movement of kids that age anymore. Maybe when they get to school age I'll improve, or maybe I'm just too old and past it. Anyway, I was thankful when I got back to find a genuine excuse for my premature flight waiting for me, so no one's feelings need to get ruffled. While I'm here I may even dot on out to California later to see my other daughter. She only has one baby, thank the Lord!"

"Rather an expensive solution to your problem," Penny commented drily.

Her companion shrugged, "Well, money isn't really an issue—for my needs I've plenty, even if I never wrote another word, and of course I have every intention of spewing on as long as there's an idea left in me. Besides. . . ," she leered at

Penny, "I can write this off to expenses. What could be more genuine research than an honest-to-God murder mystery on my former turf?"

"With your background how *did* you come to end up here and for such a long time?" Penny pressed.

"As I told you yesterday, I married a Canadian diplomat who specialized, it seemed, in the U.S.—leastways, both of the kids were born here—Deborah in Washington and Janet in San Francisco, so they're officially American. Eventually he got posted to the UN in New York and it was splitsville time. Usual story of male menopause and a twenty-year-old, big-boobed bimbo. Can't say I was devastated. The girls were in a good private school in Connecticut, England in the pre-Thatcher era was still a pretty dreary place to live, we'd often summered on the Cape and I liked it, so here I came and here I stayed. When the time came, Deborah decided to go back to my old college, St. Hughs, in Oxford and, predictably, ended up marrying an Englishman. Janet went to Brown and ended up marrying a classmate from California. So, with them gone and with things on the Cape not what they were, I thought, what the hell, time I went back home for the final stretch. This way I'm close enough to one of them to be handy if needed, and, over the North Pole, it is just as easy to get to California from England as it is from here. End of story. Phew—that was a close one!"

"You can say that again," Penny said weakly, as they missed a huge double-trailer truck by a couple of inches. "Maybe I should shut up and let you concentrate, the traffic is always ghastly from Quincy on in."

A companionable silence fell as they hurtled through the outer suburbs and reached the heart of Boston, taking the South Station off-ramp and diving into the underground parking lot of the mini-skyscraper that housed the Dimola Corporation. They were whisked rapidly up the chain of command until finally they were ushered by the now-obsequious private secretary into Alexander Dimola's private sanctum that more closely resembled a throne room than a business office.

As he rose to greet them Penny noted that he had put on a lot of weight since she had last seen him at the wedding and now bore a remarkable resemblance to the late Rinaldo. Although he greeted her amiably, she was quite unprepared for the electric effect that Jocelyn Combe's name had on him. He lit up like a beacon.

"Not Jocelyn Combe the mystery writer!" He grasped her bony hand fervently, "My wife and I are ardent fans of yours. I think we have everything you've written. Why didn't you *tell* me you were bringing such a distinguished guest?" he challenged Penny. "Had I known I'd have canceled my afternoon appointments." An invisible red carpet immediately unrolled, vintage champagne and caviar arrived, and his next appointment was put back half an hour. It was some time before Penny could cut into his rhapsodies over Jocelyn and get down to business.

As succinctly as she could she stated the background of the case and her particular problem. Alexander listened gravely and jotted down notes as she talked. "I'm really at sea in all this real estate and corporate field," she concluded. "So, if there is anything you can do to help me, I'd be very grateful."

"Yes, I think I can help," he said, scribbling away. "I'll put our Montreal office on to this Paul Robideau's background—that's easy enough. The Amdex Corporation will take more digging, but it can be done. Also, we do have a watchdog on the Cape—one of our corporate lawyers. He may have some information on any widespread purchases by a single buyer. But I warn you it may take some time."

"I understand that and I don't want to be pushy, but the sooner the better," she said. "I'm afraid the Barnstable police are about to arrest and railroad an innocent man, a Wampanoag Indian, and that could stir up endless trouble on the Cape."

He flinched as old memories surfaced. "We certainly don't

want that to happen," he muttered. "I'll make this the highest priority."

Her primary goal achieved, Penny was all set to go, but Alexander refused to part with them before he had extracted a promise from Jocelyn to come to dinner at the earliest opportunity. "My wife would love to meet you and we'd like you to autograph all your books for us," he urged with schoolboyish enthusiasm.

Penny was tickled by Jocelyn's diplomatic, yet barbed, reply as she said sweetly, "Why, I'd be delighted, as soon as this investigation is brought to a successful conclusion. You've no idea how privileged I feel to be allowed in on Penny and Toby's inner councils. So, before this is over and done with I'm afraid I couldn't possibly tear myself away."

He looked crestfallen, "Couldn't you all come for an evening—say one day next week? I could send a limo down for you."

Penny joined in the fun. "At this juncture I'm afraid we are too busy to be social. When we can see our way clear, naturally we'll be delighted to come. Shall we leave it like that?"

Reluctantly, he left it like that, and they left him barking orders over his intercom to put the inquiries in motion.

"That should light a fire under him," Jocelyn said contentedly as they rode down in the elevator. "My first tycoon fan—impressive wasn't it? Makes one wonder if the pen isn't mightier than the sword after all." They reached the car, and as they buckled their seat belts she went on, "Now what and where?"

"I could use some lunch," Penny said. "Caviar may be ritzy but it just doesn't make it as far as I'm concerned. Other than that I've nothing special in mind. Anything in Boston you want to do?"

Jocelyn pondered for a minute then brightened, "*I* know! Why don't I take you to the Genealogical Society on Newbury Street? Isn't what's-her-name doing work for Toby there?

We've managed to light a fire under Dimola, maybe we can jiggle her up a bit."

Penny looked doubtful. "I'm not sure Toby would appreciate us horning in. Anyway don't you have to be a member to get in there?"

"I *am* a member, and members can take in a one-time guest to help them," Jocelyn said, starting up the car. "One of my mysteries was set in early nineteenth-century Boston, so I did one hell of a lot of research in there for it. Book was a complete flop, as it turned out, but I kept up my membership because it's such a neat place. I used to give Clara a hand with some of her genealogical stuff from time to time, so I know my way around. Come to that, we could do some checking ourselves on Paul Robideau—what's to lose while we're here?"

"Alright, but let's eat first," Penny said.

"There's a Magic Pan just a few doors down from the Society building—quite a nice place for lunch, good omelets. Clara and I often used to eat there. The main snag is finding a parking place." Jocelyn roared out into the daylight and started to head through Boston's Chinatown at breakneck speed. Penny found it more comfortable to keep her eyes closed, until a slackening of speed indicated they were close to their destination and hunting for a parking spot. She opened her eyes just as a car pulled away from the curb and Jocelyn swooped at the gap like a hungry hawk. "Handy!" she declared. "The Society is just around the corner." As they walked up Newbury Street, she indicated the sedate red brick building bearing a discreet sign indicating opening hours. "They share the building with Sotheby's now, so that's kind of fun," she informed her companion. "And the Magic Pan is just down here on the same side."

It was well past the peak hour for lunch so the restaurant was almost empty, and they settled at a table by a corner window in the smoking section for Jocelyn's sake. They ordered and received coffee right away, and Jocelyn happily lit up as Penny sipped her coffee and gazed contentedly at the passing crowds. "Is Calpurnia Howes a Society member?" she asked idly.

"You bet your little booties! Headed up the Cape chapter of the DAR at one time; sundry Dexters in the Revolution," Jocelyn said between puffs. "She was always digging for a Mayflower connection, but never could make it. That miffed her! Caleb Crowell, who has multiple Mayflower ancestors— Hopkins, Brewster and Francis Cook, I think—used to twist that dagger in the wound occasionally, just to rile her. *He* belongs to the Mayflower Society."

"What do you make of him?" Penny said, as their omelets arrived.

"I used to think he was a closet gay, but I don't anymore. His driving force seems to be a sort of inverted snobbery, he thinks himself better than anyone else and I feel would love to throw his weight around but hasn't the money for it and is too lazy to make the effort to get it. He sort of cancels himself out, if you get what I mean."

Penny thought she did. They contentedly finished their omelets and Penny had succumbed to some shoofly pie, while Jocelyn had more coffee and another cigarette. Suddenly Jocelyn stiffened, "Well talk of the devil! Caleb Crowell is coming up Newbury Street and I think he just came out of the Genealogical Society." Penny turned and spotted his burly figure passing their window clutching a manilla folder. He then darted across the street into a small stationery and card shop that advertised a copying machine service. From this he emerged shortly, still clutching the folder in one hand and stuffing some papers into his inner coat pocket with the other, "That's odd," Jocelyn muttered, "there are plenty of copying facilities in the Society—why take stuff out? Now he seems to be heading back there. Let's follow him and see what he's up to." But Caleb's progress had been halted by a beckoning bar sign and after a moment's hesitation and an agonized look at the folder in his hand he dived through the doors of the bar. They hastily settled their bill and scuttled back toward the Society.

Once through its glass double doors, Penny found herself in an impressive marble-floored rotunda and, while Jocelyn showed her membership card to the secretary at the desk and signed her in as a guest, saw that the rest of this ground floor was devoted to the august activities of Sotheby's auctioneers. Jocelyn seized her elbow, "Now we sign the guest book and then it's on up to the library. We don't want to run into Caleb if we can help it," she hissed in full Sherlockian frenzy.

They signed the guest book standing on an antique table on the left side of the rotunda, and Jocelyn silently pointed to Caleb Crowell's signature with an eleven-thirty A.M. sign-in time beside it. Several names above Penny spotted Linda Dyke's name with a nine o'clock sign-in. "So she is here today." Jocelyn guided Penny through a portal to the left of the rotunda into a narrow passage housing two small elevators and a staircase winding upward. The tall writer pushed the up button and waited impatiently. "I swear this is the slowest lift in Boston," she sighed. "But the library is on the sixth floor so we certainly don't want to hoof it."

The elevator arrived and disgorged two preoccupied-looking elderly women and they nipped in and soared slowly upward. At the sixth floor the doors opened with snaillike slowness to reveal another narrow passage leading off to the left and the portico of the main reading room straight ahead. It was brightly lit by large windows, its walls above the bookcases studded with portraits of stern-faced Bostonians that gazed down with grim approval at the sea of earnest scholars at the large tables. Penny thought nostalgically of her mother, who must have spent endless hours here in her own genealogical quest, as she surveyed the huge crowded oak tables. Most of the seats around them were occupied by silent workers, books piled before them, heads bent over their charts.

Jocelyn steered her up to the large information desk to the left of the entrance and asked of the woman behind it, "Could you tell us where Mrs. Linda Dyke is working today?" The middle-aged woman surveyed the room. "I think she must be down in the lunch room. Members can use it after two o'clock and she usually does bring a bag lunch. Her things are still here I see. She's working at the end seat there—by the Massachusetts Vital Records. She should be back soon, if you care to wait. Is there anything I can help you with?"

"We'll be using the IGI presently, after we've had a word with Mrs. Dyke," Jocelyn murmured. "It's still on the lower level, is it?"

The woman grimaced, "Yes, but we've got a group in from out of state today and I don't think you are going to find a single microfiche machine open—but you can try."

"Now what?" Penny whispered, as they turned away from the desk, for the whole room was hushed and anything above a whisper seemed sacrilegious.

"We'll lurk in the stacks," Jocelyn whispered back, indicating an opening in the middle of the wall to their left. "I heard the lift go down again, so that might be her—or Caleb, and we don't want *him* to spot us, do we?"

Penny was quietly amused at Jocelyn, who was obviously relishing her Holmesian role and allowed herself to be bustled into the stacks full of floor-to-ceiling bookcases, some aisles brightly lit, the others in semidarkness. They lurked just within the doorway, Jocelyn peering cautiously out. "It is Caleb," she whispered, withdrawing quickly.

Penny peered out and saw him in muttered conversation with another man sitting at a small desk at the opposite end of the vast room. He handed the man a small envelope, then casually strolled along the bookcases on the wall facing the entrance. When he reached the Massachusetts records section he glanced quickly around and slid the manilla folder under a pile of papers at Linda Dyke's vacant seat. Jocelyn, peering over the top of Penny's small head, drew in her breath with a hiss. "Will you just look at that! He must have been copying her notes!"

Looking very smug, his mission accomplished, Caleb Crowell made his way swiftly out of the room and they heard the hum of the elevator. Jocelyn started forward, "Shouldn't we tail him?"

"No, I think it is more important that we talk with Linda Dyke," Penny said grimly. "I've no idea what this may mean, but we ought to know what was in that folder and whether he has taken anything."

"Why don't I go down to the lunch room and see if I can find her and you keep watch up here?" Jocelyn was eager. "Any idea what she looks like?"

"None, but I've an idea this is she coming in now," Penny said, as a small young woman with short, dark curly hair came in and made purposefully toward the end of the table. As she sat down they hurried over to her. "Mrs. Dyke?" Penny said quietly, "I am Penelope Spring, Sir Tobias Glendower's friend, and this is Jocelyn Combe. We have just witnessed something extremely strange that I think you should know about. Do you know Caleb Crowell by any chance?"

Linda Dyke was puzzled. She shook her head. "No. Why?"

"Because we have good reason to believe that Mr. Crowell has just abstracted and copied whatever you had in that manilla folder he replaced just a few minutes ago under that pile of papers. Would you mind checking it to see if he actually has taken anything?"

The puzzlement gave way to astonishment. "Why on earth would anyone do such a thing?" Linda gasped, groping for the folder and hastily flipping through it. "See for yourself, it's just my rough notes on the Dexter branch Sir Tobias asked about! I haven't even got very far as yet, because the couple he was interested in had ten children, seven of them boys, and most of those had eight or nine children apiece so it's taking a long time to check them all out. I'm hoping to finish here today and get on to Columbia Point and the more recent records tomorrow. There's nothing missing, nothing of any particular interest even, and I have not come across a single Crowell." She looked at them suspiciously. "Are you sure you haven't made a mistake?"

"Judge for yourself," Penny murmured, aware that Linda's next-door neighbor at the table was stirring restlessly at the continued hum of conversation. "Would you come into the stacks for a minute and we'll tell you?"

They related what they had seen and Penny concluded, "According to the book downstairs he came in at eleven-thirty and must have hung around until you left your stuff here and went out to lunch. Then he nipped the folder, went out and copied it, and slipped it back. I've an idea he may have tipped the man at the desk over there some cash to keep an eye on things and head you off if you came back before he had time to replace it. Do you know who that man is? I think he must work here."

Linda shook her head helplessly. "I don't know him, I think he's new here, but then I don't get in very often. What do you think I should do? It's all so crazy."

"Yes, it is puzzling, but don't you worry about it," Penny soothed. "Just go on with what you are doing and I'll let Sir Tobias know what's happened. But if you do come up with any links to any of the names he gave you, best keep them right with you and let him know about it as soon as you can."

"Oh, I certainly will now," Linda muttered and went back to her seat.

Penny looked around and discovered that Jocelyn had disappeared. She was startled, until she saw the amazing hat sprouting like an unlikely mushroom from the floor and Jocelyn emerged from the small iron staircase that led down to the lower level. She came up shaking her head. "Not a hope in hell of the IGI machines. All of them occupied and people standing hungrily around waiting to get at them. So now what?"

"I think we should get back and let Toby know of this new twist. Robideau can wait. We may have a whole new ball game, and with an unexpected player."

"I don't get you," Jocelyn said as they made for the elevator.

"One little detail I had forgotten and have not told you, because I've been so bent on other lines of investigation, but Toby remarked on it at the time. You see, when Clara was found dead in the college, her finger had been arranged to point at a map of Cape Cod, and it was pointing at Crowe's pasture in Dennis." Jocelyn stared at her blankly. "As Toby pointed out to me, 'Crowe' is the original form of the Crowells of Cape Cod. . . ," Penny said heavily.

"Then why the hell should he be interested in the *Dexters*," Jocelyn cried. "Maybe he is on the track of something himself! Maybe he's after Calpurnia. . . ."

Chapter 16

"This is certainly a strange development," Toby mused aloud. "But it does seem to indicate that I was correct in assuming that the genealogical reference had some significance. The only trouble is that it does not appear to have the slightest bearing on any of the other lines we've been following or, for that matter, any of the people we've been targeting—and I suppose Crowell has now to be added to that group. What we badly need is a common factor. . . ."

They were sitting out on the patio, drinks in hand, with both Jocelyn and Toby puffing up a storm of tobacco smoke. The frankness with which Penny had rattled off their Boston adventures had made him feel guilty about his own silence and, as a result, he had confided some, but not all, of his Provincetown discoveries.

"Well, one common factor is that they all need, or needed, money in varying degrees," Jocelyn volunteered. "Caleb and Calpurnia both would love to have more than they have already—and for much the same reason. Politicians like Fitzgerald *always* need money, Corey loved money for its own sake, and

Robideau and Norman were both hard hit by the recent recession."

"Yes, but the same could be said for most people on the hard-hit Cape," Toby pointed out. "Oh, I do agree with you that money—or the threat of its loss—may well have been the underlying motive for the *murder*, but we need something more than that; we need a link to bring all these parallel lines together. The key seems to lie in those damned books."

"Then why don't we start with Corey?" Penny put in. "After all he was the one who started the ball rolling by planting the body and the books in the college, and got murdered for his pains. That is, if we're right about him, and I think we are."

"What you need is a plot outline," Jocelyn said abruptly. They looked at her in amazement. She gazed back bright eyed. "No novel gets anywhere if it is just allowed to meander. You have to have a good strong plot outline before you even begin."

"But we're not writing a novel, we're talking about real life!" Toby spluttered.

"Same thing applies," she stated firmly. "You're meandering and getting nowhere. Give me all the facts as you see them and I can give you half a dozen or more possible scenarios using those facts. When additional information comes in it will fit into one of those scenarios better than the others—and that's the one you'd follow."

"I think I see what you mean," Penny murmured. She looked at Toby. "Why not? It's worth a try. We've an hour before we have to go to the Daniel Webster, we could make a start. You first."

"Right then. Pick your villain and your starting point and tell me why," Jocelyn challenged.

He shrugged and chuckled ruefully. "Alright, why not? I'd pick Vincent Norman, whom I believe was mixed up in a Montreal bullion robbery in 1991 and who has 'salted' the stolen bullion into the sea off Cape Cod. And I'd begin with

Clara Bacon's battle with him over his wreck identification claims and her ongoing suspicion of him, which led her to discover the source of the bullion. As possible suspects, also— Calpurnia Howes and Keith Corey, who both supported Norman's claims, possibly for a cut of the loot. Corey panics after he discovers Clara Bacon has been murdered and in turn has to be liquidated in a seeming accident. My proofs: the 'salted' wreck site, the newspaper clipping preserved by Clara Bacon, and the presence of Norman in Florida at the time of Corey's death."

Jocelyn grinned at him. "Great! And you, Penny?"

"I'd start with the character of Clara Bacon," Penny reflected. "A lonely, somewhat frustrated woman, longing for recognition, obstinate in her opinions but—above all—honest. The catalyst in this instance being the loss of her one intimate contact, namely you...," she glanced at Jocelyn. "At this point and at the beginning of this year she becomes obsessive about someone she has disliked and suspected of shady dealing for years, namely Robideau. She goes after him and uncovers concrete evidence of such dealings, but is hampered and desolated when she finds that Keith Corey, with whom she is secretly infatuated, is also mixed up in this shady business. To reveal publicly what she knows would bring about Corey's disgrace, so instead she confronts Robideau, probably with some sort of ultimatum, but gets killed for her pains. Corey belatedly discovers her murder, is conscience-stricken and so reveals the crime, but tries to keep himself off the hook and in turn is killed by Robideau.

"Another factor is the Amdex Corporation—which paid the inflated price for Corey's house—and this is where Crowell, Fitzgerald or even Calpurnia also may come in as coconspirators. My proofs: the long feud with Robideau, the payoff through Robideau on Corey's house, that registered letter that someone has been desperately trying to get hold of and which may contain damning evidence, and the presence of Robideau in Florida at the time of Corey's death."

"Wow! That's terrific," Jocelyn exclaimed. "I hope I remember all this; that would make a great 'soap.' Just to play the devil's advocate, I'll do one based on what little I know of Clara's personal life: my suspect—Stephen Brown, the missing nephew. My facts: Clara and her sister didn't get on. Her sister was deserted by her husband and she had a very hard time of it, but Clara never helped out. Stephen was a dropout—I don't think he even finished high school—and had problems. By what you've heard I'd say he was a drunk, maybe a druggie also. So my scenario is that he nurtured a growing hatred for his 'rich' relation and, driven by his need for money to feed his addictions, came to the Cape to put the arm on his only living relative, was turned down by her, and then shot her in a rage. He dumped her body in the well, expecting it to be discovered and then he'd inherit. When she wasn't found, he came back— maybe he never even left the Cape and is here now—arranged her finding and muddied the waters by leaving all those fake clues, so that when he does show up to claim her estate, which would be vast riches for a dropout, no one will suspect *him*."

"Hmm, aren't you conveniently forgetting Keith Corey?" Toby pointed out drily.

Jocelyn chuckled. "Well, his death could be just a coincidence, run down by a drunk driver, but yes, I should fit him in. Let's see, how about Keith Corey knowing of Brown being on the Cape at the time of the murder and having to be silenced before he could pass the information on. Oh, and to round thing out, and since no one else has mentioned him, there is Burrows Smith. Now in an old-fashioned detective story and as least-likely suspect, he would *have* to be the murderer—though heaven knows why!"

"Aren't you forgetting yourself?" Toby said quietly.

Jocelyn looked at him, a twinkle in her eyes, "Yes, in fact you could make something very suspicious out of me, for not only am I a least likely suspect but also have another strike against me: an iron-clad alibi. If you are right about the date of

Clara's murder, I was at a week-long mystery writers' conference in London, surrounded by a host of my peers."

"Indeed?" he murmured, "Well, having covered the field, I think it is time to head for Sandwich and sustenance." But Penny was very amused to see that he was visibly relieved.

The Daniel Webster was crowded and, since Toby steadfastly refused to accept a table in the piano lounge, they were forced to wait. Penny and Jocelyn retired to the ladies room, and as they came out into the foyer again Jocelyn recoiled and turned back. She grabbed Penny by the arm and hissed, "Calpurnia just came in with a *young* man! How very odd! Anyway, best not let them see us."

"Whyever not?" Penny was a little nettled. "This is a popular eating-out spot and what odds if she does see us?"

"But it is strange," Jocelyn persisted. "I know for a fact that at this time of year Calpurnia always entertains at the Osterville Yacht Club—just as in winter she uses the Oyster Harbors Golf Club's dining room."

"Maybe he's entertaining her," Penny said tartly, thinking Jocelyn was getting a little too carried away by her Sherlockian role.

"But who could he be? Calpurnia is definitely not the dating sort." Jocelyn was not about to let it go.

"Could be business—her insurance man, her attorney, or a visiting relative. Who knows?" Or cares, Penny thought.

"Hmm, possibly. They did have the same sort of nose. She hasn't any children, but I suppose it could be a nephew. Perhaps we should find out," Jocelyn sounded somewhat doubtful. She peered around the corner, "Ah! They've gone into the bar, the coast is clear." And they advanced toward Toby, who had been watching their antics with mild amazement and was now beckoning. "Our table is ready," he announced and started to follow their hostess.

"I'll be with you in a second," Jocelyn murmured and

headed for the reservations desk.

"What's got into her?" he muttered, as they were led into a dining room often used for public meetings and which housed a permanent podium, replete with microphones and a speaker's rostrum in the middle of its long wall. "Oh, she's in full sleuthing frenzy—spotted Calpurnia here with some man," Penny muttered back, as the hostess seated them at a table adjacent to the platform, produced menus almost the size of the table and left them with a falsely bright smile and an "Enjoy your dinner."

Jocelyn's tall figure shortly appeared in the doorway. Mercifully she had changed out of her red, white, and black ensemble, claiming it was too warm, and was now in a sleeveless navy blue silk dress, sprinkled this time with large white roses that rioted in a more sedate fashion. Even so, as she spotted them and loped toward the table, she was still noticeable enough to attract some startled stares. As she sank into a seat opposite Tony she was a little breathless with excitement, her eyes dancing and twin spots of color flaring in her brown cheeks. "You were right," she told Penny. "She *is* being taken out, but you'll never guess who by. . . ." She paused for dramatic effect. "Her escort is Paul D. Robideau."

Penny's eyes widened. "Really? Did you know they were on friendly terms?"

Jocelyn shook her head. "I'm pretty certain he's not in with the Oyster Harbor crowd—except perhaps for business. Even then he's too much of a Johnny-come-lately to have much of an in. They usually deal with the older long-established Cape firms. Of course," her eyes narrowed, "Calpurnia could be unloading her house on him—maybe for the same reason as Corey: a payoff!"

"Here they come now," Penny said, as Calpurnia and Robideau were ushered to a small table by the window.

"Oops!" Jocelyn buried her head like an ostrich in her oversize menu. "Don't want her to spot me just yet. Do you think it would be a good idea to have a word with them while they're here?"

"We can discuss that later," Toby said firmly as the waitress advanced on them, pencil poised over her order form. "But let us eat in peace."

They ate in peace, but Penny, who had the best vantage point, noted throughout the meal that their unheeding quarry were in deep and serious converse the whole time.

When they had arrived at the coffee and liqueurs stage, Jocelyn could stand it no longer. "Come on!" she urged. "Let's go and say hi. What's to lose? It may give them a jolt seeing us together."

Penny looked at her partner. "What do you think?"

"Can't see any harm in it," Toby said, waggling his brandy snifter at her. "But Robideau's your baby, not mine. I'll stay here, you two go ahead."

Muttering under her breath, Penny followed Jocelyn's determined progress across the crowded room. They were almost up to the table before Calpurnia spotted them: her stern face congealing as Jocelyn, having caught her icy eye, broke into speech. "Calpurnia! How nice to see you! I spotted you coming in and just had to come over to say hello."

"Oh, yes? I'm very surprised to see you here." Calpurnia's tone was unwelcoming but did not faze Jocelyn in the slightest. She looked inquiringly at Robideau but, since Calpurnia made no move to introduce him, went chattering on.

On closer inspection Penny saw that Robideau was not as young as he appeared at a distance: he was very slim and dark of eye and hair, but there were lines etched in his thin face and she estimated he must be somewhere in his midforties. "I know you've already met my friend here—Dame Penelope Spring," Jocelyn gushed on unheeding. At the mention of her name Penny saw Robideau's eyes narrow, as Calpurnia favored her with a stiff nod. "I felt the least I could do after poor Clara's body was discovered would be to come over and see what I could do to help," Jocelyn rattled on. "And she and Sir Tobias have been kind enough to let me in on their investigations. You knew about those, of course?" She gazed artlessly at Calpurnia.

"I understand that the police already have a suspect in custody for the murder—Burrows Smith, and that did not surprise me." Calpurnia's words dripped icicles. "So I take it the investigation is concluded."

Penny broke her silence, "Oh, far from it, Mrs. Howes. I'm afraid you have been misinformed. Burrows Smith has merely been questioned, and we are certain he has nothing to do with it. The investigation goes on, and I must thank you again for all the valuable information you provided."

Calpurnia recoiled slightly and Robideau cleared his throat. She glanced at him quickly, then said, "I don't think you have met Mr. Paul Robideau—Jocelyn Combe, the writer, and Dr. Spring. Mr. Robideau and I are discussing business, so if you would excuse us?" Robideau stood up, gravely shook their hands, and resumed his seat.

But Penny was not about to be put off that easily. With a mental apology to his redheaded assistant, she said, "Why Mr. Robideau, how nice to meet you at last! I did try and reach you at your office a couple of times, but it appears you were away in Florida on business. However, your assistant was most helpful to my inquiries."

Calpurnia looked daggers at her and Robideau's dark eyes went blank. "I can't imagine in what regard we could help you with Mrs. Bacon's murder." His deep voice still held a faint French accent.

"Oh, it was concerning Keith Corey and his involvement. Very informative," she said smoothly.

"Are you accusing the late Professor Corey of murdering Clara Bacon—how ridiculous!" Calpurnia shrilled suddenly.

"Oh, goodness no! But we have established that it was he who found and removed her body to the college," Penny said, gazing steadily at Robideau. "And we believe he was conveniently silenced for that act. But then, we mustn't keep you from your business discussion. So nice to have met you at last, Mr. Robideau, we may well meet again." And on that ominous note turned and headed back for their table, with a subdued Jocelyn hard on her heels.

"Was it wise to show your hand like that?" Jocelyn gasped as they sat down again. "I nearly had a fit!"

"There comes a time when you have to start shaking things loose," Penny informed her with a grim smile. "And I think I just did."

"You certainly stirred something up," Toby observed mildly, "He's calling for their bill and they haven't exchanged a word since you left the table. In fact, if looks could kill, they'd both be out of it. What *did* you tell them?"

Penny related what had transpired, as they watched Robideau quickly signing the charge slip and the two unlikely companions exiting the dining room in grim-faced silence.

"You must have struck a nerve. Maybe there is something in your theory about Robideau after all," Toby conceded. "But how the hell that fits in with Norman and *his* little scheme is beyond me. Let's be on our way and I'll try and get hold of Bob to see if he's come up with any information on their Florida trips."

He was spared the trouble, for no sooner had they got back to the house than the phone went and it was Bob Dyke in a state of excitement. "Stephen Brown has been found!" he announced. "He checked himself into an alcoholic detox center in Oregon two and a half months ago; he is still there."

Penny had answered the phone thinking it was Alex's nightly call. "So that lets Burrows Smith out—right?" she said.

"For the moment, yes. Birnie is now highly suspicious of Brown. Thinks his checking himself in so close to the murder date is a bit too pat."

"Rubbish! But I'm glad for Burrows' sake. Let me pass you over to Toby," Penny said. "He has some questions for you."

She handed the phone to Toby who had been lurking impatiently behind her.

Penny relayed the news to Jocelyn, who started to laugh, "There, you see! The chief of police is on my side—Stephen Brown as prime suspect. I wonder if I'm right!"

Chapter 17

The trickle of information that had started with Bob's evening call rapidly swelled to a flood in the days that followed, so that they were all but submerged by the tide as they bemusedly tried to sort out the many bits and pieces and fit them into place. The trouble was that, far from clarifying the picture, the information either petered out at a crucial point or only served to make the confused situation even more so. Only Jocelyn was at all content, as she happily scribbled away in a totally unintelligible hand at her plot outlines. She had sagaciously set up a card table on the patio as her base of operations and so was spared the constant summons of the telephone and, for that matter, the necessity to take her turn answering it.

Also in a state of high frustration was Robert Dyke, for Birnie had taken him off his continuing search for the missing letter and had given him the impossible task of tracking down the gun found in the well. Having failed to link it with Burrows Smith, Birnie was now hell-bent on linking it to some other Cape Cod Vietnam veteran. "Even with a serial number it would be well-nigh impossible," Dyke complained to the sympathetic Toby. "But without it it is hopeless, and yet the letter that may be *the* crucial bit of evidence in the case, and which *has* to be floating around somewhere in the system, he is choosing to ignore."

"Did you ask him about looking into Keith Corey's bank accounts?" Toby asked.

"Yes, and he said that he did not believe there was any connection with the murder and that, even if there was, that was the Florida police's baby, not his. On the quiet I am trying to get some info from both them and Corey's bank here."

"Since we can't make any sense of the information we have already, I don't see the point in putting Bob to all this trouble to get more," Penny fussed.

"If we can prove Corey had received any sizable payoff prior to the payoff on the house, we may be able to persuade Birnie that the two deaths are linked and get some official cooperation for the ongoing inquiry," Toby replied with heavy patience. "We can't go on putting Bob in jeopardy like this. It's just too bad his inquiries could not place either Norman or Robideau in or near Orlando or Naples, but with Norman flying into Miami and Robideau into St. Petersburg, and then both of them hiring cars—well, it still doesn't say they *weren't* there but we can't prove they were."

He was feeling somewhat disgruntled since, in their respective lines of enquiry, Penny had been receiving more feedback than he had. Dimola had been very prompt in digging out Robideau's Canadian past, even though most of it seemed to have little relevance to this present. They had learned he was divorced, with his ex-wife and two children now living in Quebec. More interestingly, they had heard he had left Montreal in a hurry and under a cloud: the outline was there but the details on it were vague. It had concerned an urban redevelopment scheme that had involved the use of strong-arm tactics to "persuade" some of the reluctant householders to sell to the corporation of which Robideau was then a director. The scheme had been successful up to a point, but then the developers had run afoul of the government's building codes. It had ended in cases against two of the partners, culminating in monumental fines and suspended jail sentences, and the consequent collapse of the corporation. Robideau had saved himself prior to these by skimming his share of the profits and running off to the States. Word was that he would not be welcome back in Canada.

"Other than showing he's a pretty shady character—which we knew already—and is not above using force to serve his ends, all that proves nothing," Penny had sighed.

On the Amdex Corporation Dimola had not gone very far, other than to find it was recent, having come into being in the past two years, and was, in his opinion, largely a dummy corporation. "Possibly a spin-off from a larger conglomerate that doesn't want all its dealings known to the rank and file. Its capitalization is very modest—about a million and a half—and, interestingly enough, seems to be secured by a Swiss bank, so its principals evidently do not want their part in it publicized," he had elaborated. There was no sign of any of their suspects involved and only one tenuous link that possibly might link Amdex with Robideau's past. On the board of directors was a Fernande Legros: on the list of Robideau's former associates in Montreal there was also a Legros. "Naturally I'm checking further to see if it's the same man, but Legros is a pretty common name." Alexander Dimola had not sounded very optimistic.

Toby's one bit of news had been more exciting and had come from Walter Prescott. "Word is going around that Norman is packing it in," Walter told him over the phone. "Says that storm has played such havoc with the bottom and the wreck that he doesn't think it's worth continuing. Apparently Fitzgerald's already made application for a final government count and splitting up of what's been found. Do you think we've spooked him?" Toby thought it highly likely, although it did not help him with his own investigation one bit.

To further their aggravation and confusion Linda Dyke had reported that Caleb Crowell had also transferred to the Columbia Point records and was working intently on some project, although he had made no effort to approach her. "What the hell could he be up to or on to?" Penny fumed. "Why don't you have a go at him, Toby? Go and get him drunk and pump him—should be right up your alley." Toby was not amused and paid her no heed.

Another weekend was upon them and a new threat lurked on the horizon. The New York invalids were all on the mend and, worse, Sonya had just got wind of what was going on on the Cape and was hell-bent on hurling herself into the fray.

"My son, the fink," Alex recounted with grim amusement on his Sunday call. "You know he's got a photographic memory? Well, he apparently overheard us talking on the phone the other night and I must have dropped something about 'your murder.' Of course off he went to his mother and demanded to know who grandma had murdered and said that he hoped it wasn't grandpa because grandpa was looking after his Tower of London. So, the cat is out of the bag. I'm stalling her by telling her she's not out of the woods yet, but—come hell or high water—we'll be up next weekend, or, if she has anything to do with it, maybe sooner. I thought I'd better warn you."

To Penny's further irritation, Toby greeted this news with amiable approval. "Ah, good! Then I vote we return to our original intention, hand over what we've got to Birnie and get back to what we're really here for. If he's too much of an idiot to do anything with it, it is not our fault."

"And let a double murderer go scot free?" she demanded hotly.

"We've still got a week, maybe something will turn up. If not...," he shrugged. "Maybe it's time we fell flat on our faces on a case; we're way beyond the law of averages as it is."

"If this is the new mellow you speaking, I think I liked you better when you were cantankerous," she muttered and went off to seek sympathy from the absorbed Jocelyn.

On Monday the dam broke. The phone went and Toby called out "Your turn." Hoping it was Alexander Dimola with fresh ammunition, Penny picked it up to be greeted by a highly excited female voice exclaiming, "I've got it, I've got it! Is that you, Sir Tobias?"

"No, it's Penny Spring, and what have you got?"

"Oh, Dr. Spring—it's Linda Dyke. The link, of course! The link Sir Tobias wanted."

"Who is it?" Penny was electrified and yelled, "Toby, get in here!"

"All of them."

"All of who?"

"Robideau, Norman, and Calpurnia Howes," Linda was bubbling with excitement. "They are *all* Dexters—cousins! That's what the D is in Paul Robideau's name—Dexter! Oh, it's far too complicated to explain it all over the phone, but Norman and Robideau are first cousins once removed and second cousins to Calpurnia, all through female lines of that Dexter-Howes marriage. It's amazing! Shall I come right back with the proofs and explain it all then?"

"Do that, and congratulations," Penny said, handing the phone to Toby. "Bingo! Believe it or not we were *both* right."

After a longer exchange with Linda Dyke and a few terse questions, he put phone down, a changed man. There was the gleam of battle in his round blue eyes as he straightened up, glared at Penny, and barked, "Right! So let's get to work with the correlation of our two lines and see if we've got enough to make a case against Norman *and* Robideau. The study, I think?"

Penny dithered. "Shouldn't we let Jocelyn in on this as well?"

"No, leave her be. She's quite happy scribbling away at

those silly plots of hers. This is serious work we have to do," he rumbled, "And I can live without her flights of fancy."

On opposite sides of the desk they consulted, correlated information, and became welded invisibly into that formidable whole which had been the downfall of so many murderers in the past. Time vanished as they labored on, until finally Toby leaned back with a satisfied sigh, lit up his pipe, and said, "So we are agreed now on this main outline of what must have happened?"

Penny nodded, "Yes, but you'd better run it through in order so that I have a clear idea of the sequence. I feel I *should* tell Jocelyn—she is an interested party and I want to get everything straight."

"Very well," he cleared his throat. "The starting point is Robideau, who flees to the Cape with his shady gains after Montreal gets too hot for him. He comes here because it is the one place outside of Canada he has any kind of contacts because of his American Dexter grandmother. To gain entrée into Cape circles for his new real estate business he contacts Calpurnia Howes, the doyenne of the Cape at the time and a distant cousin. Through her he meets other Dexter kin, including Norman, who is already talking of treasure hunting because of the current success of the *Whidah* salvage operation—I had that from Prescott. At the start it is just a get-rich-quick type of wishful thinking men kick around after a few drinks, because Robideau is doing well in real estate and Norman getting by with his boat building. Then the recession hits, and suddenly both of them are hurting badly. Robideau, from prior knowledge, hatches this daring and imaginative plan: a bullion robbery far from the Cape in Canada and then, if it succeeds, the recycling of the bullion through a salvage operation. His cousin, an ex-Black Beret from Vietnam and more a man of action than Robideau, eagerly falls in with the scheme. We know from Dimola that one of Robideau's ex-partners had been a former Brinks employee, so all the information about those regular bullion shipments to Montreal probably came from him. He may well be one of the other two men involved in the operation. . . ."

"He may be Fernande Legros," Penny put in, "and the other one may be one of the French-Canadian heavies they used on that development scheme."

Toby nodded and sailed blithely on. "To cover their tracks they initiate the salvage operation on the *Portland before* the robbery, and run into their first bit of trouble with Clara Bacon. Norman may be a man of action, but evidently no scholar or he'd have come up with a better story to begin with. The robbery takes place and succeeds beyond their wildest dreams and they get away unsuspected. They fence the jewelry and some of the untraceable securities to give themselves a sizable bankroll, set up the dummy Amdex Corporation for their eventual real estate plans and to finance Norman's operation, and start 'finding' the bullion.

"The one snag is Clara Bacon, who had her teeth firmly in the 'wreck' problem and won't give up on it. They need added support and turn on the quiet to cousin Calpurnia. If Jocelyn had spotted Clara Bacon's tender feelings for Corey, chances are Calpurnia knew of them also. Her own support of Norman's claims might look too suspect should anyone realize they were related, so she suborns Corey, who is money-hungry and gives his support for a price. It also puts Clara Bacon in a quandary and silences her outward opposition. Unfortunately for her, her basic honesty keeps her digging at the problem until she stumbles on the whole truth and has to be silenced. . . ."

"And you think that was by Norman?" Penny interrupted again.

"Yes, for three reasons: the gun, the cat, and the location. More likely that Norman, as a Vietnam veteran, would have a weapon of that kind, and, by Prescott's description of him as being big and burly, that would explain the cat's negative reaction to big and burly Birnie. Also, I doubt whether Clara would have met her old enemy Robideau on her own turf, whereas she had no such bitter feelings about Norman. So, Norman kills her, drops her in the well, and they should have been home free. . . ."

"Except for Corey," she murmured.

"Yes, their one weak link. Greed had bought his compliance, but he had not bargained on murder. Greed, however, kept him silent after he had found the body and until he thought he was safe after the payoff on his house and his removal from the Cape. Maybe his conscience bothered him, or maybe he figured if things did unravel he could not be connected with their crimes."

"And figured wrongly. You believe that was Robideau?"

"Yes, that makes the most sense. Although blood is evidently thicker than water in this case, Norman would not be stupid enough to kill twice at Robideau's bidding. This time I imagine he said, 'You take care of it.' And Robideau did, with such success that, unless someone turns State's evidence, no one will ever pin Corey's murder on him."

"Which brings us to the problem of the letter and the odd behaviour of Caleb Crowell," Penny murmured.

"Two very separate issues," Toby reproved. "On the letter we have only some rather tenuous suppositions, but the only one that makes sense to me is that, prior to her proposed departure, Clara must have hinted at or told Corey what she had in mind to do. He kept the information to himself hoping to change her mind about using her 'proofs,' whatever they were, after they were both safely in Florida. Not knowing the letter existed, Norman, after the murder, removed everything that concerned either him or Robideau from Clara's files and thought they were safe. He did a pretty slipshod job, I may add, because he left the file of newspaper clippings for me to find. But that's beside the point. . . ."

"Corey knew when she intended to leave, must have tried to contact her down there, found she had not arrived, investigated here, found the packed car and knew something was wrong, investigated further and found her body. At that stage he'd have been in a fine old panic, realizing his 'partners' were capable of murder, yet constrained by the fact he had not yet been paid off for his house and could not distance himself from the Cape for several months. His one thought would have been to get hold of that letter. . . ."

"So you think he was the one who did the Florida break-in and then tried to get the letter?" she queried.

"Yes, I do. I think he made a flying trip down there over a weekend and then, having failed to get hold of it, came back, kept mum, and sweated it out until the settlement of his house and the end of the semester. He must have been in an agony of panic all that time, wondering if he was due for a similar fate and trying to think of a way to get himself off the hook. We know the bizarre result. Not only did he want her murder revealed, but he wanted to leave clues to the culprits—albeit very oblique clues. Maybe he even had further blackmail of the principals in mind—threatening them with that letter if they should come after him. It didn't work out, although I think it was at that last confrontation with him that Robideau learned of the letter's existence, and I think that may explain this sudden packing up of the salvage operation, rather than my devious hints via Prescott. They may have altered their plans and are now planning to cut and run with the money as soon as they get their hands on it.

"As to Crowell. . . ," he sighed and shook his head, "Something you must have told him in that interview must have alerted him to the probable Howes-Robideau-Norman connection. He's been digging for it. Maybe, since he too is hungry for money, he has it in mind to put the screws on Calpurnia, or maybe he just wants to make her sweat. Unless he's careful he may be victim number three—which would simplify matters for us, of course, because we'd nab them then for sure."

"What a cold-blooded old devil you are," she said drily. "I was thinking we'd make far more tempting targets at this juncture."

"Who, us?" he scoffed. "Forget it! We're far too cozy with the police for them to try anything." He got up and stretched. "Now the only thing we have to do is prove all this. . . ."

"Oh, piece of cake!" she said sarcastically, and followed him out into the living room where he made with determination for the drinks tray. As he reached it, Jocelyn poked her head in through the patio door and said, "Ah, there you are! Can you spare a minute? There's something I very much want to talk over with you both."

"Come on in and have a drink. We've got a lot to tell you, too," Penny said.

"It's about these plot outlines," Jocelyn said, absentmindedly tucking her ballpoint pen behind her ear, "I've tried them every which way and there is only one of them that makes any kind of sense. May I try it out on you?"

Penny grinned at Toby, "Why yes, go ahead. We're all ears."

Jocelyn plopped down in the nearest chair and flourished a sheaf of papers at them. "It necessitates Robideau and Norman having been in cahoots all along, and this is the way it develops . . . ." She proceeded to recapitulate in outline the identical sequence they had just gone through so laboriously.

Penny couldn't bring herself to look at Toby, whose face was a study, lest she collapse in helpless laughter. He got steadily redder in the face as Jocelyn's high girlish voice piped on, and when she finally came to a stop and looked inquiringly at them, he gasped weakly, "And how do you account for Crowell?"

"Oh, him!" Jocelyn extracted the pen and began to suck thoughtfully on the end of it. "Blackmail, I'd say. Has got the goods somehow on Calpurnia and is about to put the squeeze on." She paused, her brow wrinkling, "There's just one snag. I've written myself into a corner. I can't for the life of me think of how to bring the culprits to book for their crimes. Any ideas?"

Chapter 18

Linda Dyke had come and gone, departing with grateful thanks and a handsome check from Toby, and leaving behind copies of all her charts and their sources over which they duly pored. The Dexter-Howes marriage that Corey had underlined had produced a daughter who married back into the Dexters and had raised a family of seven sons. The eldest son of this marriage was Calpurnia's great-grandfather, the fourth son had had several daughters, one of whom was Robideau's paternal grandmother, the other Norman's maternal grandmother, making them, as Linda had already stated, first cousins once removed and second cousins to Calpurnia. Jocelyn found ironic amusement in the fact that the Dexter who had fathered these lines had been a minister of the most rigid Puritanical sort. "Probably whirling in his grave at this lot," she commented. "Pity we can't summon him up to haunt them into confessing. Short of something like that, we've had it."

That indeed was the crux of the problem: to know what had happened was one thing, to bring it home to the perpetrators was something else. Robert Dyke had been added to their council and his contribution brought them little cheer.

"With all these new supportive facts to back up our theory, couldn't you now put it before Birnie and at least get him to put you back on tracing the letter rather than this ridiculous gun-owner hunt?" Toby demanded.

"I doubt it would do any good," the policeman sighed. "You've got some pretty big Cape names involved. Calpurnia's alone is enough to send him running for cover."

"Why is he so scared of her?" Penny chimed in.

"I'm not sure whether it's Calpurnia—who you must admit is pretty scary—or his wife he's most afraid of. And you've no real *proof* on any of them."

"How about that gun?" Jocelyn said. "I believe there's some kind of test with acid you can do to bring out the numbers on a gun even after they've been filed off. If you could find out from Army records whether Norman had such a weapon, wouldn't that be enough to start the ball rolling?"

"No, we tried that. Whoever filed them off did such a good job, the lab couldn't raise a thing."

"Well, how about bluffing it out? Pretending you've found a number and that it's his. Couldn't you haul him in and third degree him on that?" she persisted.

He grimaced. "That wouldn't do any good. All he'd have to do is to say he'd handed it back after the war or had it stolen and it would be up to us to prove differently. As to the third degree . . . ," he snorted derisively. "I'm afraid you're a bit out of date, Mrs. Combe. These days suspects have more rights than victims, and Norman isn't the type to collapse at a few pointed questions.

"No. . . ." Again he sighed heavily. "I'm afraid it looks as if this will be another Cape Cod murder where we know full well who the murderer is but can never bring him to book for it. It won't be the first time by a long shot—take, for instance, our bog murders. . . ." He looked at Penny and Toby. "Apart from yours and one other later on, which turned out to be drug-related and we got a confession, most of them remain unsolved, although in two cases we knew for certain who did it. One of them, a man who murdered his girlfriend and dumped her in a bog, is alive and well and living in California. Another one died before we even found the body of his wife, whom he'd murdered and buried beneath a cranberry bog shack. Short of a miracle. . . ."

"How about a confrontation of all the suspects?" Jocelyn said decidedly; she was not about to let go of it. "You know, gather them all together and confront them with our evidence?"

Toby shuddered slightly. "I did that once—never again! One of the most nerve-wracking experiences of my life. I felt I had been trapped in a bad Hollywood production."

"It worked, didn't it?" Penny pointed out.

"Yes, but we had a lot of official clout behind us that time *and* an ace or two up our sleeves," he returned.

"Then how about baiting a trap with one of us?" Jocelyn said. "Pretend we've found some crucial bit of evidence and are about to hand it over to the police; that might draw them out and then—whammo!"

"Like the letter? Not a bad idea!" Penny brightened.

Toby surged to his feet with a muffled roar. "No! If you are going to start talking that kind of nonsense, I'm off! The last time we were here you nearly got yourself killed doing such a damned fool thing. Don't you ever learn?"

"But it *worked*," she said stubbornly. "Even if it does not work this time, it is worth a try now that we've got this far."

"Then I shall have absolutely no part in it," he growled and stalked out, slamming the front door behind him.

Dyke got hesitantly to his feet. "Maybe I'd better be off too."

"Don't go yet, Bob, and don't mind Toby. We need some more information. I'd already been thinking along the lines Jocelyn suggested, but if we are going to use the letter as a lure, we'll have to have a feasible story. Now, what happens if you find the letter? Can the police open it right away, or do they have to have some sort of warrant or release from the post office, or what?" Penny asked.

He sat down again. "Dealing with the post office is a bit like dealing with the IRS, I've found. Everyone you talk to has a slightly different view of the rule book and, since this is a very unusual situation, no one has run into it before, but the way I understand it is that if the police track the letter we'd need a death certificate and a warrant to open it. Usually, if the addressee of a registered letter dies prior to its delivery, it is just returned to the sender. But in this case the sender *is* the addressee so that doesn't work. They *think* the procedure in that case would be for the addressee's next-of-kin or heir, or duly appointed person with power-of-attorney—like her lawyer, for instance—to present the death certificate and sign for the letter."

"I see," Penny was pondering. "So that would mean Stephen Brown or her local lawyer. Stephen is not exactly available, so how about the lawyer?"

"I'd say he would be a nonstarter. We checked with him about the will and that apparently was the only time he'd had any dealings with Clara. She didn't have much time for lawyers after her bitter experience in the Robideau land fight, and he wasn't the one she'd had for that."

"So that leaves us with Stephen Brown," she sighed.

"Or a substitute," Jocelyn broke in. "We don't know what he looks like, so neither would they. I don't think he has ever been on the Cape, and the only photo I ever saw of him at Clara's was as a teenager and with his mother—a bit weedy and seedy even then and presumably more so now if he's a drunk. So what we need is a weedy and seedy stand-in—shouldn't be too difficult to round up." Penny nodded enthusiastically.

"But that would be highly illegal!" Bob spluttered. "You couldn't do that!"

They looked at him blandly. "But none of it would be *real*,"

Penny said. "We're just setting up an act: a fake Stephen Brown, a fake letter, a fake hand-over to us, not you. So that's my next question. To 'find' it locally at this late date may arouse their suspicions, so what other options have we? Buzzards Bay? Anywhere else in Massachusetts?"

Robert came out of his startled daze. "Er, well, Buzzards Bay does have a dead letter section of sorts. I was getting started on that when Birnie pulled me off it. And I understood that in certain special cases they have a 'special-action' department of dead letters in Boston—the main post office downtown."

Penny and Jocelyn looked at each other, "That would be great!" they said in unison.

"We'll set up a meeting with our Stephen Brown there. It will give them plenty of time to get on our trail and, if they come after the letter, to make an attempt for it on the way back," Penny said. "Now, how are we going to leak this information to them without seeming too obvious? And how do we get hold of our fake Stephen Brown?"

Dyke got up hurriedly. "I don't think I want to hear this. I don't want to know anything about it. I agree with Sir Tobias—this is a crazy thing to do. I'm off." He headed for the door.

"Oh, not to worry, Bob, we'll be all right. Thanks, you've been a great help." He groaned as he went out and she grinned at Jocelyn. "Nice lad, that. Very steady. Now, any ideas?"

"Plenty," Jocelyn said fervently. "I've remembered: there's one of my ex-writing students in Boston—*ideal* for our Stephen! A really weedy, seedy type complete with scruffy beard. Very arty, does some Little Theater work, some painting, some writing—none of 'em well. I'm sure he'd play along if I offered to read his latest brain-child and stood him a good dinner. As to our leak—what day is it?" She looked frantically around for a calendar.

"Tuesday, why?"

"Oh, good, that's their bridge day at Osterville Yacht Club.

With any luck I'll catch Calpurnia there at lunch. She's a bridge player."

"I didn't know you were a member!" Penny interjected.

"I'm not, but I've plenty of friends who are. One of them can take me. I'll get right on it." Jocelyn sprang to the phone and after a few minutes conversation came back beaming. "That's all set. Now, where were we?"

"Whoa! What have you got in mind to tell Calpurnia? No sense in going off half-cocked before we have worked things out carefully."

"But we *are* pressed for time," Jocelyn cried. "It'll have to be done this Thursday."

"Why?"

"Because I'm moving over to my friends in Brewster on Friday, remember? And your family will probably be here the next day. You won't want to chance this with them around, will you?"

"You've got a point there," Penny mused. "Alex is just as bad as Toby when it come to things like this."

"So I'll try and get hold of Craig Polanski and set that up right away." Jocelyn sprang up again and this time the phone conversation was a long one. Penny retired to the study, got out Toby's notes and proceeded to type from them Clara Bacon's Florida address on to a manilla envelope, with the West Barnstable address in the upper left-hand corner. She stuffed it with some blank sheets of paper, sealed it, and was just about to stow it away in her tote bag when Jocelyn appeared in the doorway. "One 'Stephen Brown' all set to go," she announced triumphantly. "He'll meet us inside the main post office at eleven-thirty on Thursday morning—has to be at work by twelve. Quite eager and intrigued by the whole thing. Of course, I'll have to let him know about bringing the envelope . . . ."

"No need," Penny held up her handiwork. "I've got it right here. Thought I'd pop down to the post office and register it later, but won't let them mail it. We can slip it to him when we meet up with him, so that he can give it back to us in plain sight."

"Good thinking!" Jocelyn applauded. "What's in it?"

"Blank paper. More importantly, what have you got in mind to tell Calpurnia? That *has* to be convincing."

Jocelyn outlined her scenario. "You think that will do?"

"Absolutely great! Toby is always going on about my imagination—he should see a *really* fertile one in action. If that doesn't work, nothing will, and it all hangs together so convincingly." Penny sobered. "But it all depends on catching up with Calpurnia before Thursday. If that fails we're up the creek."

"Think positive," Jocelyn reproved. "Calpurnia is a creature of habit. But I'd better be off, just in case. If she isn't there, we'll have to do a quick rethink."

They shut up the house and went their separate ways: Penny to the Hyannis Post Office, Jocelyn along the shore road to Osterville, where she picked up her compliant friend and headed back for the Yacht Club, which was its usual crowded summer pandemonium. She had to run the gauntlet of "Well, what a nice surprise," and "What are you doing back here," from sundry acquaintances, before settling at a small table by the windows overlooking the equally crowded wooden patio overlooking the ocean. Jocelyn hungrily scanned the room for Calpurnia, but there was no sign of her. Her friend, who was a gifted artist and part-time writer in her own right, looked at her with wry amusement. "Not that I'm not delighted to see you, but what *are* you up to, Jocelyn?"

She giggled self-consciously, "Bear with me, Margery. I can't tell you—at least, not at the moment. Next week, if you're free, I'll take you out to dinner and tell you all about it. Now it's in the nature of a secret mission. I need to run into Calpurnia Howes and I was hoping she'd be here."

"Well, it's Tuesday so she usually is. But wouldn't it be simpler to phone here?" Margery was highly intrigued.

"No, that wouldn't do at all," Jocelyn muttered and then her heart skipped a beat and her spirits rose as she saw Calpurnia come through the glass double doors accompanied by another woman of similar vintage but less intimidating mien. "What an incredible piece of luck," she breathed as the two sought a table near the screened-off area where the bridge players would eventually go into action. "She's with Frances Dickson!"

"So?" Margery drawled, sipping the vodka martini that a college girl waitress had just put before her. "They're bridge partners from way back."

"And Frances happens to be a devoted fan of mine. I can do it indirectly. This is great!"

"Lucky you! The sort of fan to have, Frances is rolling in it," Margery said drily. "And since I've *no* idea what you're talking about, let's eat and talk about something else." They ate their seafood salads and gossiped as Jocelyn kept a wary eye on her quarry. When their coffee arrived she could not bear the suspense any longer so she got up. "If you'll excuse me, Margery, I must tackle them now, before the bridge players start to move in."

"Go right ahead," her friend said with a grin, "I've never seen a secret agent in action. Maybe I'll take notes."

Jocelyn started toward their table, thankful that Calpurnia was seated with her back to her. Before she reached it, Frances Dickson spotted her and waved enthusiastically, "Why, look who's here!" she boomed in a surprisingly deep voice, "My favorite mystery writer! What are you doing here? Come and join us." She pulled a chair away from the next table and indicated it. "Tell us what you are up to! You know Calpurnia of course?"

"Yes, hello Calpurnia, so nice to see you again," Jocelyn said casually, as she sank into the chair and focused her attention on Frances. "Well, it's all rather exciting. I came over because of poor Clara Bacon's murder—you heard about that?" Frances nodded, her amiable face becoming owlishly solemn. "I've been staying with Dame Penelope Spring and Sir Tobias Glendower over in Hyannisport helping them investigate it. And I'm on to a real scoop. My publisher is delighted and it will undoubtedly be my next book based on a real-life murder this time."

"How delightful! Remember to have them send me a dozen autographed copies as soon as the hardback comes out. Have you solved it?" Frances exclaimed.

"Well no, not yet, but we're on the brink." Jocelyn leaned forward confidingly. "This is just between us, you understand? We are about to have a major breakthrough. This Thursday Clara's nephew is flying in from the West Coast to retrieve a letter of Clara's from the dead-letter office in Boston. It is thought to contain vital evidence about her murderer." Jocelyn couldn't resist sneaking a look at Calpurnia and was disconcerted to see it did not elicit the slightest reaction from her grimly impassive face.

"He is somewhat strapped for money until Clara's estate is settled, so I arranged through my publisher to finance his trip and give him a handsome bonus into the bargain for letting me see the contents of the letter before we hand it over to the police. It's all quite legal and it will help me enormously to write it up quickly. We're meeting him at the main post office in Boston some time before noon on Thursday and then will bring the letter on to the police down here. Isn't that exciting?"

"It certainly is, but then you're always doing such exciting things, Jocelyn," Frances said wistfully. "I don't know how you manage it."

Calpurnia broke her silence. "We're here to play bridge and it is time—they're moving in, Frances. So, if you'll excuse us, Jocelyn?" She got up decisively.

A little nonplussed, Jocelyn stood up. "So mum's the word," she charged them. Frances nodded solemnly and followed Calpurnia's rigid back around the screens.

"How did it go?" Margery asked, as she got back to the table.

"I'm not sure—not quite what I expected," Jocelyn confessed. "My fish not only did not rise to the bait, she didn't even seem to know it *was* bait."

"Clear as mud," Margery said cheerfully. "Shall we go?"

Jocelyn got back to find Penny anxiously waiting. "Well?"

"Um, not very well. Calpurnia was there all right. . . ," she related what had happened. "What beats me is that she didn't show even a flicker of interest. I know Calpurnia's into iron self-control, but you'd think. . . ."

"Maybe they didn't even tell her about the letter. It's quite possible because they've only known themselves since Corey's death," Penny comforted. "The important thing is whether she passes it on. And if she is in cahoots with them I think she will."

"What if she doesn't? What if this whole thing on Thursday is a bust?" Jocelyn asked.

"Then we'd be no worse off that we are now. We'd just have to think of something else. Anyway, in your own words, Think Positive—it's worth a try. And not a word of this to Toby," Penny said with decision.

Chapter 19

"Shouldn't we take a gun or something?" Now that the crucial hour was approaching Jocelyn was getting increasingly antsy.

"Good grief, no! I've never fired a gun in my life and I'm certainly not going to start at this late date," Penny replied. "Why? Do you *have* one?"

"No, but I thought you must have one after all the murders you've been through," Jocelyn sounded wistful. "Haven't you ever been attacked or shot at?"

"Oh yes," Penny was grim. "I've been attacked sure enough."

"Then what did you do?"

"Dodged mostly, and, on occasion, thrown things. I'm not much into violence. Don't really have the physique for it, do I?"

"I suppose not. Oh, it's all so easy on paper," Jocelyn sighed. "To be a super-something, I mean: expert at the martial arts, or a crack shot or a better fighter than Muhammad Ali, but in real life. . . ," she trailed off. There was a short silence, then, "Shouldn't we have some kind of backup? I know Sir Tobias is dead against this and you don't want to tell him, but shouldn't we at least let him know?"

Penny regarded her with an enigmatic smile. "Toby and I

have known one another for a very long time, we understand each other. What Toby says and what he does are two very disparate things. He's not about to let anything happen to me; if for nothing else, the thought of being a single grandparent would terrify him."

"But you haven't *told* him our plan have you?" Jocelyn cried.

"Not a word, but he's up to something. Haven't you noticed?"

It was true: ever since he had slammed out of the house two days before Toby had been mysteriously absent most of the time, and from the latest of these absences had returned with a grimly satisfied air. He had been perfectly pleasant, but had studiously avoided showing any interest in their activities, nor had he disclosed any of his. When they had arisen on this fateful morning, it was to find he had already breakfasted and gone.

"Then perhaps we should ask the Barnstable police for an escort," Jocelyn said anxiously.

"Judging by what's happened so far, they'd only either stop us or refuse to get involved. What we're proposing is not *il*legal, but it's not exactly legal either and is nothing they officially could countenance. Besides, we'll be outside their jurisdiction and don't know for certain anything is going to happen."

"Then what will we do if they come after us?" Jocelyn fretted.

"Well, I was rather depending on your skills as a demon driver to keep us out of trouble. You *are* a demon driver, you know," Penny grinned.

Jocelyn looked at her pop-eyed, "But what good would that do? If they chase after us and we outrun them right to Barnstable police station, what would we have accomplished? They surely wouldn't go after us in the parking lot of a police station!"

"No, they'd have to make their move long before that," Penny said quietly. "Look, if this is getting too much for you—

which would be perfectly understandable—we can call it off right now. It's a long shot at best," she went on, "You could just call Polanski off and that would be that."

"It's just that I keep thinking about poor Clara shot in the back like that," Jocelyn muttered. "Such a mean way to go."

"Yes, these were mean little crimes and carried out by mean, greedy little people: greed and power—the nastiest of motives." Penny was grim. "That's why I'd like to nail these bastards. Some of the murderers we've caught I have felt a lot of compassion for—but not this lot. They murdered in cold blood two lonely old people who, whatever their faults, had led useful lives, had earned their rest, and did not deserve to die as they did."

Jocelyn's mobile mouth thinned into a grim determined line. "You're right. Time to put up or shut up. I'm on, come what may."

Penny glanced at the clock. "Then we'd better be on our way if we're going to get to the rendezvous on time. One favor I ask of you, let's not try to break the speed record into Boston. Keep your demon driving for the return trip—I don't think my nerves would stand it both ways!"

Jocelyn chuckled and went off to seek her raincoat, for the Cape skies that had been brilliantly clear for the past week were once more aboil with scudding rain clouds. This was a fortunate happenstance because they had previously agreed that the best way to pass over the large envelope to Polanski would be under cover of a coat.

As they set out at what for Jocelyn was a very sedate pace, Penny started to regale her with stories from their improbable past. "Toby is always going on about how reckless *I* am," she complained. "But in actual fact he's the one who has suffered the most injuries and taken the most risks. He's been shot at, kidnapped, clobbered on the head, broken a leg, and dislocated a shoulder. Nothing that dire has ever happened to me."

Jocelyn grinned sideways at her. "You can stop the sales

talk, I'm all right now—just a temporary attack of the jitters. Not to worry. Let's talk about something bland, like our grandchildren."

"There's nothing bland about my grandchildren," Penny said mildly, and they proceeded to chat amiably throughout the long tedium of Route 3. As they neared the city and the Boston skyline humped up before them, they returned to the business in hand. "That's a pretty crowded area around the main PO," Penny observed. "I think the best way to go about this is for us to double-park right in front of it. I'll take the wheel and drive around the block while you dive in and do your thing with Craig Polanski. We can make a production of both our arrival and departure so that we get noticed. I'm pretty sure they won't try anything in the post office itself—too crowded, and driving around I might spot someone watching, though I imagine that's a pretty dim hope. When you come out with the envelope, wait in the entrance until you see me, then run down brandishing it and we can make a quick getaway."

"I thought it might be a nice touch if I ripped it open and brandished the papers at you in triumph," Jocelyn put in.

"No, don't open it," Penny said quickly.

"Whyever not?"

"Because if they *do* manage to stop us and if they see it is still sealed they may decide not to kill us."

Jocelyn grimaced. "What a gruesome thought! But I get your point. Where do you think they'll go after us?"

"Well, if they try and run us off the road, I'm pretty sure it won't be in the city. My feeling is that they'll either try it on Route 3 before the Quincy turnoff, which would give them another escape route if anyone comes after them, or after we've crossed the Sagamore Bridge on to the Mid-Cape. There are several rest areas between the bridge and the Route 132 turnoff—they could try it near one of those. Alternatively they could have two cars involved, one chasing after us, the other lurking near the 132 exit to cut us off and between them force us off into that little side road just beyond it."

"That would be cutting it pretty close," Jocelyn murmured. "We'd only be about three blocks from the police station." She chuckled suddenly. "You do realize, don't you, that we're basing our hopes on one of the oldest clichés in the business? A car chase! I'm beginning to feel more than a little absurd."

"Granted it's a very long shot," Penny murmured, "but, so far as I can see, it's the only one we've got. If we'd had more time maybe we could have come up with something better, though I haven't the faintest idea what. One good thing we have going for us is the time of day—early afternoon is a pretty dead time on Route 3 and the Mid-Cape; if we are being followed we'll have a better chance of spotting them."

They fell silent as Jocelyn negotiated the congested narrow streets leading to the post office. "Nothing but one-way streets around here," she muttered, "When we make our getaway I'll take Federal out and go over the Sumner Street bridge. I know my way back to Route 3 from there."

"Anything you say, our fate is now firmly in your hands," Penny said cheerfully.

They double-parked in front of the post office and made a great production of changing seats: a perfect picture of two flustered old ladies in a state of high excitement. Jocelyn scuttled off into the main doors and Penny began to drive slowly, around the block. She could see no sign of anyone taking any particular interest in her or the post office itself. She circled the block three times—to the great irritation of fellow motorists—and was on her fourth time around when she spotted Jocelyn's tall figure emerge and scan the street anxiously. Spotting the car, she brandished aloft the envelope shrilling, "I've got it!" at the top of her voice. She ran to the driver's side and Penny slid over to the passenger seat as she jumped in.

"Anything?" Jocelyn said, panting slightly and buckling herself in.

"Nothing I could spot," Penny said, tightening her seat belt as they moved out into the traffic.

"That *dunderhead* Craig!" Jocelyn cried as she picked up speed. "Do you know he had actually brought his manuscript along—all five hundred pages of it—and wanted me to take it with me! Honestly, I nearly dotted him one, but instead I gave him the money to get a mailer and send it to me. I only hope no one was watching us and he hasn't blown the whole thing. I didn't see anyone I recognized."

They regained Route 3 and while Jocelyn darted in and out of the traffic, Penny kept a wary eye out the rear window. "Anything?" Jocelyn demanded again as they neared the Quincy turnoff.

"Other than a crick in the neck, not a damn thing," Penny said. "I thought a green van was following on our heels for a while, but he's just zipped past us and is heading for the turnoff, so that's a no go."

The traffic became even sparser as they passed Quincy and headed toward the Cape. They were nearing the Sagamore rotary when Jocelyn again broke the silence. "Looks like a bust, doesn't it?"

"I'm afraid so," Penny sighed, rubbing the back of her neck. "Over the bridge you might try slowing down and then speeding up again to see if any of these jokers following us do the same. There's a brown panel van with something on its side that seems to have been there since Boston, but it's hanging way back."

"Oh shit!" Jocelyn exploded as she rounded the circle and a black car pulled out in front of her from the Cape Cod Information Center nearby. "That son-of-a-bitch nearly cut into me." She accelerated and nipped ahead of it over the bridge, but once on the Mid-Cape obediently slowed down and pulled into the right lane. The black car sped past her and then settled back into the right lane a couple of cars in front. A stream of traffic zoomed past them on the left. "Has that van passed us?" Jocelyn demanded.

"No, it's pulled up on us a bit, but it did slow down when we did," Penny said with a little surge of excitement.

"Can you see the driver?"

"No, it has one of those tinted-glass windshields—can't see a thing. But I'll keep a close eye on it and yell if it starts to move up on us."

"Shall I speed up again?"

"Sure—give it a try."

Jocelyn pulled out and passed the small procession in the right lane headed by the black car.

"The van is speeding up and coming on fast," Penny said in growing excitement. "In a second it will be on your back bumper."

"So now what?"

"Pull over to the right and see what happens. I just can't believe they'll try anything with all this traffic behind us."

In a second the brown van with a scarlet band on its side was abreast of them and for a moment they were racing side by side. Then, to their chagrin, it accelerated and sped ahead.

"Follow it!" Penny said and Jocelyn zoomed into the left lane. But as she did so a new note was added as, behind them, a siren rose unsteadily into a wail and Penny looked around to see a blue-clad arm appear from the black car and a flashing red light slapped on the roof: the arm waved them down.

"Oh my God! Of all the turn-ups—a cop car!" Jocelyn gasped. "What will I do?"

"There's a rest area just up ahead. Pull off into that and as near the road as you can. That's an unmarked car and it's all a little too pat—I think this may be it," Penny said tightly. As they swerved off into the tree-shaded rest area, her fears were confirmed when she saw the brown van was already there and rolling slowly toward them. Jocelyn slammed on the brakes and came to a shuddering stop. "What'll we do?" she said frantically.

"Do exactly what they say—and pray that the cavalry isn't too far behind." Penny muttered as things began to happen with the speed of light. The black car drew up close beside them and the van rolled to a stop behind, effectively screening them from the cars speeding along the Mid-Cape. A figure in the dark blue uniform of the Barnstable police emerged from the black car, gun in hand—but he was no cop, for his face was shrouded in a stocking mask. "Out!" he commanded, waving the gun, and as they scrambled to obey, the door of the van slid open and two large figures jumped out—one with a gun and both masked. Incongruously the painted faces of Ronald Reagan and Richard Nixon grinned vacantly at them.

"You're no policeman! How dare you! What is the meaning of this?" Penny quavered, knowing she had to play for time. Jocelyn stood like a frozen statue on the other side of the car. "The envelope. Give!" the fake cop said.

"Shut up, you old bag, and hand it over," the burly figure with the gun spat out. "And be quick about it!"

"That envelope is the property of the Barnstable police," she shrilled. "You'll be in very serious trouble over this."

"Not half as much as you'll be in if you don't hand it over. Five seconds and you've had it." He raised the gun.

She dived into the car and emerged clutching the envelope to her plump breast. He snatched it from her hands. "What'll we do with 'em?" His companion demanded.

"Take 'em with us and lose 'em later."

A new voice broke in, coming muffled from the inside of the black car. "Is the envelope open?"

"No, still sealed." Please God, don't let them open it here, Penny prayed silently, or we've had it.

"Then don't complicate things. Leave them here. Take the car keys and lose them." The stocking-masked man climbed into the car and on emerging hurled the keys into the scrub woods edging the paved rest area, as the man in the Reagan mask cocked his head and rumbled. "I hear a siren—and coming fast. Let's get out of here."

"Back in the car," Richard Nixon's face ordered. "And stay put and keep mum if you know what's good for you. We know where you live and we know where your family is. Remember that!"

Penny scrambled back in and dragged the frozen Jocelyn back into the driver's seat. "Lock the doors," she muttered, "And if shooting starts—duck! I think the cavalry is coming." As she spoke a state police car roared by and then did a violent turn into the exit of the rest area, while another shot like a rocket into its entrance and screeched to a stop. "Drop your guns and put your hands behind your heads," a megaphoned voice ordered.

The stocking-masked man gave an inarticulate cry and made a dive for the black car, then whirled around and loosed off a shot toward the nearest police car from the shelter of its open door.

"Get the women!" A hand wrenched at the handle of the locked door. "Duck!" Penny cried and they scrunched down on the floor as another shot rang out. They heard the revving of the van motor, another shot, and then a confused melee of shouting and running. "Remind me never to get involved in anything like this again," Jocelyn begged through chattering teeth. "I've aged twenty years in the last five minutes and I don't think my legs will ever function again."

"Just keep your head down and hope for the best," Penny muttered, straining to understand what was going on outside: she could hear another siren growing in volume and then dying suddenly with an angry squawk. A curious quiet settled, then the handle on her side rattled and there was a tapping at the window. She peered cautiously up to see Toby's round face gazing anxiously down at her. "You all right? You can come out now," he boomed graciously. "It's all over."

She prodded Jocelyn in the ribs. "It's okay, we can get out."

"For which relief, much thanks," Jocelyn quoted dazedly and hoisted herself with a groan back into the driver's seat. Penny opened the door, got out, and looked up at Toby. "I was beginning to think that this time you really had left me to hang and wither on the vine."

"And it would serve you damn well right if I had," he said with a grim smile.

She looked around at the hectic scene: a young man in the gray uniform of the state police who looked vaguely familiar was reading their rights to the two burly men, now unmasked and handcuffed by the van. Another state trooper was doing the same thing to the occupants of the black car, while two troopers from the third police car kept the scene covered with their guns. Robert Dyke, in civilian clothes, was standing by the van with the manilla envelope clutched to his chest. As he saw her emerge he walked over to her, gave her a meaningful grin, and said in a loud voice, "I must thank you on behalf of the Barnstable Police Department for bringing us this vital evidence safely intact. I apologize for the jeopardy you suffered."

"Who got nabbed?" she asked.

He jerked his chin in the direction of the van. "One of them is Norman, we don't know who the other one is yet. Robideau was in the black car, the other guy is one of our bent cops that got bounced in the great clear-out some years ago. We've got them on a nice assortment of charges: assault with a deadly weapon, resisting arrest, theft, impersonating a police officer, attempted kidnapping. . . ." He dropped his voice. "Enough to keep them on ice until (please God!) we come up with some real evidence or we can get one of them to rat on the others. As you can see, this is the state police's baby now. I'm here unofficially, but after you've made a statement to Detective Eldredge over there, I'll give you a lift back and fill you in."

She was momentarily baffled, "But that's not *our* Detective Eldredge!"

"That's the son of retired Inspector Eldredge who, luckily for us, followed in his father's footsteps and has been most cooperative. So nice to have friends in the right places," Toby purred blandly. "I'll tell you about it later—over a drink."

"You really are a most ingenious old devil," she exploded.

"I know," said Sir Tobias Glendower.

Chapter 20

"Knowing it was useless to talk your mother out of her wild scheme, I naturally had to move fast to save her from the usual dire consequences of her foolhardiness. I knew I would get little help from the local police, so applied to my old friend and former fellow-sufferer Detective Eldredge of the state police with, as you have gathered, very satisfactory results...," Toby droned, fixing his son-in-law with the hypnotic eye of the Ancient Mariner in full cry.

It was an idyllic family scene, set within a Sunday Cape Cod at its most beneficent. The sun shone brightly from a sky in which the cotton-wool puff of the occasional bright, white cloud only emphasized its azure blueness and was mirrored in the glass-calm waters of the bay beneath, fringed with a foam of tatted lace as it lapped sibilantly at the tiny Hyannisport beach beneath them.

As befits a patriarch, Toby was the central figure of the family group on the patio. Mala, ensconced firmly on his lap, gazed dreamily out to sea, although on occasion she would lift a plump hand to pat her grandfather's cheek and reassure herself of his presence. To his left Sonya reclined gracefully in a chaise lounge. After an initial Slavic snit at having missed out on all the action, she had recovered and was now listening to her father's lengthy exposition with absorbed interest, or so it appeared, for she was wearing a large-brimmed straw hat which completely shadowed her vivid face.

Penny, who had heard it all before, had abandoned the group and was down on the beach assisting Marcus in his creation of the Bloody Tower, now assuming vast proportions and becoming, in his enthusiasm, more like the Leaning Tower of Pisa: she was listening with only half an ear. This left Alex, hatless and upright in a fan-backed chair and hence Toby's most vulnerable target. Lulled by sun and surf and totally relaxed, he was having considerable difficulty keeping his eyes open as Toby rumbled on. He looked with deep envy at his daughter, whose golden eyelashes, lulled by the reassuring reverberations of her grandfather's chest, gradually drooped over the dark blue eyes and she slumbered peacefully.

" . . . then I thought it wise to have a quiet word with Caleb Crowell," Toby went on. This sparked a response from the beach. "You *did*? You never told me that," Penny called, "What on earth for?"

Toby transferred his attention to her and Alex thankfully let his eyes close and his head fall back. "Well, yes. Considering we'd already had *two* murders I felt that we could be in for a third, if Crowell went ahead and tried to blackmail any of our principals. So I warned him off—in a nice kind of way."

"How did he take it?"

"He professed not to understand what I was talking about, but I got the message across all right, even though he seemed in an alcoholic daze, poor fellow. I got the impression he was disappointed, but not defeated, if you follow me? I wouldn't be at all surprised if he puts some pressure on Calpurnia—not for money but for their own little power spheres."

"Serves her right if he does," Penny said stoutly. "It doesn't look as if she'll be called to account for anything else, the way things are going."

Toby cleared his throat and Alex hastily opened his eyes to see his father-in-law gazing reproachfully at him. "Not boring you, am I?" Toby said, an edge on his voice.

"No, not at all!" Alex forced his eyes wide open. "Fascinating—all very clever!" Something between a snort and a giggle emerged from under Sonya's hat and this was followed by the faint chimes of the doorbell.

"That must be Jocelyn Combe. She said she'd drop in. Anxious to meet you," Toby said, gazing helplessly at the slumbering Mala and over at his unheeding partner.

"I'll get it," Alex said thankfully, leaping to his feet and loping away.

They could hear Jocelyn's high voice growing in volume as she approached the open French windows, but when she appeared they gaped at her in blank amazement, for she was dressed in an extremely smart black and white outfit and with a daring, high-fashion hat perched jauntily on her salt-and-pepper hair. When she saw the look on their faces, she recoiled and looked down at herself in dismay.

"Oh dear, I knew this was a mistake!" she cried. "Terrible isn't it? My daughter insisted I get it, even though I told her it wasn't *me* at all. But I thought with your daughter being so smart and all . . . ," she trailed off.

Toby got his voice back first. "Not at all, Jocelyn! You are looking very nice, very nice indeed."

"*Very* nice," Penny echoed from below. "Straight out of *Vogue*!" Sonya tipped her own hat back and joined the chorus, "You are très chic, madame. It suits you to perfection."

Jocelyn still hovered doubtfully on the threshold peering down at the ensemble. "It's so plain," she muttered. "Myself I *do* like flowers on things."

"Come out, sit down, and meet the family," Toby boomed, every inch the jovial host. "Forgive me for not getting up, but you see how it is." He looked proudly down at the slumbering Mala, who opened one eye, glared balefully at the intruder and burrowed her golden curls more firmly into her grandfather's chest. Alex ushered Jocelyn to a chaise lounge on the other side of Sonya's and introductions were made all around. To everyone's surprise Marcus abandoned the Bloody Tower, climbed the wooden steps and gravely bowed over Jocelyn's bony hand like some eighteenth-century courtier. "That's basso Boris!" his parents explained in unison.

"I was just telling them how we cracked the case," Toby explained to their guest. "Shall I continue?"

"I'll get us some drinks," Alex said hastily and made a quick exit.

The door chimes sounded again. "Who on earth can that be?" Toby exclaimed. "Not expecting anyone else are we?" Penny, who had joined the group on the patio, shook her head. The chimes resounded more urgently. "Oh, well," he grumbled, seeing the womenfolk were not stirring, "I'd better see who it is." He dumped the slumbering Mala into her mother's lap and proceeded, rather stiff-in-the-joints, to the door. "I'm coming, I'm coming," he called testily as the chimes pealed on, and swung the door open.

Ernie Birnie, resplendent in his full chief's uniform, stood on the threshold. "I need a word with you, Sir Tobias." His eyes strayed to Alex, who had appeared pushing a laden drinks trolley, nodded and added, "In private—if you please."

Toby recoiled slightly, for the chief's manner was semi-belligerent but, by contrast, his expression very smug. "Er, of course, Chief Birnie. My family is here, but we can go into the study where we won't be disturbed. I was planning to have a word with you myself—about the crucial and very helpful role that Bob Dyke has had in all this. Highly commendable. . . ."

"You can say that again!" Birnie agreed to his surprise, as Toby steered him into the study. They seated themselves on opposite sides of the desk and Toby eyed the chief warily.

Knowing that bringing the state police in on the final confrontation would be considered a slap in the face to the Barnstable force, he decided that attack might be the best defense and sailed into action.

"I hope you understand, Chief, that with Dr. Spring and Mrs. Combe in possible great physical danger, I had no choice but to go to the state police for aid, and I hope and trust that it has had no unfortunate repercussions on you," he said loftily.

He was amazed when Birnie dismissed this with an airy wave of his hand. "Oh, that! No, I've got all that straightened out with Eldredge. Silly stunt, but fortunately no harm done, even though it was totally unnecessary."

"*Unnecessary?*" Toby said on a rising note. "But it worked! It solved the case for you."

"No way!" the chief smirked. "Merely the icing on the cake. We had the evidence to pull them in two days before that. Could have used a couple more days to firm things up, but that stupid attack just made it easier."

Toby gaped at him as Birnie chuckled and shook his head reprovingly. "I knew from former experience that if I warned you off, Dr. Spring and you would go at it all the harder, and once I saw Smith was a nonstarter and the nephew was out of it and that *you* were probably on the track of the right suspects—well, you made the perfect decoys. . . ."

"*Decoys!*" Toby exploded. "And how on earth did you know what we were working on? Did Bob. . . ?"

"Bob told me nothing. He was as much in the dark as to what I was up to as you were and I meant to keep it that way. How I knew does not matter. . . ," but the chief did squirm uneasily in his chair at that. "You've got to realize that Cape Cod is really a very small community and nothing is secret for very long. Fact is I did, and the way you were going about your investigations I was pretty sure *they* did too. So I wanted to keep their attentions focused on you and Bob and not on me.

"That's why I pulled Bob off looking for the one vital piece of evidence we had to have—the letter—and sent him on that wild goose chase after the gun." Birnie's face tightened. "I know damn well there are a lot of leaks in the force—and some heads are going to roll after this, I can promise you! So *nobody* knew what I was up to except my second-in-command, whom I've known for twenty-five years and who knows how to keep his trap shut. I did it all through *my* personal contacts and with the help of the Canadians."

"But the letter. . . ." Toby spluttered weakly.

"Had it since Wednesday," the chief said with irritating smugness. "Got a cousin who works in the Buzzards Bay center. It was there all along. Took a lot of digging, but he found it. Got a nephew in the records office and he did the Amdex Corporation tie-in. They obviously had something major in mind for Mashpee: bought a chunk of properties already and had options on one hell of a lot more. Waiting for the bullion salvage money to come in, they were. And we've got them cold."

"For the murder?" Toby demanded.

The chief looked at him, his face grave. "I'm still talking with the DA about that. But I don't think so." He heaved a sigh. "I'd better explain something, Sir Tobias. It's about our justice system. What we have on them now is probably enough to put Robideau and Norman away for the next forty years. We're thinking of letting the Canadians have first crack at them as they aren't as tender about armed robbery—particularly one of that magnitude—as we tend to be. That's good up there for twenty years at least, and then we'd have them back here for the rest of it. There is no statute of limitations on murder and our biggest hope would be if one of them cracks and rats on the real culprit in hopes of a lighter sentence this end. As it is. . . ," he heaved a deep sigh, "we have an awful lot of liberal judges here in Massachusetts, and our crooks have only got to keep their mouths shut—which they seem to be doing—and we'd have one hell of a time proving *which* of them did it right now. I think they might get off on Clara's murder, and we've never had a hope on Corey's."

"I see," Toby mused, "But what about the statute of limitations on their other crimes down here? Wouldn't that run out while they were in prison in Canada?"

"Ah, that's what we're negotiating right now," Birnie said. "What we'd do is that *while* they were serving their Canadian sentence, the Canadians would send them down to stand trial here and, if convicted, as they will be, they would just be handed over to us by the Canadians at the end of their sentence there to serve the rest of their time here." He smiled faintly. "That harebrained scheme of Dr. Spring's will be useful in adding to that—armed highway robbery and attempted kidnapping. Should be good for another ten years on top of everything else."

"But how about your witnesses? We may all be dead by then!" Toby fussed.

"You're forgetting Bob," Birnie retaliated. "He's a young one and, hopefully, will still be around. No, I'd say they're good for forty years hard time at least."

"The price of two lives," Toby murmured, his tone bleak.

Birnie looked him in the eye. "Not ideal maybe, but the best we can do. The main thing is we've done what Clara had in mind and wanted—we've stopped their mangy schemes for good." He got up.

Toby felt he had to get in one final dig. "And what of Calpurnia Howes?"

Birnie's face was inscrutable. "I doubt that Calpurnia will ever be put on trial for anything, but I'd say she is in for the worst punishment of all. The Cape is a small place with a long memory, I'd bet that everything meaningful in Calpurnia's life is already over."

"Fair enough," Toby said, getting up in his turn. They solemnly shook hands. "Thanks again," the chief said gruffly, but with a twinkle in his eye. "You've been a very great help."

"Oh, delighted I'm sure," Toby made a wry face. "I can hardly wait to tell Dr. Spring about our real role." Chuckling, he showed Birnie out.

He was still laughing inwardly as he rejoined the group on the patio, although his face was as solemn as a judge's as he took Alex's vacated chair. Penny looked across at him inquiringly. "Birnie's nose out of joint? Bob in any trouble?"

Toby's face quivered and grew red as he struggled to fight down the laughter, but it was hopeless. "Ho-ho-ho," he chortled. "We've been had! What did you call Birnie—a hick cop?" He doubled over in paroxysms of mirth and tears started to stream down his face. "What a pompous old ass I've been! We've been right royally *had* by your hick cop."

As they gazed at him in growing astonishment, Mala, who was now in her father's lap, hastily scrambled down and rushed over to Toby. She climbed in his lap and put her arms around his neck, looking anxiously up into his streaming eyes. "Don't cry, Grandpa!" she charged, "*I'm* here."

"Oh, Grandpa's not crying, my darling, he's laughing," Toby sobbed between chortles, mopping at his glasses with his handkerchief. "It's all so unbelievably funny. Red herrings, that's what we've been—a p . . . p . . . pack of silly red herrings, patsies all the way. Oh my. . . !"

Mala turned to her father, blue eyes flashing, "*Do* something!" she shouted in perfect imitation of her mother's voice.

"I'll get Grandpa a drink," Alex said and, suiting the action to the word, handed Toby a stiff brandy and soda and reclaimed his enraged daughter.

"Thanks, I can use that," Toby snuffled, massaging his aching ribs and taking a large gulp. "Haven't laughed this much in years."

"I've *never* seen you laugh like that," his partner reproved. "So if you're quite finished, how about sharing this huge joke with us?"

"The joke's *on* us," Toby corrected with a happy sigh. "And I will, I will indeed." And he did.

By the time he was finished Penny was laughing almost as hard as he was, their respective offspring grinning. They became belatedly aware that their guest was not joining in the mirth and looked over at Jocelyn, whose face was red, mouth agape and eyes starting out of her head. Seeing she had their attention she gasped out, "You mean I risked my neck in that damned car chase and then got scared out of ten good years for *nothing*? That it wasn't *necessary*? And you think that's *funny*!"

"I'm sorry but I'm afraid I do," Toby snorted. "You said you wanted to partake in our investigation, and now you can see what crackerjack detectives we really are. Oh my, what a humbling experience! This should put you off real-life detecting for good."

Jocelyn stood up, a grim smile on her face. "You can say that again! Once is quite enough. From now on I stick to paper. Well, I must be off to Brewster. Although. . . ," she turned to Sonya, "I'll see you tomorrow, right?" Sonya nodded enthusiastically and they all got up and saw her to the door.

Later that night, when the twins were in bed and soundly off in rosy and pallid sleep respectively, and their parents had also retired early for some connubial cooing, Toby sneaked out of the house for a quiet smoke before going to bed himself. He was startled to see Penny down at the edge of the water, her small form hunched at the shoulders, hands in her pockets and gazing steadfastly out to sea. He ambled out to join her and peered down into her preoccupied face. "What's up? Anything the matter?"

She roused herself with a sigh. "No, nothing. I was just thinking how extremely fortunate we both are."

"Granted. So? And. . . ?

"Well, but it could have been so very different," she burst out. "Surely you've seen the similarities? But for the Grace of

God I could have ended up like Clara and you like Corey, with nobody to care, nobody even to notice we were alive or dead."

He nearly retorted, "Never in a million years!" but restrained himself; instead he said mildly, "But we didn't, so what's your point?"

"Oh, I don't even know that I've got one, but I feel so *wretched* about all those lonely old people out there," she waved a hand wildly at the horizon. "Like those silly old people we saw on the beach the other day? How many of them will end up the same way? Lying dead for days, weeks, or months with no one even noticing? It is not right—and it would never happen in a *primitive* society!"

"Again granted," he agreed. "But there is nothing you or I can do about that, except on an individual basis, just as we have done in this case—and with success. You should feel pleased, not depressed." He puffed vigorously on his pipe, so that it spouted red sparks like a miniature volcano. After a sideways glance at her troubled little face he went on. "You know what's wrong with us? Too much sweetness and light, that's what." He looked up at the darkened house and lowered his voice. "I tell you what, let's move on down the beach so that we don't wake anyone up and let's have a damn good row about something. Clear the air and settle us both down?"

Penny brightened instantly. "Just like old times!" she exclaimed. "Yes, let's." They started to move off and a calculating gleam came into her eye. "Such a good idea of Sonya's, don't you think? She's going shopping with Jocelyn and give her some fashion advice, and in return Jocelyn is going to give her driving lessons. I think that's a great idea, don't you?"

"*What*! With that driving maniac? Absolutely absurd! I won't hear of it," Toby trumpeted, and they were off and running as they walked the moonlit strand.